"Something wrong, Kes . . . ?"

She jumped, startled, then managed a smile for Aren Yashar.

"Nothing's wrong, really, it's just—Now that she had to articulate it, Kes felt foolish. Still puzzled, she reached out to touch the odorless purple flower.

Her hand went right through it.

Kes gasped, turning to face Aren, a question on her lips. The words died as she saw that he had something metallic and dangerous-looking pointed directly at her.

La critica más que by individual consumers. For discounts on bulk purchases, please contact our marketing of 10 or more copies to fit your needs for special quantity for premium use. For further details, please write to the Vice-President of Special Markets, Pocket Books, 1230 Avenue of the Americas, New York, NY 10020.

For information on how individual consumers can place orders, please write to Mail Order Department, Simon & Schuster Inc., 200 Old Tappan Road, Old Tappan, NJ 07675.

STAR TREK®
VOYAGER™

MAROONED

Christie Golden

POCKET BOOKS
New York   London   Toronto   Sydney   Tokyo   Singapore

This book is a work of fiction. Names, characters, places and incidents are products of the author's imagination or are used fictitiously. Any resemblance to actual events or locales or persons living or dead is entirely coincidental.

An *Original* Publication of POCKET BOOKS

POCKET BOOKS, a division of Simon & Schuster Inc.
1230 Avenue of the Americas, New York, NY 10020

STAR TREK is a Registered Trademark of Paramount Pictures.

A VIACOM COMPANY

This book is published by Pocket Books, a division of Simon & Schuster Inc., under exclusive license from Paramount Pictures.

ISBN: 0-671-01423-4

First Pocket Books printing December 1997

10 9 8 7 6 5 4 3 2 1

POCKET and colophon are registered trademarks of Simon & Schuster Inc.

Printed in the U.S.A.

This book is dedicated to my agent,
Lucienne Diver.
A writer could have no better companion
on a trek to the stars.

PROLOGUE

KULA DHAD HASTENED DOWN THE CROWDED SQUARE, HIS cape folded tightly about his tall, bony frame despite the warmth of this city's midday. The courier was more accustomed to conversing with his commander in the comforting, familiar surroundings of gleaming metal, deep, soft chairs, and regulated temperatures. But the commander had selected this out-of-the-way corner of an out-of-the-way planet for their rendez-vous, and who was Kula Dhad to object?

Dhad brushed against the people he had been surgically altered to resemble, forced himself to smile and apologize when bodies collided a tad too harshly. They returned the smile, not realizing its falseness, and moved aside, these witless, technologically poor beings, their slitted eyes blinking much more rapidly than Dhad's.

And the smell! Shamaris expressed their emotions through scents as well as gestures and vocalizations. Dhad had been around them long enough to realize that the nearly choking odor that wafted up from the groups of humanoids represented a state of pleasurable tranquillity. It had been difficult to figure out a way to emulate that form of communication; still, they had managed. But oh, he'd far rather breathe the fumes of the guara pits of Burara Six than that reeking scent of happiness that emanated from the contented Shamaris.

He swallowed hard and continued on, folding his nostril flaps closed against the stench.

Up ahead, the commander had told him, would be a weaver's stall. There, Dhad would meet someone who would send him on to the formal meeting site. Dhad could see it now, the brightly colored fabrics contrasting vividly with the pale purple sands. He closed his eyes briefly in relief. The end of his journey was almost at hand.

Four strong fingers closed on his shoulder. Dhad gasped as he felt the cool metal of a weapon—what kind he didn't know and wasn't about to inquire at this juncture—pressing into the puffy flesh of his neck.

"You have been identified as a courier of the Ja'in," a voice rasped in his ear. "Come with me, please."

Dhad closed his eyes, wishing he'd had the foresight to bring something, anything, with which to end his wretched existence before questioning. Amiable as they were at most times, the Shamari loathed the pirates with an intensity that matched their smell, and Dhad knew that to fall into their hands—paws?—would mean pain beyond belief.

He thought about struggling, ending it quickly, but as if reading his thoughts his mysterious captor said, "The weapon stuns only. You will not escape our wrath, courier."

Dhad considered the options, then complied. No one seemed to notice anything amiss, and he wondered at that. It was almost as if his captor were as anxious to avoid discovery as he was, and that could only mean . . .

"C-Commander?" Dhad asked in a voice that quivered. Laughter was his reward, a cool chuckle, cool as the metal that was now removed from his tender throat.

"Ah, there is no fooling you, is there?" replied the Commander of the Ja'in as he stepped around to face Dhad.

He was as unrecognizable as Dhad himself was. Both now resembled the members of the Shamari merchant class they pretended to be. There was no hint of the normal good looks of the pirate leader about that homely face now. He slipped a comradely arm about Dhad and the latter breathed a slight sigh of relief that he had remained silent. Had he confessed to the "Shamari law enforcer," his commander would have slain him on the spot, no matter what treasure he carried.

There was no room for a traitor among the Ja'in.

Dhad followed as his leader guided him down the winding streets, at last into a rundown stone building that appeared from the outside to be nothing more than a humble Shamari's home. The commander nodded to what seemed to be a pair of beggars, dropping shu-stones into their hands and waving aside their effusive thanks. Dhad didn't recognize

3

them, but he would have bet a year's haul of goods that they were guards, and he would not have lost.

Inside, in the cool darkness, was a jumbled collection of machines and gadgets that would have stunned the low-tech Shamaris. Lights blinked on and off; soft, whirring sounds hummed through the room.

The commander pulled off his cloak and straightened to his full height of just over two meters. He lounged in a chair and reached for one of the orange, spiky fruits on the table. Biting into it, he wiped at the juice that flowed down his chin and ordered, "Show me what you have for me, Dhad."

The courier hastened to obey, dropping a tiny square piece of metal into a hologram unit and activating it quickly. Then he stepped back, hardly breathing, with a desperate hope that his master would be pleased.

On the table before the commander appeared the image of a ship. Its lines were smooth and sleek, the metal of its hull softly illuminated by tiny pricks of variously colored lights from within.

The Ja'in leader frowned. "I've seen this vessel," he rumbled. "Several months ago, in fact. Your gossip is hardly timely, Dhad, if this is all you have for me."

Dhad began to feel nervous. "But—it is headed toward this sector, Great One, and our spies report that it has heard nothing of the Ja'in."

The commander laughed. "What use is that to me?"

"With a ship like *Voyager,* Great One, you could conquer the whole quadrant!"

"And how, pray, would I be able to conquer *Voyager?*" the pirate shot back. "No ship I have could best it, and I will not jeopardize the base for it. If I have learned one thing in my four millennia, it is caution. No, Dhad, have you nothing better to show me?"

Dhad swallowed hard and resisted the temptation to brush at the sweat that started to dapple his gray-green brow. "Perhaps my master has not seen the curiosities that are aboard *Voyager,*" he said, with a ghastly attempt at nonchalance.

He fiddled with the machine and images appeared. The commander leaned forward, his slitted eyes narrowing, the orange fruit forgotten. Hope flickered inside Dhad.

"This hologram was made secretly, when members of the crew of *Voyager* took shore leave on Tajos Prime several weeks ago." Emboldened by the commander's interested reaction, he added, falsely, "Three lives were lost in getting this to you."

The commander shot Dhad a look that instantly deflated him. "That, I doubt, Dhad. Who and what am I seeing?"

"This female," and Dhad pointed at the Rhulanoid woman whose thick hair was pulled back and clasped at the back of her neck, "is the captain of the vessel. She is from a species known as human. Most of her crew are humans. This is her security officer. Members of his race are called Vulcans."

"Vulcans," repeated the commander, and smiled. "A pleasing name on the tongue. Oh—and this one. What is it?"

Dhad could taste the promotion. "That is a half-human, half-Klingon woman. She is the chief engineer. That funny green-blue one is a Bolian. And this,

5

Great One," and Dhad touched a button that changed the scene, "is a being called an Ocampa."

A ten-centimeter–high vision of feminine grace stood on the tabletop. Her hair was long and yellow, the golden ringlets coyly hiding ears that appeared to curl in on themselves to form a point. Slim was her body, and wise were her eyes. She moved with a deep grace that touched even Dhad. The pirate leader stared, as if transfixed.

"By the Makers," he breathed, "she's—"

"Beautiful?" prompted Dhad eagerly.

The commander shook his head, never taking his eyes from the girl. "No. More than that. Perfect. What is her name?"

"She is called Kes. And," Dhad puffed himself up, about to utter the words that would clinch his promotion, "her race lives only nine years!"

"What?" gasped the commander, dragging his eyes away from the hologram. "If you are lying to me—"

"No, Great One, I swear! I heard her talking. Only nine years."

The commander fell silent, watching the miniature woman, his eyes roving over her face, her figure. "You say *Voyager* is approaching this sector?" Dhad nodded. "Then we must welcome them properly. You did right to show this to me. I think you deserve a reward, Dhad. I think I shall enlist your aid in my quest."

"Then, you will try to take *Voyager*?"

The commander shook his head, his gaze drawn inexorably to the tiny, delicate girl-woman on the table.

"No. I will take Kes."

CHAPTER
1

"OH, LOOK, CAPTAIN! THE CYMARRI'S FINALLY STARTED to bloom!"

Kes clapped her hands together delightedly, radiating pleasure as she hastened to the fragile blossom that was only just beginning to unfurl its petals. She reached to touch the trembling purple plant with gentle fingers.

"I've been wondering if this would happen at all. Six months is a long time in the life cycle of this plant." She chuckled self-deprecatingly. "I was worried I'd killed it."

"You?" It was Captain Kathryn Janeway's turn to laugh. "You were born with what my mother would call a green thumb." Janeway permitted herself a moment to look around at the wonders Kes's diligent care had wrought. Though the Ocampa's "garden"

7

was a feast for the eye, it was the fruits—and roots, and leaves, and berries—of these plants that would eventually become real feasts. Kes's work here was, in its own way, almost as vital as the tasks she performed in sickbay.

"Mmmmm," Kes breathed, closing her eyes as she pressed her face into the flower. "It smells so beautiful. Captain, you must smell this!"

"What you and I both must do is head over to transporter room one," Janeway chided, feeling a smile creep onto her face nonetheless at Kes's rapture over the flower's fragrance. It was a pretty picture, no doubt, this image of the fragile, elfin girl surrounded by a riot of colorful plants. "The administrator is waiting for us."

Kes nodded her comprehension, all business now, save for a last, lingering touch of the cymarri's soft petals. As they left, the door hissed quietly shut behind them.

"I'm rather looking forward to this," Janeway said as the two strode down the corridor. "We haven't seen all that many space stations here in the Delta quadrant."

"Are there many of them in the Alpha Quadrant?" Kes queried.

"Oh, yes. They're quite common indeed."

"Why do you think they're not so numerous here?"

Learning. Kes always seemed to want to be learning. It was as if, Janeway mused with a sudden, unexpected pang of sorrow, the Ocampan were trying to cram a dozen lifetimes into the nine brief years allotted to her species.

"We've yet to encounter an organization comparable to our Federation out here. Without a unified group of planets deciding to support a station, there's really no point in having one. Oasis, though, is right in the middle of a cluster of class M planets, and at least according to Administrator Yashar, it seems to be doing well enough. If that's the case, then I'm hopeful they may have some star charts to sell."

They turned a corner. Janeway nodded in greeting to a young ensign who hastened past. In the back of her mind, Janeway noted that the youth looked tired. Yashar had mentioned that Oasis would be a pleasant spot for some shore leave. Depending on what the away team found, that might not be such a bad idea.

"I'm particularly looking forward to the greenhouse that Administrator Yashar mentioned," said Kes, interrupting Janeway's thoughts.

"You haven't seen all that many," Janeway replied. "It's logical, when you think about it. A space station can be pretty cold and sterile. Something green and living—that can brighten the spirit a great deal. And it might be particularly important to the local culture. Many civilizations have sacred groves or their equivalents." She glanced over at Kes, her eyes dancing. "Like your garden, for example."

Kes caught the teasing and laughed. Together they entered the transporter room to find the other members of the away team, B'Elanna Torres, Tom Paris, and Neelix, waiting impatiently.

Still smiling to herself, Janeway stepped lightly onto the platform. "Energize."

* * *

Their host's voice floated to Janeway's ears even before she had finished materializing.

"May I be the first to welcome you to Oasis, Captain Janeway."

The captain turned to greet Aren Yashar, the station's administrator. He bowed deeply, and Janeway and her crew members imitated the movement.

Janeway had already conversed with Administrator Yashar via the ship's viewscreen, but she always looked forward to the first personal contact. Much could be negotiated without two parties ever meeting, and often was, of course, but Janeway liked to size up friend and foe alike in person when she could.

Yashar did not disappoint. Tall, elegant, the Rhulani administrator of Space Station Oasis was almost completely human in appearance. Long, blue-black hair fell down his back, elaborately bound with variously colored ribbons. The nails on the ends of his fingers were painted and filed to points. It was only when one looked closely that one noticed that the eyebrows were much thinner and placed higher on the forehead than was common with humans. The most startling difference was also subtle—the Rhulani race, of which Aren was a member, had iridescent webbing between those sharp-nailed fingers. He wore full-length robes of shiny material, and stood straight and tall. Despite the courteous bow, Janeway got the impression that Aren considered her an equal. She liked that.

"Thank you, Administrator Yashar, for inviting us."

He held up a hand in mild protest, the webbing

flashing brightly for an instant, then disappearing. "Ah, please. I prefer Aren. Among my people, the use of the second name denotes extreme formality or hostility, neither of which, I hope, will set the tone for our relationship."

Janeway nodded her head slightly. "As you wish, Aren. Allow me to introduce the members of my away team. This is Lieutenant Tom Paris, one of our flight controllers; our Chief Engineer, B'Elanna Torres; Neelix, our chef and morale officer; and Kes, our medical assistant and resident expert on various plants."

Janeway glanced around as her crew exchanged pleasantries with Aren, and her smile faded somewhat. Her initial impression, gleaned from her earlier conversations with Aren, was that this was a space station operating at full capacity. She was wrong.

They had noted three ships already docked at the station prior to *Voyager*'s arrival, and there was the steady hum of voices in the background that indicated a number of beings. Certainly, many individuals of a variety of races made their busy ways along the open area that was, apparently, the merchant's row of the station.

But several stores were closed or in a state of disrepair. Despite the crowds, the place . . . *felt* vacant. Janeway could sense her crew's disappointment, a mirror of her own, as they took in the curving white metal walls, the honeycombed ceiling in which were set soft, glowing orbs of light. Too big for the number of people here; too empty for the number of shops with closed doors and covered windows.

"Not what it once was, I'm afraid," said Aren, bringing the captain's attention back to her host. Clearly, he had followed her gaze and seen her reaction. "I apologize. Would that Oasis were the thriving port it has been in the past, but it can be again, Captain, which was why I was so eager for you to visit us."

"Was there some sort of trouble?"

Sorrow and something a touch harder made the administrator frown. "Trouble. Yes, that word will do as well as any other," he said somberly. "Come and walk through the Tradesman's Sector with me and I will tell you what happened. But first," and with a smile and a flourish Aren produced a small, shiny oval from a pocket hidden somewhere in his voluminous robes, "here are the star charts you requested."

Janeway accepted the smooth—crystal? stone?—with pleasure. "But Aren, we haven't yet negotiated a trade for this."

"Your presence and that of your crew will be trade enough. You have seen the stores standing empty. Do you not think those merchants who are able to reopen their shops would be thrilled to have your crew purchasing items from them? Honest trade, Captain, with honest people—that is all Oasis is about; all it has ever been about. Not so long ago, I could rent out the smallest stall here for a thousand kuristos, and the merchant would call it cheap at four thousand. But ever since the Ja'in came . . ."

He sighed. "Will you walk with me, and at least see what Oasis has to offer? Everyone here has heard tales of our visitors from a far distant part of the galaxy.

Your patronage would heighten station morale beyond price, I assure you."

A quick glance at her crew showed her that they were as curious as their captain, so Janeway nodded and indicated that Aren should proceed.

"Ah, I am grateful, Captain. Now, where was I?"

"The Ja'in," prompted Torres. "What happened? Was there a war?"

"Of a sort," replied Aren. He clasped his hands behind him and began to lead his visitors along the rows of shops. For the first time, Janeway got a brief glimpse of his back. Two large lumps below the shoulder blades marred the otherwise sleek, long back of the Rhulani administrator. Almost immediately, Aren gracefully maneuvered himself so that the unsightly protuberances were no longer visible.

It was a subtle gesture, but Janeway was used to picking up on subtleties from alien races. Aren was uncomfortable with her seeing the malformations.

A deformity? Janeway wondered. A trait of his race not meant to be shared with outsiders? Whichever it was, it piqued her curiosity and she made a point of not discomfiting her host further by staring.

"But you cannot have a war without an opponent, and the shopkeepers, patrons, crew, and staff of Oasis could hardly be called that. Oasis is neutral in any conflicts between the five planets of the Oryma system, and has been that way ever since it was established. We were certainly attacked, but it was a very one-sided war.

"The Ja'in, you see, are pirates."

There came a decidedly inappropriate snort of

laughter from the direction of Tom Paris. Aren frowned, and Janeway caught a glimpse of something hard beneath the friendly surface. Janeway couldn't blame him, and shot Paris a warning glance. The young lieutenant composed himself at once, but Janeway wasn't going to let him get off so easily.

"Something amuse you, Mr. Paris?" she asked in a deceptively conversational tone.

"No, Captain, nothing at all. I apologize. Please continue, Administrator." A blush warmed his cheeks.

Taking pity on him, Janeway turned to Aren, who still looked angry. "Where we come from, we are fortunate that piracy is very rare indeed. Most of us think of pirates as something from antiquity—quaint, rather than formidable. Lieutenant Paris was no doubt thinking of ribald tales rather than something very real and very dangerous."

"Ah, a cultural difference," said Aren, calming visibly. "It has been so long since anyone truly alien to us has visited Oasis, I forgot how one can occasionally brush up against such things. I quite understand."

He granted Paris a smile and had just opened his mouth to continue when a woman's angry voice cracked like a whip.

"I don't *care!*"

Despite herself, Janeway turned her head to discover the source of the outburst. Two young Rhulani leaned up against one of the white, curving metal walls. The female had her arms folded across her chest in a posture that, in humans, signaled both defense and defiance.

The male ran his hands through his long hair in exasperation. "Dear one, I swear to you, that relationship was over a long time ago."

The girl pouted. "Not the way she was touching you, it wasn't!"

"Now, that's not my fault."

"Oh, really?"

"If I wanted to be with someone else, would I be giving you this?" The youth produced something that glittered, that caused the young woman to squeal happily and embrace him.

Janeway felt a smile curve her lips, and caught Aren smiling as well. They exchanged a knowing look. "Cultural *similarities*," said Aren.

Janeway's smile became a full-fledged chuckle. Some things, it would seem, were indeed universal.

"Anyway," Aren continued both his walk and his story, "you may take it from me that *these* pirates were brutally efficient. Even after all these years, you can see the results of their handiwork. They hit us hard and left many dead. It is fortunate that Oasis is as valued as it is. In fairly short order a display of combined force from all of the nations with a vested interest in this station managed to drive the Ja'in from our space. But we are only now starting to recover economically. *Voyager* is one of the first visiting ships to enter our space since we reestablished business activity on the station. We occasionally do business with the Tlatli, but," he smiled, "insectoid races don't generally require the same things that we do.

"Now," and he looked around at the away team,

"perhaps you can tell me what your interests are and I can steer you in the right direction. We're at the heart of the Tradesman's Sector now and you can see all the open shops from here. Perhaps you are hungry?" he asked, hopeful.

"A little thirsty," said Paris. "Is that a, uh, tavern of some sort?" He gestured at a dimly lit establishment where several patrons were lifting glasses.

"It is indeed. Jakrig's, is the name. Ask about the Rhulani flower liquor. And—B'Elanna, is it? I believe your captain said you were interested in speaking with one of our repair personnel."

"That's right," began Torres, "we were wondering if—"

"I do apologize," a voice interrupted. A smaller, rounder Rhulani scurried up to them, consternation on his face. "Administrator, I'm afraid there's been a malfunction in our system. All the accounts have been affected, and—"

Aren groaned. "Not that again. I just corrected— Never mind. Captain, you must excuse me. If I don't straighten out these accounts at once, I'll have some very unhappy merchants on my hands. Would you and your crew like to reschedule your visit, or do you feel comfortable enough to continue exploring on your own?"

"We'll be just fine, thank you. Now that we're here, I wouldn't mind doing a little shopping." *And if these star charts are as accurate as I'm hoping, it'll be a fair trade indeed,* she thought. Neelix had done an admirable job the last few years of playing native guide, but they had exhausted even his extensive knowledge of the Delta quadrant. Star charts of the area would be a lifeline.

And besides, her quarters could use a little something colorful.

Aren brightened at her words and executed a deep bow. Again, Janeway caught a glimpse of the lumps on his back as she bowed in return. "Lieutenant Torres, the repair sector is along that corridor and—Kes and Neelix, yes? Our hydroponics arboretum and grocery is right over there. We're rather proud of it here on Oasis; if you're interested in fresh foodstuffs, please tell the gardener on duty that I sent you. Again, my apologies. Perhaps I'll be able to finish this quickly and catch up with you, though sadly, I doubt it."

He turned, clasping the smaller man by the shoulder, and walked quickly away, listening to his assistant explain something about lost data and glitches.

"I take it then, Captain, that we may consider ourselves off duty for a bit?" asked Paris, looking hopeful at the prospect.

"You may, Mr. Paris, but don't drink too much of that Rhulani flower liquor. I expect you back on the bridge and up to speed within the hour." She glanced around at Torres, Kes, and Neelix. "That goes for the rest of you, too. We don't want to overstay our welcome this first time. As for payment, I advise you to remember that whatever you purchase comes out of your rations unless it's something specifically for the ship. Other than that—enjoy. Dismissed."

She gave them a warm smile as the four immediately dispersed. They looked like schoolchildren hearing the bell for recess. Paris headed straight for

Jakrig's, Torres moved with a determined stride down the corridor in the direction of the repair facilities, and Neelix and Kes moved in tandem to the arboretum. They were chatting excitedly at the prospect of what they might find there, and that, more than anything, made Janeway glad. Their love for one another had once been very strong, so strong that she'd have sworn nothing could come between them. But of course something had, and everything was different now. The violent possession of Kes's body by the alien Tieran had changed the Ocampa, ripping much of her innocence from her and altering all of her relationships with those close to her. Her love affair with Neelix had been the most extreme casualty; they had broken up soon afterward.

Janeway worried about it at first. At times she thought of *Voyager* as the proverbial ship in a bottle, except it was more like a ship *as* a bottle. They were all they had out here, and a thousand shore leaves and a million adventures could not change that one fact. Anything that affected an individual affected everyone in such a situation—especially when it concerned the morale officer.

She soon realized that she'd underestimated both Neelix and Kes. She wasn't privy to their most private thoughts, of course, but it was plain to see that they were determined to let passion mellow into a rich, deep friendship. That was never easy, but, Janeway knew, if such a thing could be done, it was always worth it.

She watched them enter the arboretum, thought about joining them, then remembered a beautiful statue she'd glimpsed in a little shop a few stores back.

She'd leave Kes and Neelix alone, let them amble about in a tranquil, lovely place that brought them both joy. Meanwhile, she'd see if she couldn't get a deal on that statue.

How clever, thought Kes as they entered, *using these trailing leaves as the doorway!*

She extended a small hand and gently pushed the drooping fronds from an alien tree aside, holding them back so they wouldn't catch poor Neelix in the face. "Isn't this lovely? If only I could have something like this in my hydroponics bay!"

"It reminds me of the tree the humans call the weeping willow," said Neelix, looking about. "Goodness, what a lot of plants."

"We do our best," came a voice from behind them. "I'm the gardener, T'loori Hro. Is there anything in particular you're looking for?"

Kes turned, saw no one, then glanced down. T'Loori Hro was just shy of a meter in height with pale purple skin and large, black eyes. She had no discernible nose or ears and only a slit for a mouth. Her body was round, but the small appendages that served for legs and arms seemed adequate to perform tasks. With such a lack of facial features, it was difficult to read her expression, but Kes's commbadge had translated the voice as feminine and friendly.

"We're from the starship *Voyager,*" Kes replied, dropping to one knee to be closer to Hro's height. "I'm Kes, and this is my friend Neelix. We're particularly interested in any fruit-bearing plants or vegetables you might have to sell."

Hro waved a stubby arm. "Please don't feel you need to crouch, Kes. My people have been dealing with you Talls for centuries. Please," and she waved Kes back to her feet.

"Your station administrator Aren Yashar directed us to you," said Neelix.

"Ah!" There was no change of expression, but the voice was obviously pleased. "Then he'll be wanting me to show you some of the special fungi I keep back here. Which of you will be preparing the meals?"

Neelix stood a little straighter. "That's my job," he said solemnly. Hro bobbed her small head in acknowledgment.

"And clearly you are aware of the responsibility," Hro replied with equal seriousness. "Aren has chosen well. I think you will do justice to my fungi. Will you come with me, please?"

Neelix shot Kes a pleased grin, and she smiled back. The Talaxian took his job as morale officer aboard *Voyager* very seriously, and preparing meals was his favorite aspect of the position. He looked on it as a life-giving task, a way to both nourish and nurture the crew, and he was always disappointed that most of his carefully prepared meals were underappreciated.

Kes herself loved everything Neelix cooked. Perhaps tastes were simply different in the far-distant Alpha quadrant. She shared his excitement at being shown new and exotic foodstuffs and was as delighted as he with the opportunity.

She, however, was much more interested in a

strange-looking tree back in the corner. Its bark was dark blue and its serrated leaves were almost as pale gold as her own hair. One giant, purple blossom unfurled as she watched.

"Oh," she gasped, and strode forward to bury her face in the flower.

She frowned. There was no smell. That in itself was not unusual; some flowers had scents that were imperceptible to the Ocampan olfactory system. But the scentless flower suddenly made Kes realize that *nothing* in this arboretum smelled. At all.

"Something wrong, Kes?" She jumped, startled, then managed a smile for Aren Yashar. The man was as quiet as a pad-footed *siaa*.

"Hello, Administrator. Nothing's wrong, really, it's just—" Now that she had to articulate it, Kes felt foolish. But still, surely, not all the plants in here were scentless. Still puzzling over it, she absently reached to touch the odorless purple flower.

Her fingers went right through it.

Kes gasped, turning to face Aren, a question on her lips. The words died as she saw that the administrator had something metallic and dangerous looking pointed directly at her.

"It's time to leave, my dear. And if you utter one word, Hro has orders to murder your friend."

CHAPTER

2

Tom Paris had entered many a bar in his day, and all of them, he had discovered, had a few things in common.

Beverages of varying potencies were always served. A large member of the predominant race lurked by the door, ready to eject customers who had overindulged in those beverages. The lighting was dim, and some kind of game of chance was usually being played.

He found all of these traditional elements to be present in Jakrig's establishment, and a faint smile touched his lips. In the midst of strangeness, there was always something familiar about a bar. He knew what to expect and how to behave.

Much talk was going on as he entered the darkened room, and way in the back some creature that looked unsettlingly like a praying mantis busily worked a variety of instruments to produce something that was clearly meant to be music. Paris winced at the discordant sounds, but there was a small crowd gathered around the mantis, and they were nodding their heads and clearly enjoying themselves.

One man's junk is another man's treasure, Paris thought, then winced again—but not at the music. He was cringing from the thought of what he had done to Aren Yashar.

Treasure . . .

It was definitely time for a drink.

He moved through the crowd and headed toward the center of the room. A thin, bony humanoid stood behind a circular bar. Bottles of various liquids hovered in the air, supported clearly by some sort of gravitational field. The bartender could clasp the floating bottles with ease, but as Paris watched, someone else tried to help himself and the bottle floated away tauntingly.

"Come on, Swha, you know better than that," the bartender chided. He wagged a remonstratory finger at the sad-looking alien who had tried to filch a free drink.

"But Jakrig," the drunken alien pleaded, his four eyes blinking slowly, "I don't get paid until—"

"Then you don't drink until," Jakrig replied, nodding at a large being who stood quietly beside the door. The entity, who looked like the ghastly product of a union between a Cardassian and a Denebian slime devil, moved purposefully toward the bar.

"All right, all right," slurred the pale blue, four-eyed alien, slipping off the stool to land on the floor. "Been comin' here for years now. Y'd think somone'd take my word for somethin'."

He managed to crawl out, right past Paris's feet, somehow retaining his dignity. Paris admired that and marveled as he watched the alien, still muttering, creep outside. He headed for the stool the alien had vacated, slipping onto it with a bit of maneuvering. It was clearly not designed for human anatomy but he could sit on it all right.

"So, this is your establishment, I take it?" he asked the bartender.

"I'm Jakrig, if that's what you mean," the other said guardedly.

Paris smiled his most winning smile. "Your station administrator, Aren Yashar, recommended your place. He told me that I was to inquire about something called Rhulani flower liquor."

Jakrig's face, similar to a human's but for the disconcerting slitted purple eyes, lit up. "Ah, a connoisseur! By all means, presuming you have the, er, wherewithal to purchase such a delicacy?"

Payment had not yet been agreed upon, but Aren had seemed so certain that the shopkeepers would be happy to conduct business . . . "Well, I'm from the starship *Voyager,* and it was my understanding that something would be worked out."

Jakrig held up a three-fingered hand. "Say no more, friend, say no more. Administrator Yashar has mentioned your ship." He reached, plucked a floating, corked globe, and poured liquid from it into a small bowl. "I hope you have a strong head for such things, friend," he warned.

Paris grinned to himself. He'd handled Saurian brandy, Romulan ale, chech'tluth, good old Earth Scotch, and more types of alcohol than he could pronounce. Something called flower liquor shouldn't be too bad.

"A strong enough head to be able to manage a second cup a bit later, friend," he replied in kind as he took the small, cool bowl.

It smelled wonderful. He sniffed appreciatively, his mind suddenly traveling back to his days at the Academy. He remembered strolling through the gardens with some very lovely women. Smiling at the recollection, he took a small, cautious sip.

Oh, this would be no problem at all. It was warm on the tongue and down the throat, yes, but there was no kick to it that boded unusual strength. Nevertheless, Paris lingered over the drink, savoring the sweet flavor as he brooded over the earlier encounter with Oasis's administrator.

Why the hell had he laughed when Aren had mentioned pirates? He knew better. Rogue forces had decimated whole star systems; he'd seen what they could do. Piracy was no laughing matter.

But Paris had only that morning finished programming a holodeck program for himself, Harry, and B'Elanna—provided that they could talk her into it—that revolved around just that theme. Bottles of rum, yo-ho-ho, planks to be walked, swashes to be buckled—Tom was certain that this playful, rather silly program would be one of the most physically challenging and mentally relaxing recreations he'd yet attempted. No one save holograms would be hurt in this scenario. Lots of blades would clash, lots of snarling, quaint oaths would be uttered, but it was all in good fun.

His mind had been on that kind of pirate, not on

the dangerous and brutal pirates of this century. So, when Aren had used the word, he'd laughed at the unbidden image of Blackbeard and Captain Hook swarming over the space station buying clothes and inspecting glass statuettes.

He took another sip, a larger one this time, and blinked. This stuff *was* unexpectedly potent, wasn't it.

"So what kind of flower is this distilled from?" he asked, but what came out of his mouth sounded much more like "Swa kfla zizfro?" He tried again. His second attempt was even more garbled, and worse, his fingers seemed to declare rebellion and dropped the cup. Pale yellow liquor began to spread over the counter.

Paris forced his suddenly heavy head to look up at Jakrig and found the alien smiling. But it was not the wry amusement of a bartender at the expense of a drunken customer. This smile was triumphant, cruel.

Just as Paris's head took a sudden downturn to land with a thump on the wet counter, the lieutenant realized with a flash of impotent fear that there had been something far more sinister in the drink than he ever could have imagined.

Kula Dhad talked tech and matched B'Elanna Torres stride for stride. She respected that in a man.

She let him talk, nodding her head occasionally, as he explained the facilities available for passing ships. Certainly she and her trained crew would be better able to execute the needed maintenance and repair of *Voyager* than any of the Oasis crew, but spare parts that could be adapted to the Starfleet vessel were hard to come by. Oasis might be just what Torres had hoped for.

The corridor ended and Dhad paused in front of a large, circular door. He punched in a code on a lighted keypad on the wall with his oddly thin, webbed fingers and the door irised open with a faint breathy sound, almost like a sigh. Smiling politely, Dhad extended his hand, indicating that Torres might precede him. She stepped briskly through the door—

—and froze.

There was a large docking bay, all right. But there were no ships, no parts of ships, and no maintenance crew at all. The door sighed closed behind her. Torres had just started to turn, angry questions on her lips, when a terrible pain crashed down on the back of her head and she saw a blinding light, then nothing at all.

A thin line of annoyance appeared between Janeway's brows. She was fairly certain that the little statue shop had been just a few stores back down the way they had come, but she had apparently been mistaken. Almost a half hour had gone by in her fruitless search.

Finally, she turned a corner and smiled. There it was! And the lovely, six-centimeter–high orb of polished stone still sat in the window. It really was quite pretty, its softly glowing surface decorated by an equally beautiful carving of a humanoid female head. Janeway stepped forward to get a better look at it.

"Ah, greetings," a cheery voice welcomed her. Janeway glanced up to see a squat, red-faced, multi-eyed being hasten up to her, its moist snout twitching with what she assumed to be pleasure. "I see you have very good taste. What ship are you from?"

"Voyager," Janeway replied. "Your station administrator Aren Yashar has made us feel quite welcome."

"Ah, one of Aren's friends!" the ugly being exclaimed. Its snout twitched even more vigorously. "Someone special, I see. Why don't you accompany me to the back of the shop and let me show you some of the items I keep in the safe?"

Janeway had just opened her mouth to accept when suddenly, an angry female voice interrupted her.

"I don't care!*"*

Janeway frowned and looked around. Right beside her was the young Rhulani couple she had heard arguing earlier. They apparently had managed to find something else to quarrel about. The female had her arms folded across her chest, just as she had before, and looked every bit as unhappy.

The male ran his hands through his long hair. "Dear one, I swear to you, that relationship was over a long time ago."

The girl pouted. "Not the way she was touching you, it wasn't!"

A chill ran down the captain's spine.

"Now, that's not my fault."

"Oh, really?"

It was the same conversation. *Exactly* the same conversation, word for word, gesture for gesture.

"If I wanted to be with someone else, would I be giving you this?" The youth produced something that glittered, that caused the young woman to squeal happily and embrace him.

Something was very wrong here. Janeway stared at

the young couple, a terrible suspicion beginning to form in her mind.

"Captain Janeway?" It was the shopkeeper, looking as if he felt a sale slipping through his fingers. Another something wrong. Janeway hadn't introduced herself. She knew with a deep certainty that she was not about to set one foot in that shop.

She smiled easily, as if nothing at all were the matter. "Thank you, but I don't think so. I'd like to wander a bit, do some comparison shopping. You understand."

"There's no store on Oasis that has items as attractive as this," the shopkeeper insisted, a touch forcefully.

Again Janeway smiled. "The customer is always right," she chided, and walked away, slowly, not drawing attention from the shopkeeper, ignoring the young couple who, after some kissing and cuddling, once again erupted into their routine—programmed?—argument.

As she walked, not too slowly, not too fast, she touched her commbadge. "Janeway to Chakotay."

"Chakotay here, Captain. How do you like Oasis? Is it a shopper's paradise as advertised?"

She didn't even bother to explain. "Scan for life forms aboard the station."

"Aye, Captain." Not for the first time, Janeway realized that her first officer was a godsend. There was puzzlement in the calm voice, but Chakotay wouldn't waste precious time in questions, not with her own voice as icy and precise as it was.

A beat, then: "Captain, we're reading only five life

signs, all but one of which are from our ship. Wait. Make that four. When we first arrived, there were at least a hundred people on the station. What's going on?"

The young couple had kissed and made up. Janeway knew that if she strode up to them and tried to talk to them, they would be completely unable to interact with her. Holograms. Everyone here but her crew members was a hologram.

Suddenly Janeway fully registered all of what Chakotay had reported. "You said four. Who's missing?"

A brief pause, then: "Kes. And every ship but *Voyager* has left."

Briefly, Janeway closed her eyes, gathering strength. "Lock onto all life forms and beam them aboard immediately. I'll explain when I'm on board."

The first thing Janeway noticed when she materialized in the transporter room was that every other member of her away team lay limply on the floor, unconscious. There were no marks on the still forms of Neelix and Paris, but Torres's head bore a nasty gash at the base of her skull.

"Emergency beam out to sickbay, all of us," she snapped at the startled looking young woman who had transported them aboard. Immediately the world around Janeway shimmered, and when it became clear again she was standing in sickbay.

The doctor immediately rose, all brusque efficiency. He glanced briefly at his captain with a raised eyebrow. She nodded her head; she was fine. "Well, at least one of you has managed to avoid the usual—" One look from Janeway changed his mind about finishing the comment. In a more constructive vein he said, "Captain, if you don't mind I could use some help getting them on the tables. What happened?" he demanded as he flipped open his medical tricorder.

"I'm hoping you can tell me. We separated about forty-five minutes ago. Are they—"

"They'll be fine," he replied, not taking his dark brown eyes off the readings. "I'll let you know what I find."

Janeway had already turned and was heading for the bridge. If her suspicions were correct, then they couldn't afford to waste any time.

"Status report, Mr. Chakotay," Janeway demanded as she stepped out of the turbolift.

"There are no life forms aboard Oasis at all any more," Chakotay replied. "All of the ships departed some time ago. Captain, what happened down there?"

Janeway didn't answer at once, instead approaching Ensign Harry Kim and handing him the small, shiny oval stone that she had thought contained star charts but now, she suspected, bore more vital information. "Mr. Kim, you need to get someone on translating this immediately."

"Aye, Captain," the young man replied.

"Mr. Tuvok, I understand that the other ships docked at Oasis departed some time ago. I need you to get to work on tracking them."

The Vulcan nodded his comprehension. Briskly Janeway strode to her command chair. "There's an old Earth term for the roles in which we were cast, Mr. Chakotay, and that term is sucker."

"I'm afraid I don't understand."

"I wish I didn't." She tapped her commbadge. "Bridge to sickbay. What happened to the patients, Doctor?"

"A variety of things," came the doctor's dry voice. "Mr. Paris was drugged, Ms. Torres was bashed over the head with a blunt object of some sort, and Mr. Neelix, in a curiously satisfying bit of irony, was poisoned."

"How are they doing?"

"They're all fine, though Mr. Neelix seems quite agitated that Kes did not return with the rest of you." A pause, then: "I confess, I share his concern."

"We all do, Doctor. Please tell the away team to report to the conference room the minute you're able to release them. Bridge out."

No doubt the doctor sensed the urgency of the matter, for within five minutes the senior officers were gathered in the conference room. Janeway took a few seconds to size them all up before voicing her concerns and suspicions. Tuvok's dark visage was as calm as ever. Paris looked a little haggard, but the predominant expression on his handsome face was worry, a worry that was nakedly manifested upon Neelix's plain, blunt features. Torres was silent and thin lipped with controlled anger. Kim and Chakotay looked puzzled but expectant.

Janeway took a deep breath, then summed up what had happened to her on Oasis. Neelix, Torres, and Paris each took a turn, explaining the mysterious attacks perpetrated upon them.

"I suspect I narrowly avoided such an encounter myself," said Janeway. "If it hadn't been for the holograms of the two young lovers and their argument, I'm sure I would have gone to the back of that shop without even thinking about it. Mr. Kim, any progress on translating the information that Yashar gave us?"

"Yes, and it's puzzling, given what's happened," Kim replied. "It's exactly what he said it would be. Star charts. No message, nothing."

"It could be that Aren Yashar thought we might translate the information at once," volunteered Tuvok. "He would not want to tip his hand by delivering a gloating message without being certain of his success."

"What happened while we were away?" Janeway asked Chakotay. "Anything unusual?"

"Absolutely nothing," her first officer replied. "None of the ships made any hostile moves. We weren't even scanned."

"So the only thing that's happened is that three of us were temporarily put out of commission—and clearly they would have had the captain, too, if they could have—and Kes was taken," said Paris. "Is that it?"

"Isn't that *enough?*"

The voice was Neelix's, the words a hurt, aching cry.

"Neelix—" Janeway began, gently.

"No! I won't be calmed down by being Neelixed, not this time. Kes and I may not be together as we once were, but that doesn't mean she isn't dearer to me than life itself!"

"Neelix," said Janeway, more harshly this time, "Everyone here cares about Kes a great deal. And we'll do everything we can to find her once we figure out just what is going on."

"It's so odd, so elaborate," said Torres. "All the holograms, the shops, each of us being attacked but no attempt made to kill us, no attempt to take the ship. It just doesn't make sense."

"It makes perfect sense!" Neelix exploded. "Don't you see? We travel along as if *Voyager* is the best ship in the quadrant. We assume that everyone is like the Kazon, that they all want a piece of our wonderful technology. And it is wonderful, but it is not everyone's ultimate goal."

Everyone was staring at him now. Janeway held her tongue. Neelix obviously needed to speak and she was wise enough to let him air his grievances before they moved on.

"Someone set a very elaborate trap, that's for certain. But you know what? It wasn't for our technology. It wasn't for *Voyager*. This whole thing was orchestrated for just one purpose, a horrible purpose that was completely achieved. *And that one purpose was to kidnap Kes!*"

CHAPTER 3

CAPTAIN'S LOG, STARDATE 50573.2. A SECOND AWAY TEAM has confirmed our first theory. Nearly everything on Oasis, save the most dilapidated of internal structures, was holographic. It would appear that no one save Kes's abductors had been on Oasis for years. We found hundreds of emitters, each programmed for a different scenario. Some, like my pair of young lovers, were very straightforward and never designed to interact with living beings, while others, such as Lieutenant Paris's bar, were extremely complicated. Though this indicates an extremely high level of technology, the fact that some of the holograms were so simple indicates a limited number of resources. This station was no real base for anyone, merely an ideal location for a trap.

Much as we aboard Voyager have learned to value Kes's contributions, we remain utterly at a loss as to why someone would set up so complex a trap for one *member of the crew, and indeed, a member with the least amount of useful knowledge of our technology. Perhaps they were in need of her medical skills. But in that case, why not kidnap the doctor? They obviously are familiar with holographic emitters and could use him very effectively.*

Armed with as much information about our enemy as we can glean from the ruins of Oasis, we are attempting to track the vessel that absconded with Kes. However, some things are easier said than done.

Harry Kim sighed, leaned back, and knuckled his reddened eyes.

"I don't understand it," said B'Elanna Torres for the umpteenth time. Her fingers drummed an impatient tattoo on the console. "They can't simply have vanished."

Anger and frustration simmered in her voice. The incident had shaken the entire crew. Torres in particular had reacted badly, with embarrassment and contained rage combined in a vitriolic brew. Somehow, she seemed to think that she should have expected the attack, even though there hadn't been the slightest reason to believe anything was amiss on Oasis. Somehow, she seemed to think she should have stopped it, prevented Kes's kidnapping, and saved Neelix and Paris in the bargain.

Kim started to reply, also for the umpteenth time, that the ships could have some sort of cloaking technology, but he closed his mouth. Torres would then answer, as she had repeatedly, that they had looked for that and found no indication of it. And he would then insist, again, that perhaps these aliens had different cloaking technology that could remain undiscovered by the Federation's tachyon detection grid technique and . . .

Isn't it amazing, thought Kim with a good deal of sarcasm, *all the conversations you can have without ever opening your mouth.*

Torres sulked a moment longer, than sat erect in her chair. She squared her shoulders in a gesture of stubborn defiance. "Let's take a look at this one more time."

Inwardly, Kim groaned.

The chief engineer pointed to the colorful schematic on the computer screen. "Okay. This is what Oasis looked like when we entered into orbit."

Kim stared dully at the images of the slowly turning space station with the three ships of varying types snugly docked in the port. They blurred around the edges as he gazed at them. He blinked hard to clear his vision.

Rapidly Torres tapped on the computer keypads. The image shifted. "This is approximately forty minutes later." The three ships disengaged, almost simultaneously, and headed off in three different directions. "And about thirty minutes after that, Captain Janeway found out that something was wrong. So they've got a half-hour lead on us."

"Half hour," repeated Kim, his voice slightly slurred with exhaustion. "B'Elanna—"

"We tracked the first one's warp particle trail. Dead end. Second and third, the same. How is it possible, Harry?" She turned her dark-fire eyes upon him almost accusingly, as if he had the answers. "How could they just *disappear?* There's not the slightest trace of tachyon emissions or anything that would even hint at the activation of a cloaking device!"

Harry felt his head droop and he jerked it upright. "B'Elanna," he began, as gently as he could, "it's oh three thirty. We've done pretty well on Neelix's coffee thus far, but if we keep this up much longer I'm going to start seeing white rabbits with pocket watches running around."

She narrowed her eyes. "What the hell are you talking about, Starfleet?"

Kim was suddenly embarrassed. "You know," he stammered as he felt his face grow hot, *"Alice in Wonderland.* Didn't your mom read that to you when you were a kid?"

A shadow fell on Torres's face. "My mother never read to me," she replied softly.

Kim closed his eyes. Foot in mouth again. "Well, anyway, it's a children's story. Alice was chasing the white rabbit and fell through the rabbit hole, and . . ."

His voice trailed off. He looked at B'Elanna, confused. Her eyes were suddenly distant, unfocused, and he knew that was a sign that her mind was working at warp speed.

"Fell through the rabbit hole," she echoed softly. She rapidly keyed in some information and gazed at the schematic. "There's something out of the ordinary going on here, Harry. Not a wormhole, no, but something else, something that we haven't thought of yet." She turned to him, grinning. *"Alice in Wonder-*

land, huh? Tell me more." At Harry's look of utter confusion, she added, "This is what we call brainstorming, Starfleet. Get our minds out of the rut of the typical. C'mon, what else?"

"Torres, you have totally lost me."

"Nothing new there." She softened the words with a friendly wink. "So, what else?"

Kim took another swig of the bitter concoction that passed for coffee and thought. Surrendering to the situation, he began to simply spout images as they came to him.

"Queen of Hearts. Caterpillars on mushrooms, the Mad Hatter. Dormouse. Um, *Through the Looking Glass.* Off with their heads . . . um, tea party—"

"Wait. Looking glass. That's a mirror, right?" Kim nodded. "Okay, let's run with that. Reflection, funhouse mirror, distortion—oh, my god, Harry, that's it!"

He started to ask what, and then he knew. All hints of sleepiness evaporated as he suddenly realized he *knew.* "They're somehow reflecting their true path, putting us on a false trail!" he cried.

He was crowding Torres at the computer console, anxious to test their newfound theory that had come to them via Lewis Carroll. But Torres had the edge and was already tapping in information. Harry gnawed at his lower lip. The fraction of a second that it took for the computer to input the new information seemed to last an eternity. This was more than an intellectual exercise. Being able to track these alien ships quickly might mean the difference between life and death for Kes.

Tiny, almost undetectable traces of warp particles appeared, but not leading off from where the ships had apparently come to a dead end. This trail—for indeed there was only one, along which all three of the alien vessels had traveled—led in a fourth direction, in a line as straight as the others had been winding, indicating a single purpose and a clearly defined destination. Had Kim and Torres not searched specifically in that location, they would never have found it.

"Tricky devils," breathed Torres. "But we've got you now." Her eyes sparkled with triumph.

"Not a cloaking device—some kind of displacer technology. They're able to give the impression that they're in one place when actually they're somewhere entirely different," said Kim. "If our equipment hadn't been as advanced as it is, we'd never have found them."

"We'd never even have thought to look for this if you hadn't remembered your Alice in Wonderland story," said Torres.

"Next time we're stumped, I'll make sure I consult *Winnie the Pooh.*"

Torres looked puzzled but Kim was too busy laughing—much harder than his joke called for—to respond. It was good to laugh, though; good to know they were finally doing something that would bring them closer to Kes. These last few hours had been filled with nothing but growing resentment and frustration at their helplessness. No longer.

"It makes perfect sense," he said. "B'Elanna, I think we may be dealing with—what did Aren call them—pirates."

"The Ja'in," said Torres. "You're right. It makes sense that a group of pirates would focus their knowledge to develop this kind of technology. I mean, think about it. What do they want most, other than finding targets to attack? The ability to shake pursuit."

"And until we came along," Kim finished excitedly, "they probably got away with it every time."

"It's going to take some doing to reconfigure the sensors to compensate for this—this displacer technology. Otherwise we'll be guessing every time they take a turn," said Torres. "How about it, Starfleet? Still want to call it a night?"

"Not on your life," Kim retorted. "I'll get us some more coffee."

As usual, Captain Janeway was incredibly proud of her crew. Kim and Torres had woken her early—at 0512—but she hadn't minded a bit, not with the news they had for her.

"They've been using some kind of displacer technology," Kim's crisp voice told Janeway as she sat up in bed, her whole body straining to listen. "Something that made them appear someplace they weren't. But Lieutenant Torres and I have been able to reconfigure the sensors to compensate. They may try it a dozen times, but we won't fall for that trick again."

"Mr. Kim, you and Lieutenant Torres are a wonder. How did you ever think to look for that?" She was up, brushing her hair vigorously, staring out at the stars streaking past her window but not really seeing them.

There was a pause. "Mr. Kim?"

"We—we made a series of logical calculations based on the information we had at hand, Captain." His voice was not as certain as his words, and Janeway grinned as she moved toward the sonic shower.

"Of course you did," she said with false heartiness. "I'd expect nothing less from my crew. Notify Commander Chakotay and the rest of the senior staff. There'll be no more sleep tonight for any of us. Kes's kidnappers have a sizable lead and I want to close that gap. Give me fifteen minutes and I'll meet you on the bridge."

"Aye, Captain."

She'd gotten there in ten, pleased to see that the rest of the officers were either there or on their way. "Where are they, Mr. Kim?" asked the captain.

"Now that we know what to look for, they're leaving quite a trail," Kim replied. Janeway noted the circles under his eyes, but his body posture and voice bespoke attentiveness. "Their course is zero point four six mark five."

"Mr. Paris—"

"Laying it in, Captain," replied the blond lieutenant, anticipating Janeway's request. His slim fingers flew across the controls.

"I want us on that trail like bloodhounds, Mr. Paris. Warp eight." She glanced over at Chakotay, shared a quick grin with him. His dark eyes shone and as he smiled, they crinkled at the edges. She'd compared them with bloodhounds, but she thought that Chakotay—and herself, when she'd admit it—were more like wolves on the hunt. The Ja'in, for so it probably was, had stolen one of their own, one of their cubs. And the alpha pair of this particular pack was going to get her back.

Janeway craned her neck to look at Ensign Harry Kim. "Mr. Kim, you look tired. Have you and Torres been up all night working this out?"

His boyish face fell. "Y—yes, Captain. But I feel fine," he added quickly.

"Adrenaline will do that to you," Janeway agreed. "But sleep is better."

"Captain, I'd much rather remain at my post. What if they try another trick?"

Janeway permitted herself a chuckle. "You've done extremely well, Harry. Get yourself a cup of real coffee and tell B'Elanna to do the same. My treat," she added.

"Yes, Captain. Thank you!"

As the hours ticked by, Janeway wondered if Harry was changing his mind. A couple of hours of sleep would have done them all good. She had thought that warp eight would have closed the lead the Ja'in had, but apparently not.

"Captain," came Tuvok's calm voice, "I'm detecting a great deal of matter up ahead."

"On screen."

There was nothing, save the white lights streaking past them.

"Long range," Janeway said.

This time, something did appear.

"What the hell—" breathed Paris softly.

This area of space was a graveyard. Debris from dozens of ships floated in the cold darkness of space.

Some pieces were small; others were still complete ships, whole save for the holes in their sides gaping open like wounds. Shadows cast by *Voyager's* lights played eerily over the ruination, illuminating letters in a language they did not know that doubtless spelled out the names of these once-proud vessels.

Chakotay found his voice first, and when he spoke it was in hushed, respectful tones.

"How many?"

"The best estimate is over ten thousand ships or pieces of ships," Tuvok replied in his normal cool voice. "But that is only within our sensor range. There is every indication that this—" he paused, and Janeway wondered if, beneath his calm Vulcan exterior Tuvok, too, was moved, "—this collection of debris continues on for several thousand more kilometers."

"Mr. Kim," said Janeway, her voice and expression revealing none of the sense of loss the sight engendered, "does the trail of the three ships take us through this collection of debris?"

"Aye, Captain. Directly."

"In that case, maintain course, Mr. Paris. Drop to impulse when we get within a few hundred kilometers of the first bits of flotsam and jetsam."

"Walk softly," said Chakotay, quite unexpectedly. Janeway knew the rest that Chakotay did not say: For you walk among the dead. She'd heard him utter the respectful words before, when they had come across bodies or a burial site, but she'd never heard her first officer say the words on the bridge, referring to the aftermath of a space battle. Yet it seemed appropriate in the face of such devastation.

To distract herself, Janeway turned her attention to her own console and began to analyze the debris. She raised an eyebrow. This was no recent battle. The wreckage had been turning quietly in space for decades, perhaps centuries.

Something penetrated her muted grief over the dead ships. "Mr. Tuvok, is there any way around this site?"

"Not readily, but yes, if we were to go out of our way."

The nagging voice of warning in her head grew louder. "Why would they come through here if they could go around? They'd have to slow their speed in order to safely maneuver through all this debris."

"The shortest distance is between two points," Chakotay pointed out. "And if they're familiar with the area, they may be willing to risk it. Perhaps they think it might deter pursuit."

Janeway sat upright in her chair, her slim body tense. "They're familiar with the area, all right. I'm willing to bet a year's rations this is a trap. Shields up. All hands, battle stations. Red alert!"

At once the bridge lights dimmed and a scarlet light bathed the area. Janeway stared at the screen, her heart thudding inside her chest with excitement, her body tense and her mind focused.

"Keep us going, Mr. Paris, but be ready for an—"

Before she could utter the word *ambush,* eight small ships—much smaller, newer, and more lethal than the derelicts that had provided such fine concealment—leaped into action. Blue bursts of energy exploded from the ships, pounding *Voyager's* shields relentlessly.

"Shields holding," said Tuvok.

"Captain, none of these ships are the ones that were docked at Oasis," said Chakotay. Abruptly the ship rocked from the latest barrage.

"Captain," added Kim, "If these ships weren't on Oasis, then Kes can't be on them. Once we found them, we were able to track them every step of the way. They've encountered no other vessels up till now and there's no evidence that they have transporter technology."

"Besides, anyone who went to all that trouble to get Kes wouldn't put her in the line of fire," added Janeway, nodding an acknowledgment of Kim's words. "Good. Then return fire at will, Tuvok," ordered Janeway. "I was right. They were expecting us and we walked right into it."

"Shields at eighty percent," said Tuvok.

"Tom," barked the captain, "Stay on our original course. No evasive maneuvers."

"Captain?" Normally, Paris didn't question Janeway's commands, especially not in the heat of battle, but she forgave him under the circumstances.

"The longer we're delayed here fighting these ships, the more time the other ships have to get away."

Again the ship rocked. "Casualties coming in," reported Kim. "Decks fourteen and fifteen report damage."

"Keep firing, Tuvok." Scarcely had the words left

her lips than one of the ships took a square hit and flew apart before her eyes. She slitted her eyes against the brightness of the explosion.

"Harry, can you still follow the trail of the original three ships?"

Kim hit several buttons, then shook his dark head. "Negative, Captain. The trail ends here."

"Then they're not fleeing—not yet," said Janeway, digging her nails into the arms of her chair as *Voyager* shuddered beneath the attacks.

"They're hiding," said Chakotay slowly. "They're using the bigger pieces of wreckage as protection while providing a distraction."

"Tuvok, could the combined forces of those eight ships defeat *Voyager?*" Janeway queried, her eyes still fastened to the screen.

"Unlikely. But they could cause severe damage. I suggest we tarry here no longer than is absolutely—"

This time the ship did more than rock. It bucked and heaved, listing violently before a scrambling Tom Paris, half out of his seat, brought it back to an even keel. Janeway herself tumbled out of her chair, striking her head against the arm. She heard her crew cry out as consoles sparked and flamed. For a wild instant the bridge went completely dark, then the emergency backup system kicked in.

Janeway's head throbbed violently and blood trickled into her eyes. She blinked, clearing her vision, and wiped the distracting red fluid away with one hand as she reclaimed her seat. "Report!" she cried, staring at the small ships that darted back and forth on the viewscreen.

"Shields at fifty-six percent," said Kim. "Casualty reports up to twenty-seven now. They're making up in persistence what they lack in technology."

Janeway's mind raced as she caught her breath. "Mr. Tuvok, concentrate fire on any dead ships large enough to conceal smaller ones. Glancing blows. I want to flush them out, not hurt them."

"Aye, Captain." The Vulcan's fingers tapped calmly on the controls. As they watched, red phaser energy sliced through space yet again. But this time, no ship with a living crew suffered. Tuvok had trained the weapon on a huge, hulking piece of gray metal. Part of it blew off, spiraling wildly into space, but most of the ship remained intact. At least, as intact as a dead ship could be.

"Again," ordered Janeway. Lord, but her head hurt.

Tuvok obeyed, concentrating on the other end of the ship. The smaller ships continued their attack, and Janeway listened with half an ear as Kim recited a litany of damage. She was right, she knew she was. She had to be.

She didn't need to tell Tuvok to continue on, directing the phaser fire at every piece of wreckage large enough to serve as a hiding place for the ship that had bolted with Kes. But as piece after piece was blasted, and as the stubborn little ships persisted in their attack, Janeway wondered if she shouldn't back off. She was still convinced that her tactics were the correct ones, but the question was, did they have the time? Could she continue to put her crew's lives at risk on a hunch?

You're out there, you bastards. I know you're there.

And we're going to flush you out like an Irish setter does a quail.

But if they were, they weren't showing themselves. Grimly, Janeway wondered if perhaps her ploy had worked too well, if, despite her caution, Tuvok's fire had destroyed the ship with Kes aboard as it hid in the ruins of larger vessels.

The pain in her head had subsided to a dull ache, and the blood had dried into a crust. She took a deep breath. "Mr. Tuvok—"

"There they are!" yelped Paris, unable to contain himself in his excitement. And sure enough, three small ships, of a design unlike any of those currently attacking *Voyager,* suddenly swooped out of the belly of a dead ship.

"Follow them!" cried Janeway.

Tom Paris needed no urging. His mouth set in a thin, grim line, he swung the ship hard to port and brought it around in hot pursuit. The three ships made no move to defend themselves, though the eight originally embroiled in the battle increased their attack.

The three ships were fast, Janeway had to give them that. *It's like chasing swallows,* she thought as the little vessels dipped and dove. *Voyager* had a great deal of maneuverability for such a large ship—Paris had once quipped that piloting it was like riding a tiger— but their quarry were almost acrobatic. Paris was on them, though, and Janeway knew he'd rather be in a locked room with a phaser on overload than let them get away now.

She knew exactly how he felt.

"The eight ships have abandoned pursuit. They've split off in eight different directions," said Chakotay.

"They're trying to lure us away," Kim volunteered. "They're activating their displacer device in an attempt to confuse us."

"Don't let those three ships out of your sight, Mr. Paris," warned Janeway.

"Don't intend to, ma'am," retorted the lieutenant.

"Begin firing, Tuvok. Aim for their engines. We want them disabled and boardable if possible. Remember, one of them's got Kes."

"Aye, Captain."

The next fifteen minutes seemed to last fifteen years. *Voyager* kept firmly on the tail of the ships, despite all attempts the aliens made to shake the pursuit. Two of them fired back, closing ranks to protect the third.

"How are we doing, Mr. Kim?"

"Not good, Captain. We can't keep this up much longer."

"It looks as though we won't have to," said Chakotay. "The battlefield is thinning. We should be in open space in a few seconds."

"Keep firing, Tuvok. We've got to disable them so they don't jump into warp once we're clear of the debris. Concentrate your fire on the one in the middle."

But the stubborn two escort ships prevented any damage to the vessel they were protecting. They took the phaser fire themselves, and one of them spun off out of control to collide with the hull of an ancient ship in a blinding explosion.

They were running out of time. Paris and Tuvok worked together as a team, the young helmsmen skillfully maneuvering *Voyager* to bring it into position for the clearest, most effective shot, and the Vulcan security chief taking complete advantage of every opportunity thus provided.

"We'll be clear of the debris in ten seconds," said Kim. "Five . . . three . . ."

And space suddenly opened up, peculiarly liberating after the close, dangerous confinement of the wreckage through which they'd been maneuvering. Tuvok got off one final phaser blast, but the remaining escort ship, in a move worthy of a twentieth-century kamikaze pilot, placed itself between the fleeing ship and the phaser fire. It was blown to pieces.

The single remaining vessel went into warp, and was gone.

"Stay on it," said Janeway. Simultaneously, expecting her response, she heard Harry say miserably, "We can't, Captain."

"Why not?" Disappointment filled Janeway, but she was not about to let it show.

"Every time they go into warp, they set up the displacer equation." His fingers continued to move on the console as he spoke. "It's an algorhythmic equation, different every time. We know how to break it, but it'll take a few minutes. I'm sorry, but each time they do this, we've got to figure it out all over again."

Janeway leaned back in her chair. "I know you and Torres are working as fast as you can, Ensign. Carry on."

"Captain," broke in Chakotay's gentle voice, "You should probably take advantage of this lull to have that injury checked out." He nodded at the wound on her head. It was, ironically enough, in the same spot as the first officer's tattoo.

"I will," she promised, "but let's let the doctor treat the more seriously injured first." She hesitated, then said, "He'll have his hands full without Kes to help him. Mr. Paris, once upon a time I had you training with the doctor as a field medic. Think you remember enough to help?"

"I know enough to distinguish a medical tricorder from a standard one," Paris quipped, a hint of his old jauntiness returning to him as he gave Harry a friendly wink.

"Then get yourself down there. I'll let you know when we need your expertise back here." Paris left quickly, his movements full of contained energy, eager to do something—anything—to help.

Janeway could feel the restlessness on the bridge. No one was brash enough to say anything, but they all chafed at the imposed inaction. They wanted Kes back.

Suddenly Janeway thought of someone who probably wanted Kes back more than anyone else on the ship. He'd been wonderful so far, keeping out of their way and letting them do their jobs. But he had to be hurting.

"Commander, you have the conn. I'll be down in the mess hall." She gave Chakotay a sad little smile. "Enjoying a pot of Neelix's coffee."

CHAPTER
4

THERE WAS THE FAMILIAR SOUND OF BANGING AND CLANG-
ing as Janeway entered the mess hall, and odors—
some pleasant, some not so pleasant—assaulted her
nose. Just like the rest of them, Neelix was bent on
carrying out his duties despite Kes's absence.

But there was no one in the mess hall to either eat
the food the Talaxian prepared or push it around on
the plate; the rest of the crew was at their stations. No
one on the ship took a break to visit the mess hall—
except the ship's captain.

"Hello, Neelix," she said softly, gazing at him with
compassion.

He turned around quickly at the sound of his name,
and her heart sank even further to see what had
happened to him. His muttonchops hung limply. No
time—no desire?—to spruce them up this morning.
His face was gray and slack, so unlike Neelix's usually

animated visage that Janeway felt a twinge of concern for his welfare.

"Oh, good morning, Captain," he said, but there was no warmth and enthusiasm turning the greeting into a verbal hug. The words held no real welcome. "What may I get you?"

"Just some of your coffee, please," Janeway replied. Hoping to enliven the conversation, she added, "Kim and B'Elanna spoke quite highly of it this morning. Said it gave them what they needed to work through the night and figure out a way to track the ships."

Like water on a thirsty plant, Janeway's words worked wonders. Neelix's head came up and his eyes brightened. "Really? They can track the ships now?"

No thought for kind trivialities about the cooking, Janeway mused. *His only concern is Kes.*

She accepted a mug and downed a swallow, managing not to grimace. It did have a kick like a mule, though, and she was in need of it right now. "Yes indeed. We've been on their trail for the last few hours. We just had a fight with them, too. Perhaps you noticed?"

He frowned, and to her pleasure there was some of the old Neelix annoyance in the expression. "Oh, I noticed. I've spent the last fifteen minutes picking up broken pieces of cookware. And my tulari bulbs— bruised beyond salvaging." His chatter broke off, and the mourning and fear settled on him again. "Kes loved—loves—these. I had hoped to prepare them specially, when we got her back."

Janeway laid a hand on Neelix's, the gesture stilling its restless, aimless movements. "Of any ship in the

galaxy," she began, "the crew of this one most understands what it's like to lose a loved one. We've all left
someone behind—a friend, a parent, a child, a
spouse." *A lover,* her mind added. "And we've all
grown closer as a crew as a result. We're all we've got.
There's not a person on this vessel who hasn't felt
Kes's caring touch as she tended them in sickbay."
She smiled. "Except maybe the doctor. He never gets
sick."

But Neelix did not chuckle at the joke. He was
looking at her now, his yellow eyes glued to hers,
drinking in her words of hope. Briefly, Janeway
thought of those she had loved and lost: her father,
her fiancé Justin, her mother and sister, and dear
Mark; two to death, three to distance. She'd had to
come to grips with their absence from her life, and
even as she formed her next words, she said a silent
prayer that events wouldn't make her a liar. She didn't
want to lose Kes, and she didn't want to see what that
loss would do to the chipper Talaxian.

"We will get her back," she promised, articulating
every word clearly and with determination. She
gripped his hand. His stubby fingers closed around
hers, so hard they hurt. She didn't mind.

With her free hand, she pushed the cup across the
counter toward Neelix. "How about a warm-up?"

The call that they had once again been able to
successfully decipher the Ja'in's tricks came shortly,
and Janeway headed back to the bridge after reassuring Neelix a final time. As she left, his humming was
literally music to her ears.

Stepping onto the bridge, she raised an eyebrow to see the doctor frowning at her. "When Mohammed will not come to the mountain, the mountain must come to Mohammed," he quoted, "and this mountain is rather annoyed that he had to come all the way from sickbay while Mohammed was relaxing with a cup of coffee in the mess."

"It's Neelix's coffee," Janeway protested halfheartedly as she obediently stood still while the doctor quickly treated her injury. "It was hardly relaxing."

"There," he said, a hint of pride tingeing his voice. "The wound is healed. You get to wash the blood off yourself, though."

"I think I can manage that." Automatically she reached to touch the crusted blood on her forehead. "Status report."

"We're back on the trail," Chakotay replied. "Heading four zero mark seven, warp six."

"Let's bring her up to warp eight," said Janeway. "I want to catch them, not just follow them." She stepped briskly toward her ready room, planning to run some water and wash away the blood, when she realized the doctor was following her. "Something on your mind, doctor?"

He looked uncomfortable, so she waved him into her room. The door hissed shut behind them. She indicated that he might have a seat while she ducked into her private head and began to clean her face. "What is it?"

"Captain," he began, ignoring the invitation to sit and pacing restlessly instead, "I need to know. What is your honest opinion about the possibility of recovering Kes?"

She patted her face dry with a towel and stepped back into the main room. "I have every hope that we will."

"It's vital!" the doctor exclaimed, then, as if ashamed of his outburst, amended, "We need her. I was designed as an emergency medical backup system in case something happened to the primary ship's doctor. We need Kes as *my* emergency backup."

"Of course we do. And you miss her as much as any of us, doctor. I understand. We—"

The door hissed open. Chakotay stood in the doorway.

"What is it, Commander?"

"Captain, I think we've reached the end of our trail."

Janeway narrowed her eyes at his hesitant tone and tossed the towel on her desk. "I don't like the sound of this." She hurried outside, followed by the doctor and her first officer, and turned her attention toward the screen.

Before her was a planet, but even the one quick glance she'd had was enough to make her heart sink. A thick, gray-green cloud swirled around it, blocking any clear glimpse of the planet's natural surface. The whole picture was a miasma of sickly colors.

"Ion storm?" she guessed with the knowledge of years spent as a student of science.

"Aye," Kim affirmed.

Janeway felt an almost physical pang of bitter disappointment. The storm roiled with a savage intensity. A tempest that size had almost certainly stripped away any atmosphere the planet might have had.

"Any life signs?" she asked.

Kim shook his head. "None."

Tuvok broke in. "Captain, on the opposite side of the planet I am detecting several vessels."

"Bring *Voyager* around," said Janeway as she seated herself, hope returning to her with a slight flicker. "Let's take a look at them."

But these, too, brought only disappointment. The ships were ancient vessels, long since abandoned and locked in a decaying orbit. Hulking and ugly, they bore no resemblance to the small, easily maneuverable pirate ships *Voyager* had been chasing. A quick glance at her console revealed that they, too, were devoid of life.

"I don't understand," said Chakotay, frowning. "The trail leads here. They have to be here. Kim, could it be that you and B'Elanna somehow miscalculated? Took us to the wrong place?"

Kim again shook his head. "No way, Commander. It's tough to get it at first, but it follows a completely logical and predictable pattern once you've laid in the equation. This is where the ship went, I'm certain of it."

"Then let's look for other options," said Janeway firmly. "If they're here, then we should be picking up signs of life. Therefore, something is blocking our ability to do that. Let's take a harder look at this storm." Her eyes narrowed as she analyzed the graphic on her computer screen. "It's not moving in a normal pattern at all, now that I look more closely at it. It's stationary."

"As if it's deliberately engulfing the planet," added Chakotay. Their eyes met over the computer. "Are you thinking what I'm thinking?"

"I think so," replied Janeway. "Mr. Tuvok, search for any signs that this storm might be artificial—a cover."

"Captain," yelped Kim, "I've got it. There's some kind of distortion field around the planet as well. It didn't register at first because the ion storm made it difficult for our sensors to get a lock on it. There is an atmosphere down there." He ran his fingers lightly over the console and added, "It can support life."

"How convenient," mused the captain, her eyes narrowing speculatively as she gazed at the viewscreen. "A planet with a stationary ion storm and a distortion field that hides any signs of life from prying eyes. Mr. Paris, I understand you're familiar with pirates."

"Uh," stammered the helmsmen. He didn't turn around, but he didn't have to for Janeway to sense his embarrassment; the tips of his ears turned pink. "I've, I've done some research on eighteenth century Earth pirates recently, yes."

Janeway exchanged smiles with Chakotay. "I thought so," she said. "What's your opinion of the present situation?"

"If I were a pirate in this system, I'd want a base that no one would think to look for."

"Exactly. Then take us into orbit, Lieutenant. I think ion storm, not X, marks the spot where we should look for our particular treasure."

Voyager slid smoothly into orbit. That was the last time anything went smoothly. Almost immediately the ship pitched and rolled as if it were under attack.

"Captain, the storm—" began Paris, his voice vibrating with the movement of the ship.

"Compensate!" cried Janeway. A tiny flame of anger began to burn deep inside her. She was tired of being jolted and shaken, her Starfleet vessel being worried like a rat in a terrier's mouth. When they caught up with these pirates—

"Captain, the sensors are going crazy!" If she hadn't known better she would have said Kim's voice had an edge of panic to it. "The readings—nothing's making sense any more!"

The ship was hit hard. The lights dimmed and then flickered wildly. Suddenly Janeway felt herself rising from her seat. She knew what had happened and immediately gripped the arms of her chair hard, even as her lower extremities continued to float upward.

"The artificial gravity has been disrupted!" she cried. "Everyone, hang on! Mister Kim, get it back *now!*" She felt a gentle pressure on her legs and craned her neck, peering upside down at the doctor. The hologram alone had been unaffected by the loss of gravity and was pushing her legs down, gently guiding her back into the chair. She felt a sudden surge of gratitude toward the troublesome twentieth-century meddler Henry Starling. If he had done nothing else, he'd given them the autonomous holographic emitter that enabled the doctor to perform his tasks with much more effectiveness. She was glad he was on the bridge.

"Trying—" Kim had locked his legs around something and was furiously punching controls. Something he did worked, for Janeway abruptly dropped eight inches into the seat of her command chair. The crashes and grunts she heard around her indicated that not everyone else had had such a soft landing.

"Doctor, if there are no serious injuries, get back to sickbay now," she ordered, not even bothering to turn and look at him. There was a pause of a few seconds, presumably while the doctor assessed the situation, and then she heard the soft hiss of the turbolift door opening and closing.

"Tuvok, what hit us?"

"An ion pulse. Unusual, but not unheard of. This storm system appears to be rife with them. It is extremely violent."

She heard a muttering from Paris that sounded suspiciously like "Tell me something I don't know" but chose to ignore it.

"Damage report?"

"The shields are down by forty percent," said Kim. "We've had a lot of injuries from the loss of gravity, but the doc says he's back in sickbay and is trying to handle it all."

"Tom, take us above one of the poles," Janeway instructed. "The storm should be less severe there. We'll be able to avoid the worst of it."

"Aye, Captain." But even as he spoke, she saw the crackling lights that heralded another ion pulse.

"Brace for impact!"

This time when the lights went out, they didn't come on again. The dull emergency lighting was all they had to see by, that and the red, throbbing pulse that signaled that the ship was still on red alert. Janeway swore.

"Tom, we've got to get to that pole!"

Bit by agonizing bit, the ship shook and swung until Paris got them to the planet's south pole. The storm subsided somewhat, but it still swirled angrily. Janeway caught her breath and was about to ask for a status report when Kim interrupted her.

"Captain, we're being hailed!"

"I knew it," said Janeway softly. More loudly, she said, "On screen."

The face that immediately appeared was handsome, intelligent, and bore a supercilious grin. It was also immediately recognizable. Janeway blinked, taken aback. She heard the swift inhaling of breath that told her she was not alone in her surprise.

"Aren Yashar," she said coldly. The Rhulani bowed his glossy black head in acknowledgment.

"Ah, Captain Janeway. We meet again. You impress me. I have the utmost respect for *Voyager* and its crew, but I really wasn't expecting you. Welcome to Mishkara!"

"So you're the leader of the pirates." She'd known he was in league with them, but not that he ranked so high.

Looking pained, Aren held up a webbed hand in offended protest. "Please, Captain. I am the leader of the Ja'in. Pirate is such a vulgar term, don't you agree?"

Janeway rose. Her battered body protested, but she ignored it, buoyed by righteous anger. "A vulgar term for a vulgar profession. Where is Kes?"

"Such forceful tones!" exclaimed Aren in mock horror, the smile still on his handsome face. "You needn't be so belligerent, Captain. Kes is here and utterly unharmed, I assure you. Kes, dearest." He turned and waved to someone offscreen. "Do come and say hello to your captain. She's quite concerned, and I'm anxious to reassure her."

A second later, Kes's face appeared on the viewscreen. Her eyes were large and intense, filled not with fright but with anger. "Kes," said Janeway, unconsciously taking a step forward toward the viewscreen as if she could touch the younger woman, "are you all right? Has he hurt you?"

She shook her blond head. "No, Captain. Aren is telling the truth, about that much, at least. I haven't been mistreated. Is everyone else all right?"

"We're fine," Janeway reassured her.

"There, you see?" Aren stepped forward and started to put an arm around Kes, but she twisted away violently.

That's the girl, thought Janeway with approval. *Don't let him do a damn thing to you.*

Aren reacted well, moving away as if respecting Kes's boundaries. He returned his attention to Janeway.

"I've had enough pleasantries, Aren. Return Kes to

us at once and we'll take no reprisals. You have my word."

"And as half of the Delta quadrant knows, your word is good, Captain," replied Aren smoothly. "But so is mine. Have you checked the star charts I gave you?"

"Yes," Janeway said, reluctantly.

"And were they anything other than what I represented them to be?"

"No."

"Then we have made a fair trade. Kes for the star charts." He shrugged eloquently. "I confess, I don't see the problem."

"You behave as if you know a great deal about us," said Chakotay in his deceptively calm voice before Janeway could respond. "But you know nothing at all if you think we'll leave without one of our crew members."

"Ah, Commander Chakotay," said Aren with incongruous warmth. "They talk about you, too. Pity we couldn't talk under more harmonious circumstances. But enough of this." His smile hardened and his eyes flashed a warning. He moved forward, his face filling the screen. "The trap I laid for Kes hurt no one. I could easily have killed you, Captain, you and every member of your away team. But I let them live and I gave you the information you requested. I did this to prove to you that I bear you no ill will. I have what I wanted. And if you are as wise as the rumors say you are, you will depart Mishkara," and his voice dropped to an icy timbre, "and no one will be hurt.

That is not an offer I grant many who cross my will. Take it, and respect my benevolence."

That was too much for Janeway. "Benevolence? You spy on us to learn our weaknesses. You set an elaborate trap. You drug, poison, and bludgeon three crewmembers and abduct a fourth. You damage my ship when we pursue, which we have every right to do, and injure dozens more of my people. And now you hold Kes hostage by your own admission and you still have the audacity to call yourself *benevolent?*"

"I do," replied Aren, with a stillness in his voice and body that sent a chill down Janeway's spine.

For a long moment, neither of the adversaries spoke. They stood, sizing up one another. Unconsciously, Janeway lifted her chin and narrowed her eyes in defiance.

"We should meet," said Aren finally. "I would have you see Kes's new home. I'm sure it will meet with your approval." Janeway opened her mouth to respond indignantly but Aren forestalled her comment with, "Save your breath, Captain. You may rail at me all you wish once we meet in person, but I tire of this distant form of communication. I'm certain my hospitality will convince you of my sincerity."

"Why should we trust you?"

"I've kept my word thus far. If I assure you that no one will come to harm during our meeting, you may take it to be the truth. We Ja'in are not wholly without honor, Captain Janeway."

"Silence audio," she ordered. When Kim nodded at her that it was safe to speak, she asked her crew, "Opinions?"

"I don't trust this guy any farther than I can throw him," replied Paris immediately.

"I don't either, Mr. Paris, I assure you," his captain said.

"On the other hand," said Chakotay, "I think Neelix was right. I think Kes really was what Aren was after all the time. There's been no attempt on any other crewmember, except to get them out of the way, and Aren does have a point. He didn't kill them when he easily could have."

"He may truly believe that once we see that Kes is being treated well, we will depart of our own volition," said Tuvok. "It seems in accord with his previously established moral standards."

"It may be the only way we can get Kes back," said Chakotay. "We could study the environment, determine its weaknesses. I really don't see that we have any better choices. We have no idea where she is or how to get to her."

"Agreed, though I don't like it. Ensign, resume audio." She turned again toward the screen. "Very well, Aren. We'll transport down immediately."

"Impossible, I'm afraid. If you have your Mr. Kim check, you'll see that your transporter technology won't be able to penetrate Mishkara's distortion field. You'll have to take one of your shuttlecrafts. I'm transmitting the coordinates now. And please leave your phasers on the ship."

Janeway didn't like this one bit. He knew far, far too much about them.

"Ensign?"

"He's right, Captain."

"All right, Commander Yashar," said Janeway, deliberately choosing the second name and thus emphasizing the formality of the situation. "A group of us will—"

"I will tell you who to bring," and though his voice was soft, there was an edge to it. "I would like to see you, your Vulcan Tuvok, the interesting half-breed B'Elanna Torres, Mr. Neelix—for old time's sake on behalf of my dear Kes—one of those funny blue-green people, and one other of your choosing, Captain." His eyes danced. "Pick somebody fun, Captain, somebody different, entertaining."

"Janeway out." She felt that if she continued this conversation a moment longer, she'd run the risk of losing control. And she couldn't permit that to happen. Aren opened his mouth indignantly to protest, then his face was replaced by the image of Mishkara and its surrounding stars.

"What a jerk!" said Paris.

"That, Mr. Paris," said Janeway, her own voice rich with contempt, "is an understatement." She turned to Chakotay. "Let's go, Tuvok. You're in charge, Commander. Notify the docking bay to ready a shuttlecraft for us, and tell Ensign Bokk to meet us there. Mr. Paris, you're with us. We could use a good pilot to get through that storm and besides," she added with a touch of dark humor, "Aren wanted someone unusual, and it'll make me feel better to have someone as ordinary as you to fill that final slot."

"Nice to know that my captain fully appreciates all my stellar qualities," said Paris dryly as he rose.

"A suggestion," said Tuvok. "This is likely to be a

trap. Yashar could be attempting to hold any or all of us hostage as well. It seems to be Kes that he is after, but we don't know that for a certainty."

"Go on," said Janeway. "What are you getting at?"

"If he kidnaps anyone else, it will most likely be you, Captain. In which case we will need to locate both you and Kes. I suggest implanting a subdermal modified radioactive isotope. That way if we are separated, we will have a way of tracking you."

"And it will help us to find Kes again if we're forced to make a second attempt," finished Janeway. "Brilliant, Tuvok. The sort of devious solution I've come to expect from you." Tuvok raised an eyebrow. "Very logical too, of course," she added with a barely discernable twinkle in her eye. The Vulcan did not respond, but his brow descended.

"I don't quite understand," admitted Paris as the three of them stepped into the turbolift.

"Sickbay," Janeway instructed. Then she turned toward Paris, "The doctor will implant an isotope just beneath my skin that will give out a very subtle radioactive signal. The signal is a standard Starfleet pattern, so we'll easily be able to recognize it. Everywhere I go, it'll leave a trail we can follow."

"I get it," said Paris. "Hansel and Gretel and the trail of breadcrumbs."

"Precisely," smiled Janeway. Tuvok looked from one to the other of them impassively.

"There are times when I truly do not understand human behavior," said Tuvok. Janeway wondered if there weren't a hint of exasperation in his normally modulated voice. She and Paris exchanged a grin at Tuvok's expense. Her smile faded, though, as they sped toward the shuttle bay. With the sensors inoperative, they had no idea what might be awaiting them on the hidden surface of Mishkara.

CHAPTER
5

WHEN THE SHUTTLECRAFT HIT THE ION STORM, JANEWAY briefly allowed herself the luxury of wondering if she hadn't taken Torres, Paris, Bokk, Neelix, and Tuvok on a fool's errand. The little vessel was knocked crazily about by the storm like a giant child's favorite plaything. For a few seconds that seemed like an eternity, Paris could do nothing. Then, he and Janeway managed to regain control of the shuttlecraft and direct it away from the worst of the onslaught, heading down toward the atmosphere—at least, what remained of it under the protection of the distortion field.

Gradually, the ferocity eased and at last disappeared altogether. Janeway gasped, realizing that for a brief time she'd been holding her breath, and became aware of the degree of her dishevelment. Tendrils of hair that had escaped the barrette clung wetly to her face. The place on her arm where the doctor had injected the radioactive isotope itched furiously, but Janeway didn't dare scratch. She glanced over at Tom, who looked similarly shaken, and wordlessly inquired if he had control of the vessel now. As if reading her thoughts, he nodded.

She took a moment to stretch and rearrange her hair, wiping her face. It was important that she look calm and not shaken while negotiating with Aren. Now that the worst was past, she could take a moment to assess what she could see of Mishkara.

It was not the friendliest of planets. The ion storm had shut out most of the light Mishkara received from the nearby yellow star, and everything was a dim gray-green. The land beneath them, while too far away for Janeway to discern details, looked barren. Brown and rocky, it appeared devoid of plants or indeed any signs of life.

"Goodness, what a nasty place," commented Ensign Bokk. The Bolian was peering out the window, his blue face puckered in disgust.

"Poor Kes," said Neelix, softly. "Trapped on this dead rock with that monster—" He couldn't continue.

Janeway turned around in her seat as Tom continued to take them in. "I understand that our emotions are going to be running high," she said to her away team. "But we can't give in to them. Take your cues from me and Tuvok. If Aren thinks he's got us riled and angry, it will only give him an advantage. Is this understood?"

They nodded, regarding her seriously. Janeway

returned her attention to the window and got her first good look at their ultimate destination.

When she was a small child, Janeway had been given an antique snow globe as a birthday present. She'd been enchanted with the toy, constantly shaking it and turning it upside down to make the small white flakes float down upon the tiny cabin and trees housed within the glass. But she'd been careless with the precious gift one day, setting it down too close to the edge of a table. A subsequent romp with her dog, Bramble, had resulted in both of them crashing into the table. To this day, Janeway remembered watching with horror as the globe teetered, seemed to recover, then tumbled to the floor. Its glass had broken on impact. Water filled with bits of tiny "snowflakes" splattered everywhere, and the globe landed on its side, a dreadful hole in the glass, the last of the magic bleeding away like life from a dying man.

Before her was an image of that snow dome writ large.

Clear as glass, an environmental bubble arched into the sky. Once, it must have sheltered hundreds, perhaps thousands, from the harsh natural environment of the planet. But as they descended into their approach, Janeway could see that the hemisphere had been shattered and all the protection it offered was gone. Had someone or something tried to break in— or out? Had there been a dreadful accident? These were questions that Janeway would perhaps never find the answers to and she banished them from her thoughts, focusing her attention on assisting Paris as he navigated the small vessel in through the gaping hole.

Out of the corner of her eye Janeway caught brief images of what remained of the enclosed civilization: dilapidated buildings, forgotten roadways, fields that boasted no crops. Her attention was on the landing pad that appeared a few meters ahead, seeming strangely new and colorful amid the ruins.

Paris punched a few buttons and the shuttlecraft gently began to descend, landing easily. Janeway took a deep breath, made eye contact with every member of her team, and prepared herself.

She didn't have long to wait. Barely had the shuttlecraft come to a full stop than there came the loud pounding of a fist on the walls. "Our welcoming committee, no doubt," said Tom Paris. He hit the release button and the door opened, the ramp slowly extending.

Seven armed guards, all of varying strange but humanoid species, stood impassively outside. Their weapons were trained on the away team. "Please step outside," said one in a harsh voice that turned the request into an order.

Janeway complied, with a movement of her head silently instructing her team to do the same. They followed her, striding down the ramp onto the landing platform. Janeway expected them to be scanned or perhaps even physically searched, but five of the armed aliens merely stood silently, guarding them, while two of their number disappeared into the shuttlecraft. "There is no one else inside," one of them told the leader as they emerged. "We searched thoroughly."

The tall, exceedingly thin humanoid to whom the comments were addressed nodded. "Good," it said, and Janeway's commbadge translated the voice as feminine and harsh. "Please follow us, Captain Janeway. The Commander awaits your presence."

She turned on her heel and began taking long, swift strides toward the interior of the space the bubble had once safely enclosed. The *Voyager* crew followed, having to jog from time to time to keep up. The remaining guards closed ranks about them. They no longer trained their weapons on the Federation crew, but their body language was clear: Do not try to run.

The guards' height was such that Janeway caught only the barest glimpses of their surroundings, little more than what she had first seen—buildings long since abandoned, streets not in use and cluttered with rubble. Her lungs began to heave with the mild exertion and she mentally made a note of it. *Breathable, certainly, but not oxygen rich; we can stay here but not for long.*

Their jog-walk brought them to an enormous building that towered over them oppressively. It, like all the other structures Janeway had seen, was old, but this one had been kept up better. One of the guards stepped forward and flipped open a panel. Its long digits moved, typing in a code of some sort. It felt Janeway's gaze, and moved its body so that she couldn't see.

With a groan of aged metal, a door slid upward, revealing a small room. With her weapon, the head guard gestured that they step inside. When they had done so, another guard keyed in a second code. The doors closed and the light all but vanished. The small, boxy room began to move with jerky, alarming movements.

"It's a turbolift!" exclaimed Bokk.

"Quiet," rumbled one of the guards ominously. He shifted his weapon to underscore his point, the faint light glinting off the metal. Pressed close beside Janeway, Neelix took a deep breath, but fortunately had the sense to remain quiet.

They seemed to descend forever. Janeway was silently glad of the radioactive isotope hidden just beneath the surface of her arm. She deeply suspected a trap, and was just as glad that she'd given her first officer a way to track them if necessary.

Down, down, down they went. Janeway fought an urge to rub her arms to protect against the cold. The guards seemed impervious to it, but she could tell her crew was uncomfortable.

Just when she was about to wonder if this particular voyage led to the center of the planet, they bumped to a stop. The doors opened again, and Janeway blinked hard against the light, harsh on the eyes after the comparative darkness of the dimly illuminated turbolift.

A cold prod from a weapon at her side told Janeway to move forward and she stepped out into a winding corridor, though not without a quick glance around to determine what level they might be on. There was no information to be had, and a second, less gentle poke with the hard end of the metal weapon told her she'd better quit looking around.

She strode forward briskly, her head high, sensing her crew following. The floor beneath them was padded and the sound of her boots was muffled, softened. The walls had been covered with a shimmering fabric of some sort to disguise their true barren metal. They passed various doors; Janeway counted four before the head guard came to an abrupt halt.

"The Commander awaits," she intoned, and opened the door.

Janeway had spent several years learning to guard her emotions in diplomatic situations. That was the only reason her jaw did not literally drop. However, her eyebrows did reach for her hairline in surprise as she entered the room. Behind her, she heard gasps from those less disciplined.

Nothing she had seen on the surface or underground had prepared her for the sumptuousness of Aren Yashar's private quarters. They seemed to stretch on for an eternity, almost obscenely spacious in comparison with the claustrophobic turbolift and cramped corridors down which the *Voyager* team had just come. Soft, thick carpeting of a delicate, pale blue hue covered every inch of floor. The walls were covered with exquisite mosaics. Light poured from recesses in the ceiling, a bright, natural light that imitated sunlight to perfection. Beautiful tables and chairs and pillows practically cried out to be used. Paintings and statuary and healthy green plants adorned the tables and the shelves that lined the walls. From somewhere came music—soothing and haunting—that plucked teasingly at the mind even as it caressed the ears.

Against such a background, Kes's simple loveliness might have been expected to fade. Instead, she shone more radiant than anything crafted as she stood beside the long table, clad in her simple rust-colored jumpsuit, her small hands tightly laced together, blue eyes peering out of a pale, taut face with a mingled expression of hope, fear, and determination.

"Kes," breathed Janeway, and took a step toward her.

Her movement was halted by a feathery touch on her arm. She flinched away from it and glared at Aren Yashar, who had seemingly manifested from nowhere; she refused to be dazzled by the change in his appearance.

He was still handsome, though Janeway now saw the smile as cruel rather than welcoming. He had unbound much of his hair and it flowed over his shoulders in an ebony wave. A strand of jewels encircled his throat and his forehead, and dangled from his ears. His robes were soft as silk, green as tender young shoots of grass, and revealed hints of a strong, muscular body beneath their shifting shadows. He seemed taller than he had on Oasis, taller and more in control.

Janeway straightened and stuck her chin out in defiance. "We have come as you requested. Let us go to our crewmate."

"Oh, by all means, enter, make yourselves at home! Kes is." Janeway glanced over at the Ocampan, and

Kes most certainly did *not* look at home. A few quick steps, and Kes was in her arms. Janeway embraced the girl's shivering frame and whispered into her pointed ear, "We'll get you out of here, Kes." Then the others were there, anxious to reassure themselves that she was all right—Tuvok assessing her with a speculative gaze, Paris hugging her, Bokk and Torres smiling reassuringly, and Neelix, poor Neelix, looking lost and forlorn until Kes turned and hugged him tightly. Janeway turned away from the expression on the Talaxian's face as Neelix returned the embrace.

"Now, let me see," said Aren, his voice almost bubbly. His eyes sparkled as he gazed at the crew. "Lieutenant Tuvok. A Vulcan. Suppresses emotion and relies on logic to solve all his problems. That's not a fun way to live, is it? And the ears—at first I thought they were like Kes's, but I see now they're different. Absolutely fascinating."

Tuvok's face did not move a muscle, but his eyes snapped fire. "Ah, ah, Mr. Vulcan—as Neelix likes to call you—you look as if you're getting annoyed with me!" Aren wagged a finger an inch in front of Tuvok's face and moved on to another target.

"And a Bolian. Such lovely skin. You quite match the carpeting, Ensign!" Aren threw back his dark head and laughed, a free, ringing sound. The *Voyager* crew remained stonily silent. Heavy-set Bokk shifted uncomfortably and glanced over at his captain for reassurance. "And the ridge. Is it solid or pliable?" He reached out a hand as if to find out for himself, when Janeway's voice halted him.

"We are here to negotiate for Kes's release," she said in a cold tone, "not to serve as creatures for your amusement."

"Wrong on both counts, Captain—but what a poor host I am. Please, sit, and let me get you something to drink." When no one moved, his eyes narrowed. "That was not a suggestion."

The crew turned to Janeway and she nodded, taking a seat herself at the long black table. The rest of her people complied, though no one sat comfortably. Aren busied himself with filling eight delicate glasses full of a bright orange liquor and passing them out as he spoke.

"First, Captain, let me tell you a little bit about myself, in an effort to foster mutual understanding. I am, as you know, a Rhulani." He cast a quick glance at her, his eyes sparkling impishly. "How old do you think I am?"

"You know I have no way of telling," Janeway replied, her annoyance creeping into her voice. She accepted the goblet but put it down untouched.

"Exactly. From what I've been able to determine about you humans, I probably appear to you to be— oh, let's say thirty-five of your years. In actuality, I am over four thousand, two hundred of your years. And I am still considered quite young among my people."

He paused to let this sink in, and continued handing out the drinks. "Mr. Neelix, I do hope you find this to your liking. I'd be happy to send along a few bottles with you when you leave."

Neelix's face flushed, but he bit his tongue. Janeway

admired his restraint. The offer of a few bottles of alcohol in exchange for Kes must have infuriated him. "And for you, dear lady B'Elanna. Half Klingon, half human—what a struggle everyday life must be for you! The ridges, do they hurt?"

Inwardly, Janeway braced herself for Torres's attack on Aren. The chief engineer, though, merely tightened her jaw and accepted the drink. By the way her fingers curled around the delicate goblet, though, Janeway could tell that the restraint was costing B'Elanna dearly.

It was costing them all, and she knew it. She could only hope that it was worth it.

"And Lieutenant Tom Paris. A simple human male." Tom snatched the glass, glaring at his host as Aren turned to Janeway, clucking his tongue in remonstrance. "I told you to bring someone interesting, Captain. I'm afraid another human is a bit, well, dull."

He now lay back on a pile of cushions and sipped at the drink. "When you are as old as I am, you see a great deal. There isn't much in this quadrant that I haven't heard of, and things that arouse my interest are precious and rarer than gemstones, of which, incidentally, Mishkara has a great many. When my spies brought me word of your ship—and specifically, word of Kes—I knew I had to have her."

He reached out his long fingers, and the beautiful colors of the webbing between them flashed briefly. He touched Kes's cheek softly, and the Ocampan winced and drew back.

"Much beauty have I seen; much beauty have I had,

Captain Janeway." His voice was hushed, almost reverent, and his face lost its sly calculation as he gazed at Kes. "But never have I seen nor possessed such beauty as this. And all the sweeter for its brevity."

He turned toward Janeway, almost pleading. "Nine years, Captain. *Nine years!* That's all the time she has. Isn't that staggering, humbling, almost overwhelming? How soon the flower withers, but how unspeakably lovely it is while it is in bloom!"

"That's it," said Paris, slapping his thighs with his hands and starting to rise.

"As you were, Lieutenant," ordered Janeway. "Commander Yashar, I've had just about enough of this."

"But you haven't even touched your drink," quipped the pirate leader, deliberately misunderstanding her.

Janeway rose, fighting back her temper. She planted her hands firmly on her hips and stared down at Aren. "We consider ourselves a patient people—"

"And which people would that be? There are so many types of you Alpha quadranters!"

"—but you are pushing the limits. We came here to talk." Janeway's eyes flashed. "You'd better start saying something that I want to hear."

"Or what?" Aren chuckled. "You wouldn't dare take Kes by force, not when my guards outnumber you, what, a hundred to one?"

"Don't tempt me," growled Torres.

Without even glancing back at her chief engineer Janeway raised a commanding hand. Torres fell silent.

"Return Kes," said Janeway softly, each word laden with intensity.

Aren's lazy smile grew. "Why should I?"

"I suppose the fact that it would be the right thing to do doesn't enter into your thinking," said Neelix.

Aren ignored him. "Why should I do something for nothing? What do you propose to do for me, Captain Janeway?" He rose, somehow maneuvering out of the soft, lumpy pillows with utter grace. They stood eye to eye now, the commander of the pirates and the captain of the Federation starship. "What do you offer in exchange?" He paused, seemed to think, and said brightly, "Why, how about *Voyager?*"

"You aren't interested in talking at all, are you, Aren?" said Janeway, her tones clipped and harsh. "You've no intention of letting Kes go under any circumstances. This," and she gestured at the spacious room, "this was all just to flex your muscle, wasn't it? A grand show, to impress us. We don't impress that easily."

"Captain, please!" Kes's voice, soft as ever, trembled. Janeway turned to look at her. "You're both acting as if I'm some kind of trophy or something. I'm not. I'm a person." Janeway realized abruptly that Kes was absolutely right. She stepped back, letting the young woman speak for herself.

Kes turned to face Aren, staring up at him determinedly. "Aren, this is wrong. I don't want to be here. I want to be with my friends, free to go wherever I want. This is beautiful, yes, but a cage is a cage, no matter how lovely."

"Kes," and Aren softened as he looked at her, "You

say that only because you don't really understand what I'm offering you. Give me time. You'll see."

He took a deep breath and squared his shoulders. "There were other things I had planned to show you, Captain. Our version of your holodeck. A hydroponics bay, which I specifically acquired for Kes's pleasure. This is no prison. I'd hoped to make you see that. I'd hoped we could dine together and chat pleasantly." He glanced about, and his expression became almost wistful. "So many interesting new races. The conversations we could have had!

"But you have clearly stated that you have no interest in such pleasant pursuits. I respect that, Captain Janeway, though I'm sorry. I'm afraid I must ask you to leave."

"We won't leave without Kes," said Janeway, but it was a hollow threat and she knew it. They'd have to— for now.

"Yes, you will. And consider yourself lucky that I'm not a vengeful man." He snapped his fingers and at once the armed guards who had escorted them in appeared, their weapons held loosely, comfortably, in their arms.

Janeway allowed herself one last, long, evaluating look at the commander of the pirates.

"You're letting us go? Just like that?"

"Just like that," Yashar echoed. "Captain, I am a Ja'in, not a murderer. Why shouldn't I let you go? You are no threat to me."

You've won this round, Yashar, she thought to herself, *but you won't win the next one.*

* * *

"I'm not buying this. He's really letting us go?" said Paris rhetorically even as he tapped in the commands for liftoff.

"It would appear so," said Tuvok. "Although I must admit, Lieutenant, I share your suspicions. Captain, there must be a reason Aren is permitting us to depart unchallenged."

Janeway, her eyes on her own console, nodded absently. "Agreed, Mr. Tuvok. I don't believe he's really done with us yet. He clearly seems to think that whatever weapons he has on hand are enough to handle *Voyager,* and that's an unsettling thought. We may despise him, but we don't dare underestimate him. Whatever he is, Aren Yashar is no fool."

She glanced up for a brief moment as the shuttle-craft began to ascend, looking around at the guards who, while still holding their weapons, were not aiming them at the departing visitors. The vessel rose and began to speed toward the rendezvous coordinates with *Voyager.* There had been no attempt to halt their departure, to challenge them, nor even, she mused, to follow them.

"So, Captain," came Neelix's conspiratorial voice as he edged up behind her. "What's the plan?"

Janeway sighed softly, and with a nod turned over the controls to Torres. She rose and stretched as her chief engineer silently slipped into the seat Janeway had just vacated. Sitting back down, she replied to Neelix, "I have no idea."

His face fell. "What?" And then he laughed, an uncertain chuckle. "Of course you have a plan!"

Janeway rubbed at her eyes. "Really, Neelix, I don't. Not yet, anyway. We'll come up with something when all of us have a chance to put our heads together back on *Voyager*. Estimated time to rendezvous, Mr. Paris?"

"Ten minutes, Captain."

Janeway glanced over at Bokk. This was the first away mission for the young Bolian. Ensign Bokk had performed his security duties with a minimum of fuss, and Tuvok had spoken well of him at the last evaluation. Now his eyes were on the floor, and his blue fingers drummed on his rather pudgy thighs.

"It's not much fun, is it?" Janeway asked softly.

Bokk looked up, startled. "Pardon, Captain?"

"Being stared at like a *ch'ulla* in a cage," she said, mentioning one of Bolarus IX's most famous native creatures.

Bokk shook his head. "I only wish *I* had poisoned claws and a double set of teeth," he replied in a doleful tone. Despite herself, Janeway smiled slightly. The expressive features of the Bolians permitted them to look utterly miserable when they chose. She patted him gently on the back and turned to Tuvok. The Vulcan had left his seat and was now kneeling directly behind Paris's chair. Janeway opened her mouth to question him, but he silenced her with a raised finger to his lips. Abruptly, she saw what he had seen—a small, almost unnoticeable device affixed to the base of the chair.

Bokk, too, had seen, and sat in wide-eyed silence. Neither Paris nor Torres had noticed what Tuvok was doing, however, and the half-Klingon now burst out with a growling comment: "I really, really don't like that man."

Up front, Paris snorted. "You said it, sister."

"Oh, what a pity," came a silky, sardonic voice that made Janeway's heart jump. The smug features of Aren Yashar suddenly appeared on the viewscreen. "And I so wanted us to be friends."

At once, Janeway realized that Yashar's guards had planted a listening device aboard the shuttlecraft—no doubt that same small mechanism that Tuvok had been attempting to disable. For a brief instant she felt a fierce pleasure knowing that no one had mentioned the isotope, but Aren's next words shattered her.

"A bad storm, isn't it?" Abruptly the full fury of the ion storm broke upon the little shuttlecraft. Janeway, who had been standing, tumbled to the floor as the vessel almost rolled over. She grabbed hold of a chair and pulled herself upright. Anger flashed in her blue eyes.

The tumult made her voice vibrate as she demanded, "Status?"

"We can make it, Captain," Torres replied, her own words coming out in a choked gulp.

"Two minutes till we're clear of it," grunted Paris. "Hang on!"

"Oh, so close and yet so far," gloated Aren. Before them his image shuddered and wavered, but his voice was clear as a bell. "I'm afraid I must apologize for the trick. But come, come, Captain, you didn't really think I'd let you go? Turn your ship on my poor pirate vessels? What kind of a commander would I be then?

I didn't want to bring this up in front of my dear Kes—it would upset her. I'm so sorry you couldn't see things my way, Captain. It could have been . . . fun."

"Captain," cried Torres, "There's a huge buildup of charged particle energy on our port—"

There was a sudden blinding flash of light. A deep throbbing sound assaulted Janeway's ears and she opened her mouth in a silent cry of pain. Still blinking from the light, Janeway watched in horror as sparks flew up from the console and the lights went out. For a moment she sailed through the air as the shuttlecraft went tumbling out of control. Then merciful blackness descended. The last thing Janeway heard before she slipped into unconsciousness was the triumphant laughter of Aren Yashar.

CHAPTER
6

PRISONER.

The word throbbed in Kes's mind like an open wound, imparting pain and anger and, perhaps worst of all, an aching frustration.

How often, in her brief life, had she been a prisoner? First, the subtle prison of simply living on Ocampa, being taken care of by a benevolent yet distant Caretaker, with no room for a young girl to stretch the wings of her imagination and fly. Then a more brutal life as a slave of the Kazon, her reward for trying to escape that first prison.

Her frail body had ached with blows and bruises, staggered beneath the weight of loads far too heavy for her fine bone structure and delicate frame. Nights had been easier, filled with dreams of escape, of reaching for something grander and more wondrous than she could ever have dreamed.

And Kes had also been a prisoner inside her own body, watching her small hands, commanded by Tieran's cruel whims, commit murder, feeling her lips part for rough kisses without love, hearing her mouth utter obscenities. She had lurked quietly inside her own mind, fighting Tieran's possession of her body with everything she had. She had won all of those fights, but not without cost. She had left Ocampa and its closed minds behind; had escaped the grip of the Kazon thanks to Neelix and all those aboard *Voyager;* had been able to stand against Tieran long enough for those same friends to free her.

But now Kes was again a prisoner.

True, this time the cage was beautiful and comfortable. There was good food and wine to nourish her, beauty to delight the eye, all sorts of interesting tasks to engage her imagination. And her jailer was not an elusive demigod of an alien, nor a rough and cruel Kazon, nor her own body commandeered by another. Aren Yashar was intelligent, cultured, witty—and implacable.

Prisoner.

Impotent rage rose in her, crested, and she slammed her fist down on the table. The plate and silverware jumped.

"Careful, my little bird, you'll hurt your hand!"

Aren Yashar, of course, appearing suddenly and in silence. Jailer. Kes remained silent, her gaze fixed on the colorful foodstuffs arranged artfully on the delicate plate. Her breathing was quick and tears welled in her eyes. Not tears of fear or sorrow, but tears of an almost overwhelming wrath that threatened to break her control—the legacy of Tieran.

The pirate leader sank into the seat beside her. "You've eaten nothing, little bird."

"I'm not hungry." The words were almost a growl.

"But you must eat something." He leaned forward. Kes glanced at him, saw his face, placid and tranquil, filled with the peace that a near-eternal life–span imparted. Suddenly Kes was angry at him for that, too, for living thousands of years while she could only hope to count the years of her own life–span on her fingers.

"Shall I feed you then, like a real little bird?" He lifted a spoon and brought it to her lips, an indulgent smile curving his own mouth. "Come, Kes, it's much tastier than grubs, I promise you."

Kes barely managed to keep her hands still in her lap, clenched into tight fists. The desire to strike the spoon out of Aren's hand was almost overwhelming, but she conquered it.

Don't lose your temper. Don't let him see how this is wearing on you. Kes closed her eyes for an instant, mentally summoning the inner quietude that Tuvok had taught her was always there, always within reach, anytime she needed it. When she at last looked the Rhulani in the face, her features were calm and composed.

"You don't know my friends," she said, her voice cool and soft. "They won't give up that easily."

Aren averted his eyes for a moment and was silent. "Kes," he said at last, "I'm sorry to say that . . . it is *you* who do not know your friends."

The control slipped. Kes reached for it again,

pressing her lips tightly together for a second before speaking. "What do you mean?"

"I installed listening devices aboard your captain's vessel," Aren confessed. "I heard their unguarded comments. Captain Janeway is a practical woman, and she does have the welfare of her other crew members to consider. It doesn't seem likely that they will be returning for you."

Kes shook her fair head. "No," she whispered. "No, I know them, they wouldn't abandon me." Abruptly she closed her mouth, closed in on herself, unwilling to let him have the satisfaction of knowing how the news had devastated her.

The captain risked her life to save me when I almost died at the Nakani ancestral spirit sanctuary. She underwent a grueling ritual, stepped into what might have been death. They've all risked their lives for me repeatedly! And who will help the doctor? It's a bluff, it must be, it has to be!

"I am a formidable enemy if I choose to be. The weapon capabilities I have at my command are, all modesty aside, quite powerful," Aren went on. "If it is any comfort to you, it was not an easy decision for her to reach."

He fell silent, watching her with sharp eyes. Hitherto, Aren had not displayed any telepathic powers, and Kes's gentle probing of his mind had encountered a strong will but nothing more. So why did Kes suddenly feel as though she was naked before him—physically, emotionally and mentally—when he locked those knowing violet eyes on her face?

"How fortunate you are," he said, catching Kes completely off guard. "So loved, by so many. If in truth there be gods, they have smiled upon you." His own smile grew. "And upon me, in sending you to me. This is not a cage, Kes, truly it isn't. You'll see. Once you realize you can trust me to never, ever harm you, then I can take you anywhere—everywhere!—you wish to go."

"Except back to my ship. Except back to my life."

Aren sighed, and rose. "The room in the back is yours. I realize you would like privacy from time to time. I will respect that privacy, but not forever. You may send me away on occasion, but when I wish to enter, I will."

Without another word, he turned and left her.

Left her alone. A prisoner.

Despite her will, her stomach growled. The body had its own needs. Reluctantly, Kes reached for a shining ruby of a piece of fruit, even as diamond tears slipped, slow and hot, down her face.

"Captain."

The word made no sense, though somehow Janeway knew it should have. All she knew was pain, hot and crippling, attacking her head like some sort of beast.

"Captain."

More insistent, the word. A deep, calming voice was uttering it. She knew the voice, knew it belonged to—

"Tuvok."

Her voice was weak and cracked on the word, but

92

uttering the name brought her back to reality. She blinked, and gazed up into the dark face that Tuvok liked to think was a mask of impassivity. But she'd have to be blind not to see the relief that flickered over the imperfect facade.

He held up an index finger and moved it from the right to the left. "Follow my finger with your eyes." She did so. He nodded. "Excellent. Tell me your name."

She knew what he was getting at. "Captain Kathryn Janeway, commander of the Federation starship *Voyager*." Each word was a victory.

"Good. Can you move your hands and feet?"

She did so, grimacing. She felt as if she'd been beaten with a large stick. Janeway licked dry lips, managed another word:

"Crew?"

"We have all survived the crash, though not without injuries. I believe you have suffered a mild concussion. I myself have broken my arm."

Janeway's eyes flickered at once to the limb in question, and she saw blood on the uniform and Tuvok's arm cradled in a crude sling.

Anticipating her question, Tuvok said, "There was a powerful pulse of ion energy that led to the crash. It has effectively knocked out all power systems."

"And he means all," said Torres glumly, moving into Janeway's field of vision. "Everything inside the shuttlecraft has been affected. Phasers, tricorders, diagnostic tools, you name it. The only things useful in the medikits now are the bandages and some emergency old-fashioned pain pills and ointments."

Janeway eased herself upright. Neelix was there, gently helping her lean against the bulkhead. "How bad?" she asked, as Ensign Bokk came forward and put a damp cloth on her injured head.

Torres didn't pull any punches. "Very bad. The shuttlecraft isn't beyond repair, but we'll need a lot more tools than we have available right now. The worst thing is we've got a problem with the shuttle's warp core. The nacelles were damaged by the crash and they're venting plasma. Tom and I have managed to slap something together that should contain it for the moment."

"Yeah, but only if there's not a second ion pulse," added Paris glumly. He edged back from beneath the controls, wiping his face. "We get another one like the last one and we'll have a warp core breach on our hands."

Janeway knew what kind of devastation a warp core breach would leave in its wake, and a shudder passed through her. A good chunk of the planet would be ripped away, including a handful of humanoid interlopers from a far distant part of the galaxy.

Leaning back against the reassuring solidness of the bulkhead, Janeway silently assessed their situation. The shuttlecraft was useless. They couldn't contact *Voyager*. They had no weapons, no advanced medical technology, and several of the party were injured. There was no way to predict when and where or even if the violent ion pulse that had knocked them out of the sky would recur, but should there come a second one, their quest to return home would become suddenly moot.

They were, for all intents and purposes, now marooned on Mishkara. Marooned on a planet run by a megalomaniac who held Kes captive and wanted them dead.

She could think of better situations.

Paris rose and stretched. Janeway heard the pop of stiff joints cracking. "I'm going to take a look outside and see how bad the damage is," he said.

"At least it can't get any worse," mumbled Neelix unhappily.

Paris had to manually open the door. He managed, and the ramp descended. From her position Janeway couldn't see outside, but she had a clear look at Paris's handsome features as the blood drained from his face.

It had, clearly, just gotten worse.

Paris uttered an ancient, evocative Anglo-Saxon term that Janeway hadn't often heard from him.

"Captain," said Paris slowly, "We've got visitors."

Chakotay stared at the screen, at the whirling cloud of gray-green that wrapped the planet in a shroud of gas and energy. But he was not seeing Mishkara. His mind's eye was filled with the image of Kathryn Janeway as she'd looked before stepping into the turbolift. Her eyes were narrowed with determination, her chin up in that tilt of defiance that he'd come to recognize as meaning trouble.

Chakotay didn't envy Aren Yashar one bit.

His half smile of wry amusement faded as he mentally reviewed what had happened over the last two hours. The shuttlecraft had not met them at the rendezvous point, and while Chakotay knew enough to realize that this negotiation might take time, something had aroused his suspicion. Janeway had not gone expecting to be able to talk Yashar out of his prize, she'd gone to assess the situation. She ought to have been back by now.

Unless something had gone wrong. And deep in his heart, Chakotay thought something had.

"Sickbay to bridge. Please activate your emergency medical holographic channel."

The first officer was so deep in thought that the doctor's acerbic voice startled him. Leaning forward, he did as requested. "What is it, doctor?"

"Two words: Stockholm syndrome."

Chakotay frowned. "I'm not familiar with the term."

The doctor rolled his eyes. Chakotay hated it when he did that. The doctor was so thoroughly programmed with so many varieties of information that he found it difficult to stay patient with those not quite as fortunate. An understandable attitude, perhaps, but an annoying one.

"I assume you know where Stockholm is, at least?"

"Of course. Sweden, back on Earth."

"Ah, we're making progress. The term originated in the late twentieth century. A woman was held hostage by a bank robber—"

"Bank robber?"

The doctor gritted his teeth. "Banks were places where money was kept. Bank robbers were people who robbed the place where money was kept. Understood?"

"Yes, Doctor," said Chakotay, curbing his own annoyance.

"As I was saying, a woman was held hostage by this robber of banks. By the time her freedom was finally obtained she had bonded with her captor. She became so attached to him that she broke her engagement with another man and remained faithful to her former abductor. Another woman who served passengers on early airplanes, I believe the term was stewardess, was held hostage at gun point. When the crisis ended and the man was imprisoned, this stewardess brought him gifts in jail. There are other examples that—"

"I see your point," interrupted Chakotay. "You're afraid that the longer this goes on, the more risk there is that Kes will bond with Aren Yashar."

"Precisely," replied the doctor.

Chakotay frowned. "That doesn't seem to me to be a real worry, with all due respect, Doctor. Kes is a pretty level-headed young woman, and she's been in tough situations before."

"One doesn't have to be feebleminded or psychologically impaired to suffer from Stockholm syndrome," said the doctor tersely. "The instinct for survival is very powerful. If a hostage bonds with his or her captor, the captor might come to see the hostage as a person, not as a bargaining chip, thus decreasing the likelihood that the captive will die. Few choose to do this knowingly. Stockholm syndrome is born of a very deep instinct. It could happen to anyone if the circumstances are right—you, Captain Janeway, Lieutenant Tuvok, me—well, not me, of course, actually. And we know so little about Kes's race. But it is a very real risk. I simply wanted to advise you to be aware of it."

"Thank you for your concern, Doctor. But I still don't think—"

He paused in mid sentence, all his attention suddenly diverted to the viewscreen, which showed a sudden flash of light from Mishkara. The doctor and his warning were instantly put aside as Chakotay automatically severed contact with sickbay. "Harry, what was that?"

Kim didn't reply at once, as he was occupied with analyzing the readings. At last, he glanced over at Chakotay. "Some kind of pulse, Commander. It was as if all the energy from the ion storm condensed into one spot, somehow. I've never seen anything like that before."

"Were we affected at all?"

"Negative."

Chakotay tapped his console. "Bridge to engineering."

"Carey here, Commander."

"Did you register that ion pulse, Lieutenant?"

"We sure did. Everything down here jumped, but all systems appear to be undamaged."

"Any idea what it was?"

"No, sir. I've—"

"Don't tell me," sighed Chakotay. "You've never seen anything like it before."

A pause, then, "Aye, sir, that's correct."

"Well, you might get the opportunity to see it again. Be prepared. I want to learn everything we can about it. Apparently it's not the natural behavior of your typical ion storm, and that makes me nervous. And I don't like to be nervous, Mr. Carey. Is that understood?"

"Aye, sir!"

Chakotay smothered a grin at the tone of Carey's voice. "Good. Bridge out. Lieutenant Ngyuen, bring us in closer, slowly. And Ensign Kim, let's keep scanning as we go. The more we know about this phenomenon, the better I'll like it."

"Aye, sir," replied Kim and the slender young woman who sat at the conn. Her fingers flew over the controls, and the Federation starship moved closer to the planet.

"Any new information, Mr. Kim?"

"Nothing, sir. The sensors continue to be unable to penetrate the field. The level of ionic activity remains about the same as when the captain and the away team went down. No increase, no fluctuations, certainly nothing on the scale of what just happened."

"Keep me informed, Ensign."

But Chakotay didn't need Harry Kim's sharp eyes to see what happened next.

They had analyzed the three ancient vessels when *Voyager* had first entered into orbit; analyzed, noted, and dismissed. They were ancient, they were locked in a decaying orbit, there were no life signs.

Now, they were attacking.

The alien ships sprang to life. With a rapidity that belied their bulk and their apparent age, they spiraled gracefully, tumbling into attack formation and firing energy weapons upon the unsuspecting *Voyager*.

"Shields!" cried Chakotay, but Lieutenant McKay, covering for Tuvok, had already beaten him to it. The shields deflected the attack, though the ship rocked from the assault.

"I thought those ships were dead," Chakotay snapped at Kim. "Red alert!"

As the lights dimmed and redness pulsed through the bridge, Kim replied, "They were, sir. I mean, they are. I mean—there are still no life signs!"

Chakotay had a theory. "Ngyuen, retreat at full impulse."

"Aye, Commander!"

The ship hastened backwards and resumed its former position.

The lights in the three alien vessels died, like a candle that had been suddenly extinguished. They tumbled slowly, without control, to resume their former orbits. The trap had been reset; the vessels looked abandoned, aged, utterly nonthreatening.

Slowly, the adrenaline ceased to flood Chakotay's bloodstream and his heart rate subsided to its normal steady beat. Dimly, he was aware of the damp perspiration of alarm on his brow. He did not wipe it off; the gesture might alarm his crew. "Just as I thought," he said aloud, so that he might reassure the listening bridge crew. "Once we retreated a certain distance, the ships played dead again."

"They're sentinels," exclaimed McKay, his eyes lighting up with comprehension. "Someone doesn't want us to get too close."

"McKay, are we still within firing range?"

"Aye, sir."

"Then let's fire on them now."

"Phasers at the ready, sir."

"Fire at will."

A red streak sliced through space. The ships again came to life with that disturbing unnaturalness, their shields protecting them from *Voyager*'s fire and their own weapons system firing back.

"Hold fire."

McKay obeyed. The ships fired one last volley, then abruptly died. *Like a possum, back on Earth. Playing dead until they have to fight.*

"So now we know," said Chakotay. "They'll fight when fired upon or when we get too close for someone's liking." Chakotay rose and walked closer to the screen, as if proximity would provide answers. "The question is, what are they guarding? Who put them up? Did Yashar install them to guard his pirate lair?" He shook his head. "They look too old for that."

Other questions hung, unasked, in the air. Chakotay was grateful for the discreet silence. *If they're sentinels, are they booby-trapped in some way? What will happen if we disable them—to us, and to the crew down on Mishkara? And how in the name of everything good can we possibly find them if something has gone wrong?*

Chakotay had no idea. The minutes were ticking past, and the captain's shuttle was overdue. Grim thoughts of dark cells and torture, wreckage and bloody bodies filled his mind's eye. Even worse, thoughts of Janeway and Kes, smiling and content as they hung onto Aren Yashar's arms, made the cold sweat of apprehension sheen upon his tattooed brow.

Not Kes. Not Janeway. They had strong wills.

The doctor's words haunted him: *Stockholm Syndrome is born of a very deep instinct. It could happen to anyone if the circumstances are right.*

Kathryn, thought Chakotay, *be all right. Please be all right.*

CHAPTER
7

"HELP ME UP," SNAPPED JANEWAY, IGNORING THE PAIN screaming through her battered body as Neelix and Bokk, one on each side, eased her upright. Janeway took a breath, composed herself, and made it unassisted to the shuttlecraft door.

The plasma venting from the damaged nacelles obscured her vision at first. The misty greenness turned the shapes outside into hulking, looming figures. Janeway swallowed, using years of Federation training to combat a deeper, more primal response to the creatures that stood in eerie silence, waiting.

So must the gorillas have appeared to the first men to see them; so must the white-furred mugato have loomed in the imaginations and visions of the frightened hill people of its native planet. But Janeway sensed these were not mere animals, bestial in appearance though they were. Normally she would have drawn her phaser, or at least placed one hand reassuringly on the weapon. But because of the pulse the phasers were inoperative. They were weaponless. Out of the corner of her eye, she saw Tuvok and Paris standing at attention, ready to spring into action and manually close the door the instant the situation turned dangerous. It was all they could do.

The creatures milled about in the darkness. Janeway could see a large, furry silhouette here, a glimpse of bright eyes and teeth there. She waited, heart hammering despite her best intentions. The beings had come to them. She would let them make the first move.

Finally, one of them stepped forward, and for the first time, Janeway saw it clearly.

It was enormous, about two and a half meters tall and powerfully built, along the lines of a grizzly crossed with a gorilla. It walked erect, though not easily, and leaned heavily on a thick staff that it had decorated with jewelry, leaves, and carvings. Five fingers curled around the staff, each tipped with sharp claws. The fur-covered being had no need of clothes, but wore decorative bits of cloth and gems strung about its mammoth throat nonetheless. Above the ornamented throat was a huge head, more like that of a beast than a humanoid. Tiny eyes, bright and intelligent, peered out of a long-muzzled face. Small, tufted ears twitched. Finally, the creature opened its mouth, revealing gleaming, sharp teeth.

Janeway tensed.

A grumbling, clicking, crooning noise issued forth.

With a dreadful sinking feeling, Janeway realized that their commbadges had also been affected by the ion pulse. There was no way to communicate with these creatures!

The creature cocked its head, clearly awaiting a response.

"I'm sorry," she said, taking care not to make any sudden gestures and pitching her voice soft. "Our communication devices are disabled. We don't understand your language."

The creature that was apparently the leader of the group whuffed, then tossed its head twice. It turned its head and barked out something. The others shook their own heads on their thick necks, murmuring something in reply. They did not seem surprised at Janeway's inability to communicate.

Thinking quickly, Janeway whispered, "Tuvok. Get me some water."

"Aye, Captain." With his uninjured hand, Tuvok opened a small door and removed the metal canteen within. He handed it to Janeway. Carefully, moving slowly, she opened it and drank.

The furry beings murmured, but made no hostile move.

"Mmmm," she said in an exaggerated manner, wiping her mouth with the sleeve of her uniform. "Are you thirsty?"

She proffered the canteen. The leader drew back and looked first at the metal container, then at her. It seemed to reach a decision, and stepped closer. Reaching out a clawed hand, it accepted the offer.

Janeway tried not to think of how tiny the liter canteen looked in its huge paw; how with one blow that hand could shatter her skull.

Its eyes fastened on her, it drank, pouring the water into its muzzle and downing it with a gulping-lapping gurgle. Water dripped from its mouth and a blue tongue crept out to lick the moisture from its dewlaps as it handed the canteen to one of its comrades.

Janeway felt the press of her crew behind her, though they stayed silent. Damn, but this was tense. It was a difficult situation to begin with, but not being able to speak to these creatures, to reassure the beings of their peaceful intentions . . .

The Mishkarans were moving again. The leader stepped forward purposefully and took Janeway by the arm. Its grip was strong, but not painful.

"Captain—" It was Torres. Her voice was tight.

"It's not hurting me," Janeway reassured her. "I think they simply want us to come with them."

"Oh, this is just great," said Paris. "By the looks of them they want us to be their dinner."

"Tom, that's not fair and you know it. You ought to know by now that looks can deceive." She paused, and added with a touch of gallows humor, "Or at least I hope they deceive in this instance. We've no other choice but to cooperate," she said with a glance that brooked no disobedience, even as she was led by the arm away from the shuttlecraft. "That's an order."

One by one, the crew of the shuttlecraft was escorted away from their vessel by their strange new acquaintants. The air was more wholesome once they were away from the venting plasma, and Janeway forced herself to breathe deeply. The lack of normal oxygen was telling on her, and she realized she had to make her lungs work hard and get used to the thinness of the atmosphere. She'd been skiing in Colorado, and remembered the sensation of lungs used to rich Indiana air laboring as she stood at the top of the high, snowy slope for the first time.

The gentle behavior of the great behemoths who walked with them reassured her, and any last traces of fear and suspicion were wiped away when, at one point, she stumbled. Quickly, the leader was there to catch her. It grunted, seeming to see the wound on her head for the first time, and reached a paw up to touch it. When Janeway hissed between clenched teeth at the pain, it removed its hand at once. It made a soft, sympathetic sound and rubbed her back in a circular motion with its hand instead, like an adult soothing an infant.

Janeway smiled at it, remembering at the last minute not to show her teeth in the gesture. The baring of teeth, even in a smile, might be taken as a threat. The Mishkaran leader seemed to take no offense. It lifted its head and said something to its fellows, and Janeway noticed that those Mishkarans escorting the *Voyager* crewmembers slowed their paces and looked with renewed interest at the various wounds.

There was little light, even though it was daytime on the planet's cycle around the star that served as its sun. No shadows were cast in the weak illumination. When Janeway glanced up, all she could see was the swirling greenness of the ion storm that engulfed

Mishkara. It was alarming enough to see it from the outside, from the safety and comfort of her command chair on the bridge of her own ship. Now that she and her crew were captives of aliens—benevolent or not—the constantly churning gray-green mass that served Mishkara for a sky seemed even more threatening.

It was a wonder anything could live here, that anything could grow, could thrive, beneath the unfriendly heavens. The soil, too, seemed dead. It was mostly hard rock, though from time to time Janeway saw bits of unhealthy-looking, scraggly bits of vegetation clinging to life. By the appearance of the Mishkarans' teeth, she judged them to be carnivores.

And what did they feed on? Fear brushed her again, but resolutely she pushed it aside. Fear would not serve her if the Mishkarans proved to be as nonthreatening as they appeared, nor would it serve her if they turned hostile. She'd need all her wits about her if that happened.

"Captain," and Janeway glanced down to see Neelix, trying to appear as bright and chipper as ever. "What do you think will happen?"

"I've no idea, Neelix."

The Talaxian frowned. "This is putting a serious obstacle in the way of rescuing Kes."

Janeway had to laugh. At her chuckle, her furry companion paused and glanced down at her. She looked back up at him steadily. From deep in his throat came a whuffing, grunting sound—a sound like laughter. He was mimicking her! Hope flared inside her. Fixing her eyes on the small, piggy ones of the Mishkaran leader, she said, slowly, "I am Janeway." With her free hand, she tapped her chest. "Janeway."

Still walking, it tilted its head. Its mouth worked. Finally it said, "Ain-whu." The word was garbled, harsh, breathy, but clearly understandable as her name. It pointed to itself and said, "Hrrrl."

"H-hurl," said Janeway.

It clicked its teeth twice—to indicate a negative? Janeway wondered—and repeated, exaggerating the rolling Rs and guttural intonation, "Hrrrl."

"Hrrrl," repeated Janeway, holding the syllable deep in her throat and keeping it nasal. The creature tossed its head excitedly and rubbed her back in that circular motion again, but with more enthusiasm than gentleness this time.

"Ain-way," Hrrrl growled, and this time the name came easier to him. He pointed with his staff, and Janeway could see smoke twining upward. Campfires, perhaps. "Khaank." And then Hrrrl rattled off lengthy sentences, pointing with his staff to various things Janeway couldn't yet see.

This is going to be one for the log, Janeway thought. Her sense of adventure rose, calling out to the explorer, the scientist inside her. If it weren't for Kes—and the fact that her crew aboard *Voyager* was totally in the dark as to her fate and that of the away team—she might have enjoyed this.

In a few minutes, Janeway's human vision could see what the clearly superior Mishkaran sight could—a small encampment, with a large fire around which were clustered more Mishkarans. There were no recognizable shelters. However, there was something that she had not expected to see, give the apparently primitive level of the Mishkarans—Janeway spotted what appeared to be the ruins of several old ships. As she watched, two more Mishkarans emerged from the shadowed hulk of a long-dead vessel.

Hrrrl chattered away as he led her forward. The Mishkarans at the encampment had obviously seen them coming for a while, and had gathered together into a crowd of some twenty or thirty. A few young ones, about a meter tall and with larger heads and eyes in proportion to their slimmer bodies, peered shyly around the protective barrier of their parents at the strangers.

Gently, Hrrrl pushed Janeway forward. "Djainway," he announced, following the introduction with a babble of words in his own harsh tongue. Janeway motioned to the rest of her crew. One by one, they stepped forward and introduced themselves while the Mishkarans gazed at them curiously.

Again Janeway felt pressure on her back, propelling her forward, then a push on her shoulder signaled her to sit. She and the rest of her crew complied, and she was surprised at how good the warmth of the fire felt. She'd been moving so briskly she hadn't had a chance to get chilled, but the temperature had dropped as what passed for the sun had gone down. Automatically, Janeway glanced up to see what constellations were visible from the surface. Of course, she could see none. The thick ion storm prevented that. Darkness fell about her almost as she watched, and she realized that night on this planet would be very black indeed. They had seen no moon in orbit about Mishkara to provide any kind of reflective illumination.

Hrrrl motioned, and another Mishkaran stepped forward. He held himself stiffly, as if this were a formal occasion, and carried a sack that looked to have been made out of an animal skin of some sort. Introducing himself as Rraagh, with great ceremony he placed the bag in front of Janeway. The captain hesitated, uncertain what might be inside it, but at Hrrrl's eager gesture, she took a deep breath and carefully opened the sack.

Inside, gleaming in the flickering light of the fire, was every free tool and spare part from the shuttle-craft.

Suddenly Janeway felt warm from more than the fire. She opened the bag wider, so that the others might see. "They want us to fix our instruments," she said, marveling at the innocent trust so displayed. Some of the items in the sack, while most were harmless enough things like tricorders and communicators, were phasers. A single wide-angle blast from one of those could have killed most of the tribe. She glanced up at the shaggy creature and wondered, seeing him through the eyes of a friend, how she could have thought him an enemy.

"Hrrrl, thank you. Here, B'Elanna. The first thing I want up and running is a communicator. I want to be able to thank our new friends in a way they can understand."

"Gladly, Captain," replied Torres, clearly relieved at having something useful to do. Janeway passed the sack along and Torres rummaged through it, pulling out shiny bits and pieces of metal and chips and wiring. Janeway noticed, though her chief engineer didn't, that one Mishkaran quietly and without drawing undue attention maneuvered himself so he stood over Torres. He held a staff similar to Hrrrl's. So, they weren't quite as trusting as they seemed. Should Torres bring out a weapon and point it at someone, Janeway was thoroughly convinced the sentry Mishkaran would bash in B'Elanna's head without a second thought.

Good for them, she thought. Trust mingled with sensible precautions was nearly always the wisest pose to adopt when dealing with strangers.

The fire crackled. Janeway wondered what the Mishkarans could find to feed it. Dried animal droppings, most likely, as the plains Indian tribes of the American Southwest had used. She now noticed that what she had taken for a simple metal pot on the fire was actually composed of highly advanced metals, hammered into a usable shape. An odor wafted out, strange, but not unpleasant, as one of the Mishkarans, a tiny child clinging to her leg, stepped forward and added something to the pot.

"Oh, boy, I wish I hadn't seen that," murmured Paris. Janeway shared the sentiments. What the Mishkaran cook had tossed so carelessly into the pot had been small, white, legless, and wriggling.

"It makes sense," said Janeway. "Living here has to

be brutally harsh. You eat whatever you can." She paused, and added, "Mr. Neelix, I miss your cooking."

"Thank you, Captain!" replied the little man, sitting up a bit straighter.

"I think I've got it," announced Torres, handing the communicator pin to her captain. "We'll need a good sample first."

Janeway brought the communicator up to her lips and spoke into it, locking gazes with Hrrrl. "Talk into it like this," she said, then handed it over to the alien leader.

It seemed so tiny in his paw. Following her example, he brought it to his muzzle and emitted a series of growls, clicks, and grunts. At Janeway's gesture, he passed it along to others, who also spoke into the device. Finally, Janeway extended a hand and Hrrrl returned the small object.

"Give it a try," said Torres. "That ought to be sufficient."

Janeway fastened the communicator to her uniform, and her eyes found Hrrrl's. She smiled. "Can you understand me now, Hrrrl?"

Much excited chatter broke out. And this time, Janeway could catch some of it. "At last!" "Now we'll find out—" "—ugly, but they seem pleasant enough—"

Hrrrl laughed, a harsh bark to Janeway's ears, a merry chuckle as translated through the commbadge. "Your choice of what to repair first tells me much about you, Janeway. And I like what I am learning.

Tell me," and he leaned forward eagerly, "What was your crime?"

Kes's eyelids fluttered open.

The brightness of the light made her close her eyes again, then blink, gradually growing accustomed to the illumination. She realized she was staring up at the ceiling of sickbay, and had absolutely no idea why she was lying on the bed.

The doctor's face loomed over her and he directed a light into her eyes, checking, she knew, for her pupil reaction. "Excellent," he said, nodding his bald head. "You have made a complete recovery. Not," he added with a touch of pride, "that there was any doubt, under my care."

His voice was like music to Kes's ears. For a moment, she wondered why she was so glad to see him. "Doctor," she said happily, affection turning the word into a caress. "What happened? What am I doing here?"

"Hmm," he frowned at her. "It appears you have *not* made a full recovery after all. I shall have to run a self-diagnostic later to see what I have overlooked. You appear to have suffered a short-term memory lapse. Not to worry. That's not an uncommon reaction."

"Welcome back, Kes." Captain Janeway was there, looking as crisp and efficient as ever.

Kes reached up and touched her head with gentle, probing fingers. There was no pain, no evidence that she had been injured, but of course, there wouldn't be, would there, not after the doctor had treated her.

She couldn't shake the feeling that there was something terribly wrong, however.

"Captain, what happened?" She swung her legs off the bed and faced her commanding officer.

"Another run-in with the Kazon," replied Janeway grimly. "It was quite the battle. You weren't the only one injured." She indicated with a nod of her head the other beds in sickbay occupied with those who, like Kes, were just now sitting up after receiving treatment.

Everything was just as it should be. Except, somehow, something was simply not right.

"Kazon?" Kes asked. That was one thing that didn't make sense. The door to sickbay hissed open and Paris and Tuvok entered. "I thought we left the Kazon behind a long time ago."

"I heard you'd taken a spill, Kes." Paris's expression was concerned. "You okay?"

She nodded. "Thanks, Tom. Tuvok, thank you for coming to see me."

"We will resume our lessons as soon as you are ready," the Vulcan replied—his way of expressing his concern, Kes knew.

And still the suspicion lingered, the wrongness of the situation. Janeway hadn't answered her question about the Kazon. Everyone was here that she cared about, and Kes was free to return to the job she loved any time she wanted. And yet—

"Neelix," she said suddenly. "Where's Neelix?" Surely he would have been here to check up on her if Tuvok, Tom, and the captain had found the time to come all the way from the bridge. They were no longer together, but they were still dear friends, and Kes still loved him, albeit in a different fashion. And she knew he still cared about her.

Janeway glanced over at the doctor. "Do you know what she's talking about?"

"I've no idea," replied the doctor in a tone that indicated that the thought annoyed him. "Kes, who is this—this Neelix you speak of?"

She stared at them, wide-eyed with disbelief. She couldn't have imagined Neelix, the rescue from the Kazon, the lung she had given him when he would have died without it. He was their cook, their morale officer, a friend and advisor to the whole crew! Why were they pretending Neelix didn't—

And suddenly, with the force of the physical blow she allegedly had suffered, full memory returned to Kes. The violation, the horror of what was being done to her nearly paralyzed her for an instant, and she clutched the biobed hard for balance until she realized that it, too, was false, utterly false, like everything in this room.

She fell to her knees, nauseated, slapping at the helping hands that reached to comfort her. "Aren! I know what you're doing, and it won't work! End this *now!*"

The figures of the *Voyager* crewmembers froze, shimmered, and disappeared.

"You have but to speak, my darling, and it is done." Aren appeared, materializing through a wall, a benevolent smile on his face. The smile faded. "Kes. You're crying! Whatever for?"

Kes wiped angrily at the tears of disappointment

and anger that coursed down her face. "Why?" she asked, softly, still hurting from the brutal deception. "Why did you do that to me? Why are you torturing me like this?"

He rushed toward her, kneeling on the floor. Gentle hands closed about her arms, helping her up. Too stunned to care, Kes let herself be folded into his embrace. Aren stroked her long hair and laid a cheek on top of her head.

"Kes, my dear, dear little bird, I am so sorry! I thought it would make you happy, ease your loneliness, help you get through the transition from your former life to your new life. You've no idea how difficult it was to program. I've had my technicians working on it day and night for days now."

Kes felt utterly drained by the emotional incident, and couldn't seem to dredge up the strength to protest his caresses. His heart—two hearts? She thought she heard an irregular rhythm indicative of a bi-pulmonary system—thumped against her ear, and he was warm, with a strength to his tall body that Neelix had never possessed.

She hated him with every fiber of her being.

Aren pulled away, a little, and wiped at her face. "Please, please don't cry. It breaks my heart to see you so unhappy."

Kes stared at him. It really did seem as though he hadn't realized how terrible a thing he had done to her. "What can I do, little bird? What can I do to make up for this?"

Kes reached for anger, for outrage, and found none. She was tired. She ached with hope deferred, with a weariness that made her feel as though she were as old as Aren.

"Nothing, Aren. Just—just leave me alone for a while, will you? Please."

"Anything. End simulation," he told whoever was listening, and the sickbay vanished, to be replaced with Kes's private room. "Kes, there is more to this place than these rooms. We have a marvelous computer system, a hydroponics bay, and the things you can do are limitless."

Except the one thing I want to do, Kes thought dully.

"When you tire of staring at the walls, let me know. Some variety of scene might do you some good. Again, I truly am sorry for any pain I might have caused you. For the next few years, Kes, your joy is my life." He paused, seemed about to say something more, then apparently thought better of it. With an uncertain smile, he turned and left, the door hissing shut behind him.

Kes collapsed onto the bed, wondering if there were hidden viewscreens, hidden listening devices, if everything she did or said would be heard. Even fearing that this might be so, she couldn't help the hoarse sobs that racked her tiny body for a long time.

This was the worst prison yet, because it was the kindest.

Gulping salt tears, she sat up and hugged her legs to her chest in a childish gesture. She couldn't stop shivering!

No. No. I won't let him win. I won't let him bleed the spirit out of me, bit by bit.

She took a deep, calming breath, and closed her eyes. The lashes were heavy and wet with tears. She held the breath for a moment, then let it trickle out through her nostrils. Still keeping her eyes closed, Kes opened her arms and crossed her legs, bringing her hands gently down on her bent knees. That was better. The traditional pose Tuvok had taught her helped. It was easier then to reach for the pool of quietude, drink deeply from it, take her bullied soul and wounded dreams and soothe them one by one. Replenish. Strengthen.

Renew the fight.

CHAPTER 8

HRRRL SAT UP A BIT STRAIGHTER AND NARROWED HIS already tiny eyes. "Come, Janeway, do not play games with me. You must be a criminal of some sort, or else you would not be on Mishkara!"

Janeway made the connection. "Mishkara—it's a prison planet?"

Hrrrl rumbled low in his throat, but it was a sound of confusion, not threat. "Can it be possible you are *not* criminals, then?"

"No," said Janeway earnestly. "It's a long story, but I will tell you what has happened to us if you'll tell me about Mishkara and how you and your people came here. First, though, will you permit two of my crew to take care of the ship? The—the mist it is emitting could be dangerous."

"The warp plasma, yes. I left a few of my technicians there to work on it, while we talked with you.

But of course, please send whomever you would like. You know your own vessel better than we do."

They know about warp plasma? They have technicians? Janeway tried not to let her surprise at their level of technology show. Instead, she turned to Paris and Torres. "You two, go lend some of Hrrrl's . . . technicians . . . a hand."

"Aye, Captain," said Torres. Paris rose as well.

"Rraagh, take them back to their vessel. Janeway, not to be rude, but how are your eyes?"

"My eyes? They're fine," replied Janeway, somewhat confused.

"What I mean is, we can see you plainly, could even see you quite well without the firelight. Can you see us as well?"

"No," answered the captain. "Our eyes do not function as well in the dark as yours do."

"Then take some light for them, too." Rraagh inclined his head and began to lumber purposefully in the direction whence they had come.

"Wait a minute," said Paris. "We've only got one communicator working."

"Make do," said Janeway.

Paris gave her a wry smile. "Yes, ma'am," he replied.

"They will be all right," Hrrrl assured her. "Rraagh and the technicians will let them do their jobs. Now, you wish to learn about us, then? So you shall. But first, let us share *g'shaa*. You have passed our inspection, and we would make you welcome into our family."

Janeway wondered what kind of inspection it was

they had passed, as one of the Mishkarans began to pass out bowls of the *g'shaa*. She tried not to look directly at the contents of the bowl; the maggots were all too visible. None of her crew said a word, though there were looks of great distress on their faces as they accepted their bowls.

"It is kind of our friends to share their food with us. We'll need to keep up our strength, and we are honored to share this rite of fellowship," she said, pitching her voice loud so that the rest of the crew could hear. *In other words, eat up, people, and smile while you're doing it.*

Hrrrl graciously inclined his head and scooped up a bite of the *g'shaa*. He chewed noisily, with the same gurgling, licking sound as when he had drunk the water Janeway had offered, and the mouthful vanished. "Delicious, as always, Grrua," he said, and the preparer of the meal bowed its head in acceptance of the compliment.

Janeway took a deep breath, imitated Hrrrl by making a spoon of her hand, and dipped up a mouthful. Quickly, before she could change her mind and dishonor her host, she ate, swallowing the mouthful whole. The thought of masticating the small white worms was intolerable. The slippery glop slid easily down her throat. It wasn't unpalatable, actually; kind of earthy tasting. She forced herself to concentrate on the nutritional value of the meal rather than its appearance, and continued to eat. The rest of the crew did likewise. Neelix was even smiling and nodding his head, and Bokk looked pleasantly surprised.

Hrrrl snorted with approval. "A delicacy, in this

harsh place. We will teach you what is good to eat and how to find it. You will need such knowledge, now that you are here."

"Thank you, but we don't intend to stay very long," said Bokk hurriedly.

"Hrrrrrmmmmm," murmured Hrrrl. "No one ever intends to stay. Yet somehow, everyone does. Do you think we would stay in this merciless place if we could leave?"

"Your race is not native to Mishkara?" asked Tuvok.

Hrrrl dipped his muzzle into the bowl, emptied its contents with a few quick swipes of his long blue tongue, and placed the bowl aside. He straightened with dignity, and Janeway was suddenly aware again of the ornate decorations with which he had clothed himself.

"We are the Sshoush-shin," said Hrrrl gravely, with quiet integrity. "Many years ago, our father's father's father's father's fathers were convicted of crimes on our homeworld of Hann. We are not a violent race. There was not a taker-of-lives among them. Nor would we, as a people, dream of taking lives as a punishment. Mishkara was discovered, and it was decided that all those who transgressed would be brought here, away from the others of their race." His voice softened. "A fitting punishment, for we are a social people.

"So, here they were brought. Mishkara could support life of a sort already, and we used terraforming technology to make it more fruitful, better suited to our needs."

"The distortion field, was that part of taming

Mishkara?" asked Janeway. She finished her meal and set the bowl aside. She did not, however, lick it clean with Hrrrl's obvious relish. Enough that the food stayed down.

"Yes, that was our doing. At first, our great-many-past fathers and their guards lived in a place called New Hann. It protected us from the worst unkind-nesses of Mishkara. You can see the ruins of it if you look toward where the light is greatest in the morn-ings."

"The broken dome," said Janeway. She had a brief flash of memory, of the dead fields, the empty streets, the buildings that housed nothing and no one.

"Once, it was not broken," continued Hrrrl. "There we lived, and ate, and slept, and mated, and worked the mines. Mishkara is cruel on the surface, but it houses a great deal of mineral wealth. Our great-many-past fathers harvested the fruits of the deep earth. You can see them everywhere," and Hrrrl waved a hand extensively. "Jewels of untold value, for the Sshoush-shin to trade for goods. Minerals that powered our ships. We even have the beautiful and rare crystals that make warp drive possible here on Mishkara. All harvested through the labor of our great-many-past fathers, under the watchful eyes of the guards. And I would trade all of them for one crop that grows strong and healthy."

The bitterness in his voice was undisguised. Jane-way couldn't blame him.

"Were the guards cruel to your ancestors?"

"Sshoush-shin are not a cruel people," Hrrrl replied. "We needed each other. The convicts mined Mishkara's wealth and the guards gave us food, shelter, and protection from the hostile creatures who call Mishkara their true home. You were lucky we found you first, Janeway. Many others you could encounter here are not as benevolent as we are. And in addition to the native animals, you were also in danger from the descendants of other convicts who were brought here."

"Other races besides the Sshoush-shin?"

"Many other races," growled Hrrrl. "Many who were takers-of-lives, who liked to hurt for pleasure. We assumed that their governments must have traded many goods for permission to deposit their criminals on Mishkara.

"With the coming of other criminals, not the Sshoush-shin, the security increased. Everyone suffered then. There was no trust, no mutual back-and-forth any more. More security measures were installed. There was an attempted rescue from outside powers, so they installed unmanned, automated, limited-range sentinel vessels in orbit around Mishkara. No one lived outside of New Hann, so an artificial ion field was created. It could be manipulated from a vast control center inside New Hann. When the storm was not active, ships could land with new loads of prisoners or supplies. If a ship attempted to land without giving the correct code, security would not deactivate the field. When the ship entered the atmosphere or tried to leave the atmosphere under these conditions, it would generate a powerful ion pulse. This pulse would render the ship useless. So you see, Janeway, your situation is nothing new to us. That pulse is what happened to your ship."

"I see," replied Janeway grimly. She glanced over at Tuvok. "Aren would appear to have most of the cards. Please continue, Hrrrl. How did the dome get broken? How did your people get free?"

Hrrrl glanced down at his hands, flexing his powerful fingers with their sharp claws. Janeway believed him when he said his people were essentially peaceful, and that they were not "takers-of-lives." But not so long ago, they were not so peaceful, if their claws and teeth were any indication. She suspected that they, like the Vulcans, had chosen to overcome an innate tendency toward violence by willingly embracing a culture of peace.

"It was better before," he said softly. "Better, when the guards and convicts coexisted without fear of one another. The new, strange races, with their cruelty, brought about the advanced security measures. These in turn made us even more isolated. With the artificial ion storm in place, little could grow, be nurtured from the sun's light. With the new fear the guards had toward the convicts, they were terrified of a violent escape attempt. So the guards were not permitted any ships of their own, lest the criminals break free and steal them. We were utterly dependent on the supply ships, both convicts and guards. All of us."

"The logical conclusion is that something did happen," said Tuvok. "At some point, for whatever reason, the supply ships ceased to arrive."

"And a dark day that was indeed," said Hrrrl. "We

had heard rumors of war with the Tlatli—an insect-oid race that the great-many-past-fathers had never even heard of." He wrinkled his nose and his voice was wry. "In a prison, there are always rumors. But we knew little more than simple, whispered gossip. To this day, no one knows what happened, but the ships stopped coming. Prisoners and guards alike grew anxious, and anxiety bred fear. Encouraged by the more violent races, the great-many-past fathers joined in a revolt."

Hrrrl's ears twitched, betraying his discomfort with the revelation. "It is not something we Sshoush-shin are proud of, but it is a part of our history and we will not deny that it happened. The guards were heavily outnumbered. They barricaded themselves in the control center, far beneath the surface of Mishkara. They could and did defend themselves, and have done so to this day. The prisoners fled, out into the harshness that was Mishkara. We have divided our-selves into sects, small groups that cling to life. We trade with a few, but many we avoid. We cannot afford to let hostile strangers into our midst."

The eyes crinkled, and Hrrrl cocked his furry head. "You have passed our inspection, as I said. We saw the bright green streak of plasma against the skies, and knew that another ship had been disabled by the ion storm. We sought you out. Had we not approved of who we found, you would have been driven away."

"We were lucky indeed," said Janeway, sincerely. It was easy to believe that this harsh planet was brimful with hostile life-forms.

She took a deep breath, again feeling that lightheadedness that she was determined to overcome. "Hrrrl, may we ask a few questions?"

He spread his arms wide. "What we know, we will tell you."

"You say the guards—Sshoush-shin guards—still live at the ruins of New Hann. How do you know?"

"Over the years, a few of our scouts have seen them emerge from the broken dome. We think they need to forage for food, just as everyone must, now. But now that you mention this, they have not been seen for a while." He shrugged his massive, furry shoulders. "You must forgive. There is little way to reckon days here. We have no seasons, only the swirling, green skies."

"I understand." Once, these people had been perhaps almost as advanced as humankind. But now, even more abandoned than Janeway, they had had to choose survival over sophistication. "How is it then that your generation understands ships and technology?"

"You are not the first to crash since the dome was shattered," replied Hrrrl. "Always, since we first fled into the wilderness, there have been interlopers with new technology. Many come thinking to exploit Mishkara's wealth, but the guards have other plans. The pulse, though, renders everything useless, at least for a time, if it is not protected by being hidden away deep in the earth."

"The soil and rock of Mishkara shields technological devices from the effect of the ion pulse?" queried Tuvok.

"Yes."

"That's good to know," said Janeway. "Once Paris and Torres have effected repairs, maybe we can enlist the Sshoush-shin in temporarily burying it beneath the rocks and soil."

Hrrrl nodded. "We could help, yes. Now, Janeway, we have told you of our history. Tell me of yours."

Janeway paused, thinking how best to approach this. Finally, she sighed. "Hrrrl, much of our recent history is tied in with yours."

Before she embarked on the tale of Aren Yashar's betrayal and *Voyager*'s subsequent chase to Mishkara, Janeway told him a little bit about the Alpha quadrant, and how *Voyager* and her crew were trying to get home. The furry alien leader grew pensive as he listened.

"Home," he echoed. "It seems that many are striving for it, doesn't it?"

Janeway nodded. She then told Hrrrl and the rest of the Sshoush-shin, who crowded forward eagerly, ears pricked attentively, to listen, of Kes's abduction. Janeway spoke more quietly of the cautious voyage through the graveyard of dead ships.

"On the station, Aren Yashar spoke of an insectoid race called the Tlatli. Believe me, I don't have any difficulty suspecting that everything Yashar utters is a lie, but he did speak about the Tlatli having a strong presence in that sector of space. And there wasn't any reason—then or even now—for him to lie about that."

Murmurs hummed through the crowd. The captain continued. "While following Yashar and our kidnapped friend, the route led through a graveyard of vessels. It looked like a terrible war had taken place long ago. What we saw could have been the remains of the Sshoush-shin defense line."

"Then it is true," said Hrrrl, his big, shaggy head drooping in despair. "The Tlatli won, and Hann as we knew it is no more. We few, here on Mishkara, the many-great-past children of prisoners, are all that is left of our race."

"It is far from certain," Tuvok reminded him. "We do not know the location of your planet, or—"

"But it is likely," said Hrrrl.

"It is *possible*," corrected Tuvok.

Hrrrl was silent for a moment, then he threw back his head. His mouth, crammed with those sharp teeth, opened, and a dreadful howl issued forth. Immediately, the rest of the Sshoush-shin assembled joined in, and for several long moments the thin air of Mishkara echoed with the raw sound of a devastated keening. Neelix clapped his hands to his ears, as did Bokk. Tuvok, who had extremely sensitive hearing, made no movement to shield his ears. Neither did Janeway. This ear-shattering sound of grief was meant to be heard—heard, acknowledged, and respected. Though Janeway half feared that at any moment a thin trickle of blood would start from her pained ears, she listened, and mourned along with them.

Finally, the sound faded and died. Hrrrl lowered his head, and gazed again at his honored guest. "Let me see if I can piece together the rest," he said, with more calmness than he had displayed hitherto. "After—after our planet fell, the supply ships of course stopped coming, which then led to the revolt.

Other ships we have seen have been pirates, probably under command of the man you seek. They have taken charge of the underground control center, and they probably killed the Sshoush-shin guards who remained, which explains why they have not been seen recently."

"This is what we believe has transpired," Tuvok confirmed quietly.

"These star-robbers"—not for the first time, Janeway smiled at the translator's laborious attempts at accurate communication; it was a poetic term, far more poetic than *space pirates*—"have made Mishkara their base of operations. They are probably mining for the wealth, as once we did. They permit no one but their allies to land."

And suddenly, though she should have seen it before, the full depth of the urgency of their situation broke upon Janeway like a thunderclap. Horror stricken with the sudden realization, she turned at once to Tuvok. Though she knew he couldn't read minds without invoking the traditional Vulcan mind-meld ritual, comprehension dawned in his eyes as if he had read hers. Perhaps he did, after a fashion; she was certain her thoughts were plain enough on her face.

"We've got to get out of here before Chakotay sends another shuttlecraft after us," she breathed.

"Agreed," said Tuvok. "Any attempt to penetrate the ion field without giving the proper code to deactivate it would cause another of the disabling pulses—"

"—which would ignite the plasma that's already vented from our shuttlecraft," finished Janeway.

"There wouldn't be anything left of us for *Voyager* to rescue."

There seemed to be only one solution, and Janeway didn't like it one bit. Before she uttered the sure-to-be-disliked plan, she tried one more thing. "Hrrrl, you mention that you have some technology left of your own. I don't suppose you have anything that could send a message to our ship, tell them we're alive and warn them not to attempt to send down a second vessel?"

Hrrrl shook his head. "We have nothing that advanced. We never did. Nothing can get past the ion storm unless it is sent from the control center."

A crunching of booted and padded feet on earth came from beyond the circle of the firelight. Janeway tensed, but Hrrrl, with his superior vision, merely raised a welcoming paw and beckoned Paris, Torres, and their escorts closer.

"Status report?" demanded Janeway.

Paris and Torres looked tired but pleased with themselves. "We've managed to lock it down," replied the chief engineer as she plopped herself on the ground. "Those technicians of yours, Hrrrl, really know their stuff. They picked up on what we were doing right away and sped up the process greatly." She turned to look at them and smiled. "Thanks," she said, plainly glad to give them the gratitude they deserved now that they had a means of communication.

"There's still a lot of warp plasma drifting about, though," put in Paris in a tired tone of voice. "It's still extremely dangerous."

"We've learned a lot while you were gone," said the captain. "I don't have time to go into it now, but the main thing is, like it or not, we're going to have to return to the dome and get at that control center."

"What?" gasped Torres. Bokk, Neelix, and Paris began protesting at once. Janeway silenced them with a raised hand.

"We are several hours overdue already for our rendezvous with *Voyager*. Commander Chakotay is not the type to sit idly by and hope we'll show up one day. Sooner or later—and I hope to high heaven later—he'll send down another shuttlecraft. From what I have learned from Hrrrl, the ion storm and that pulse that disabled us are artificial. Aren Yashar controls it from the complex we were just in. If another shuttlecraft attempts to land, he'll activate the ion pulse."

Paris's eyes went wide with understanding. Torres grimaced, but clearly she, too, comprehended what Janeway was getting at.

"Well," said Neelix, as ever trying to make the best of a bad situation, "at least we know the pulse isn't random."

"It would appear that our only chance to avert catastrophe is to return to the control center," said Tuvok, saving Janeway from being the one who had to deliver the bad news.

Janeway nodded. "Agreed. We'll either have to warn Aren not to activate the ion pulse, for his own sake as well as ours, or else we'll have to break into the control rooms and deactivate the ion storm ourselves. One way or another, we've got to go back."

"And get Kes!" exclaimed Neelix, his face lighting up. "I knew you'd have a plan, Captain."

"Neelix, we will deal with recovering Kes afterwards. This is much more important. Thousands of lives are at stake here, Kes's among them."

"But—"

"No buts. I think you know how much Kes means to all of us. But right now, simply living long enough for us to rescue her has to take precedence. I don't want to hear another word about it," she added as Neelix opened his mouth to continue the argument.

"Captain, do you think Aren Yashar will actually listen to us?" queried Bokk.

"I don't know. But we've got to try. Our only other option is to sit here and take bets as to who will kill us first, Yashar or our own people."

The crew fell silent. No one liked it. But no one had to. It was the only option.

"You—you wish to return to New Hann?" asked Hrrrl, clearly disbelieving. "Perhaps the translating device—"

"There's no malfunction with our communicator," said Janeway. "You heard correctly. And you've heard our reasons. The Sshoush-shin are in danger as well. You'd have to move a lot farther away than this to escape the danger if the warp core on our vessel ruptures."

"But—" Hrrrl clicked his jaw twice, indicating his disapproval of the plan. "This Aren Yashar who has taken over New Hann, surely he must be aware of the danger the ion pulse must pose. He has downed other vessels before, many of which have warp cores."

"Perhaps," Janeway acknowledged. "But he doesn't know how badly the shuttlecraft was damaged. He doesn't have the schematics of the vessel, to judge the likelihood of something like this happening. And regardless of Aren's knowledge or lack of it, our crew in orbit around Mishkara is most certainly in the dark. And I promise you, our people are not the type to abandon friends."

"Nor are the Sshoush-shin," said Hrrrl, unexpectedly. "There is much distance between here and New Hann. The journey will not be easy. If you do not know what to eat and what to fear and how to fight, then you will not survive. We will escort you safely, Janeway. You are willing to undertake the risk to help save us, surely we owe you that much."

Surprise and pleasure filled Janeway. Once again, the old cliché, "You can't judge a book by its cover," had proven true. The Sshoush-shin were frightening in appearance, yet intelligent and gentle. And their leader had promised assistance on a dangerous mission out of friendship. She smiled at Hrrrl.

"Thank you, Hrrrl. I don't know how we can repay you."

He laughed, a harsh, barking sound. "If you can manage to talk a star-robber out of protecting his plunder, then you can move mountains. We will think of a way for you to repay us. In the meantime, I will send someone to hide your shuttlecraft, for it is certain that Aren will wish to confirm your demise. Until morning, I suggest you rest. You will need all your strength to cross the wilds of Mishkara."

CHAPTER
9

"WHAT DID YOU SAY?" AREN YASHAR LOUNGED IN HIS soft chair, sipping a hot beverage, his face deceptively composed.

Kula Dhad fought to keep his anxiety from showing. Yashar had an eye for weakness, and like any other predator, was wont to metaphorically tear out the throats of anyone he perceived as being weak.

"I said, the scouts have not yet found the shuttle-craft."

"That," said Yashar, taking another leisurely sip of his drink, "is what I thought you said. But you confuse me, Dhad. This simply cannot be correct."

Sweat beaded across Dhad's brow. He'd gloated to himself and others about being promoted from a lowly courier to the elite echelon of Yashar's most valued men. Now he wished that he were back with the peaceful Shamaris, breathing in the stink of their happiness, and had never clapped eyes upon the little girl-woman named Kes.

"I, I regret to inform you that it *is* correct. However, we have found some damaged parts, near the western mountain range. It is possible that they survived and managed to drag the shuttlecraft to—"

Dhad gasped as hot liquid splashed into his face. It wasn't hot enough to do damage, but it startled and frightened him. He knew better than to wipe it away, and simply stood, letting the beverage cool on his face and drip down his neck, soaking his high collar.

"You've seen the Alpha quadranters!" snapped Yashar, rising with that uncanny grace of his to stand with his face barely an inch away from Dhad's wet one. Angrily, he threw the empty cup down on the pale blue carpet. "Do you think they could manage to pull something as heavy as that shuttlecraft to safety?"

"N-no," stammered Dhad, averting his eyes. "But the only other solution is that your scouts are foolish, and you know and I know that is not the case!"

He blanched suddenly, willing the words back. But it was too late. They had been said, and they hung out there, almost resonating.

To his shock, Yashar suddenly appeared thoughtful. And when the commander raised his hand to his fellow Rhulani, it was not to strike Dhad, as he half-expected, it was to pat him on the shoulder.

"You are right, Kula," he said, invoking the less formal name. Dhad closed his eyes in relief and his shoulders sagged. "My scouts are most assuredly not fools. But, equally certain is the fact that Janeway and her pathetic crew couldn't have moved the shuttle-craft or even hidden it unaided. Therefore, they must have had help." His purple eyes narrowed, and Kula Dhad almost did a dance of pleasure in that his master's anger was not directed at him. "Sshoush-shin help. There's a settlement out that way, isn't there?"

A desire to say what the commander wished to hear warred with uncertainty. Rationalizing that Aren Yashar would be more displeased at a lie than an admission of lack of knowledge, Dhad licked his lips, tasted the sweet, cooling liquid still upon them, and blurted out, "I don't know, Great One, but if you will give me leave I shall find out at once!"

A slow smile spread across his commander's face, and Aren chuckled. "You continue to please me, even as you vex me. Go and clean yourself up first, then find out everything you can on the area where the debris was spotted. I do not like the thought of them wandering about. I intended them to die, and die they shall, if not from the ion pulse than from a more direct and personal blast of energy. As long as my precious Kes thinks they will come for her, she will never surrender to my will."

Just at that moment, the door to the back room opened a crack. Kes stood there, the soft light from the room making her features glow and turning her gold curls into a halo. It also cast unkind shadows beneath her large blue eyes, eyes that to Dhad seemed somehow haunted.

"Aren," she said in her soft voice. "I—I'd like to leave, if I may. The room . . ." her voice trailed off.

Aren's face softened, brightened, as he looked at his newest acquisition. "Of course, my dear," he told her. "All you ever had to do was ask. What would you like to see first, the hydroponics room, the terraforming controls, the—"

"It doesn't matter." Kes's voice was like the soft sigh of the wind in the trees. "Whatever you would like. I just want to move a little." She shrugged her slim shoulders eloquently. "That's all."

"Then move you shall, my dear." Dhad couldn't help himself, but stared, rather rudely, at his commander. This Kes girl was really upsetting things. Not that Dhad couldn't see the appeal, of course. Who couldn't? All Rhulani had an eye for beauty, for precious things. It was one reason why so many of them turned to piracy with such ease; a desire to see, to hold, to own, things of surpassing loveliness. Kes was almost heartbreaking to look upon.

But still, but still—she was making Aren do rash things, putting them all in jeopardy. And the way Aren looked at her, his face softening like that—why, if Dhad hadn't known better, he might have suspected that the little Ocampa female meant more to the pirate leader than a few years of pleasurable amusement. But of course Dhad did know better. He'd seen lovely females come and go out of these apartments. He'd even brought most of them to Yashar's attention in the first place.

But this one . . .

"You are dismissed, Kula," said Yashar, and there

was the old coldness, the old strength and power, in his voice. Reassured, Dhad bowed and scurried out.

He didn't want to be around the uncanny Kes longer than he had to.

It felt unspeakably odd to Chakotay to be the one leading the discussion in the conference room. He was used to Janeway, her eyes bright with attention and her mouth set in that firm line, taking control with practiced ease. Chakotay was no stranger to command, of course, having captained his own crew for a not inconsiderable length of time, and the mantle of the final decision that weighed on his shoulders now had a familiar feel about it.

But not here. It wasn't his mantle, wasn't his responsibility, and to assume it made him feel that Janeway was beyond aid.

Chakotay didn't like that thought one bit.

The senior staff—what was left of them—were already assembled by the time he stepped into the room himself. *Great spirits,* he thought, keeping his shock from showing on his dark face. *Great spirits, so few of us left?*

Harry Kim and the doctor were the only members of the senior staff seated at the long table. Janeway. Tuvok. Paris. Torres. Neelix. And of course Kes, whose abduction had set off the chain of events that led to a paucity of officers aboard *Voyager.* Gone, all of them.

He felt his spirit guide, warm and reassuring, in the back of his mind. *And what about you, Chakotay,* she reminded him, soft as a sigh. *You are still here. And they need every bit of wisdom you can give them.*

In other words, thought Chakotay, *quit feeling sorry for yourself, is that right?*

He could see her, in his mind's eye, cocking her head a little in amusement. Hmmmm, she said, noncommittally, but with a hint of mirth.

Chakotay met every pair of eyes, and for a moment, but for the gentle curves of a Starfleet vessel about them and the bicolored Starfleet uniforms they wore, he could almost have been the Maquis captain again. Nearly everyone here had served under him before he and Janeway had formed their strange, but vital, alliance. Lieutenant Chell, big and bulky in his yellow and black security uniform, his blue, ridged face turned up to Chakotay's. How ironic that he was here representing Tuvok; Chell, who had been a particular thorn in Tuvok's side not so long ago. Young Garan was here, too, his earring removed, ready to offer his recently acquired scientific knowledge to help his fellow crewmembers, his face older, stronger than it had been before.

Henley leaned back in her chair, her arms crossed across her slender body, her lively tongue bridled and her eyes alert. Maquis, all of them; or at least, they had once been. Wryly Chakotay realized there were more former Maquis in positions of power aboard *Voyager* at this moment than Starfleet officers. Once, that would have been a cue for mutiny, when Seska had been here.

But Seska was gone, dead in a misguided attempt to

seize *Voyager,* and the crewmen now assembled had long since learned to live under Starfleet rules and tender their own talents to all their benefit.

Chakotay wanted to tell them, these rough-and-tumble upstarts from once upon a time, how very proud he was of them, but he decided against it. Time enough to give them pats on the back when they were relaxing in the artificial sun at Neelix's resort, or at Sandrine's over a game of pool.

He decided to cut right to the chase as he sank down into a chair and folded his hands.

"The shuttlecraft with the captain and the rest of the senior staff aboard is now nearly twelve hours overdue. I'd be lying if I said I didn't suspect foul play. We can't follow standard procedure here. The ion storm has cut us off from initiating any contact with Aren Yashar, though we're sending an automatic hail every ten minutes. He's not responding. We can't beam down because of the distortion field, and we're also unable to send down an investigative team aboard another shuttlecraft because the sentinel ships won't let us get close enough." He managed a wry grin. "I'd appreciate any and all suggestions at this point."

"Lieutenant Carey and I have done some investigating," said Kim. "And after talking with Garan, it's our theory that the captain's hunch was right, this ion storm is indeed artificial,"

Chakotay raised an eyebrow and turned to the young Bajoran, who suddenly looked uncomfortable at being the center of attention. Nevertheless, when he spoke, his tone of voice was certain.

"A natural storm does follow certain patterns," began Garan. "But because it is a naturally occurring phenomenon, every storm should be different. This one operates like clockwork." He glanced over at Carey.

"If I may?" asked the curly-headed engineer.

"Please proceed, Mr. Carey," replied Chakotay.

Carey tapped in a program, and a holographic image of the planet manifested, floating above the conference table. "We've been monitoring the storm constantly since we first arrived. Here's the first image we have. Keep an eye on it, and then watch this second image." Another miniature planet, complete with swirling ion storm, appeared in front of them. The green mist ebbed and flowed, apparently random. Suddenly Carey hit another button and the storm froze.

The pattern was identical to the first one.

"This is what the storm looked like four point seven hours after we arrived. And four point seven hours after that—" A third holographic, palm-side planet appeared. The storm was again in the same position.

"If Mr. Tuvok were here," said Garan with a slight smile, "I'm sure he'd rattle off the odds of this occurring naturally without even thinking about it. We had to rely on the computer. The odds of this being a natural storm are—" he paused, glanced down at his padd "—forty-two million, nine hundred thirty-two thousand, seven hundred fifty-two point eight to one."

"What about the distortion field?" Chakotay asked Carey.

"Captain Janeway was right about that as well. It's probably artificial too. We know that it protects the atmosphere from the ion storm, and if the ion storm is a construction—"

"Then the need to protect the atmosphere from the ion storm has to be a construction," finished Chakotay. "I'll buy that. A storm and a distortion field that are both artificial and three apparently derelict vessels that spring to life when we get too close. This is an elaborate security operation, yet it's designed to look natural, as if whoever set this up didn't want to be noticed. Someone wanted Mishkara well protected, but overlooked."

"I'd say that would be an ideal situation for the Ja'in," said Kim, "except those relics look very old."

"We don't know how long the Ja'in have occupied this area of space," Chakotay countered. "It's an interesting question, no doubt about it, but our primary need is to get to our people down there on Mishkara. And that means somehow getting past the sentry ships, whoever placed them there."

Kim and Carey exchanged glances. Chakotay didn't miss the gestures and inquired, "Do you have a solution for me, gentlemen?"

"I'm not so sure it's a solution," said Kim, "but it is a suggestion."

"Suggestion, idea, proposal, initiative—whatever you want to call it, Mr. Kim, I'd welcome it."

"Okay." Kim laced his fingers together and leaned forward. "The most important problem facing us right now is how to get around those sentinel ships. We can't do anything else until we do that. I've discussed this with Lieutenant Carey, and he thinks we might be able to pull it off. What I'm suggesting is, we beam over teams to each of the sentinel ships. Once there, we can start analyzing them, see if we can't figure out what makes them tick. With any luck, we'll be able to determine how to deactivate their programmed attack response."

Chakotay frowned. "That's a pretty risky solution."

Kim managed a wry grin. "I said it was a suggestion, Commander."

"So you did." He rubbed his eyes tiredly. The tension and worry were beginning to get to him, and he thought rather grimly that it would get worse before it got better.

"How do you propose we do this? Those ships have shields, not to mention very effective weaponry."

"The shields, like the weapons, only activate when we get within a certain distance," said Carey. "Here's what I think we should do."

Chakotay did not like the plan, but it was the only one they had. He realized, as he sat in Janeway's chair, that both his hands had clenched into fists. He took a deep breath and forced his fingers to uncurl.

"Bridge to engineering."

"Lieutenant Dalby here, sir."

"How is the reconfiguration of the transporters coming?"

He could hear the pleasure in Dalby's voice as he replied. "Beautifully, sir. We've managed to readjust the targeting scanners to permit differing destinations. The only problem is, in order for this to work, the transporter operators will have to use the joystick to manually target the controls for the third ship. It's going to slow things down a bit, as well. Rematerialization is going to take approximately eight point four seconds."

"What about the range?"

"Well, I'm afraid that Carey was right when he said the diffusion of energy would decrease our minimum range. We've got to get within ten thousand kilometers of the ships before we can begin transport."

Chakotay punched up a few schematics on his console and swore underneath his breath. The ships had "come alive" when *Voyager* was approximately ten thousand kilometers away from them.

"We are going to be cutting this one close," he said aloud.

"Aye, sir," replied Dalby.

Chakotay nodded to himself. He'd much rather have beamed the three teams to the derelict ships in three different sessions, keeping their distance from the dead and deadly vessels, but time was of the essence now. The window was extremely narrow, and he doubted they'd get a second chance. Truth be told, he wondered if they'd even get a first one, but they had to try. He made a mental note to bring Dalby's good work to B'Elanna's attention when she returned.

If she returned.

He frowned and banished the negative thought from his mind.

"Commander," said Henley from her station at ops, "The three away teams are assembled as you requested, we have four people in transporter room one and two in transporter room two."

Her crisp tone made him smile a little. "Henley, do you have faith?"

"Sir?" she asked, clearly puzzled.

"Faith. Do you have religion?"

"Well," Henley replied, still confused as to what he was getting at, "I was raised Catholic, if that's what you mean."

"We've never tried this before and it's one of the riskiest ventures we've ever undertaken. I think any prayers to any deity couldn't hurt." He moved to catch her gaze, give her a reassuring smile. Ops was not her primary station, and right now, he knew she was nervous about pulling all these differing things together. Henley smiled back, relaxing just a bit.

"Understood, sir."

"Mr. Chell, bring us up to half impulse. Distance to the ships?"

"Fifty thousand kilometers and closing."

"Get those shields up, Henley."

"Shields up, sir."

They moved closer, maneuvering around the planet until the three vessels came into view. Chakotay shook his head. That anything that derelict could be at all operative, let alone as efficient as the three ships had proved they were, was a marvel. Someone, long ago, had been possessed of some very good technology.

"Range is forty thousand kilometers and closing," reported Chell.

"Take it to full impulse, Mr. Chell. Approximate time until we reach ten thousand kilometers?"

Chell's stubby fingers moved over the console. "At full impulse, we'll be there in thirty seconds."

"Red alert." The lights dimmed and a crimson glow pulsed through the bridge. "Bridge to transporter rooms one and two. Prepare to energize on my command." His whole body was tense, his eyes fastened, unblinking, on the viewscreen as the three ships moved closer. They were going to have to perform a near-warp transport, something tricky even under normal situations. With this reconfiguration of the transporter, factoring in the manual targeting of the controls, why, it really *was* like commanding his old ship again, complete with an utter reliance on miracles.

"Thirty thousand kilometers," intoned Chell.

"Shields down," snapped Chakotay. "Stand by, transporter rooms—"

"Twenty thousand . . . fifteen thousand . . . ten—"

"Energize!" cried Chakotay. "Chell, hard to port! Keep us at least ten thousand kilometers distant!"

The ship veered off to port, maintaining the distance, but not without cost. Cries of pain rang throughout the bridge, and Chakotay himself nearly lost his seat. He dug his fingers in tightly, willing himself to stay in the chair. He heard Henley swear, and Chell flailed wildly before regaining his balance.

"Shields up! Retreat, Mr.—"

But the command came almost too late. When Chell had lost his balance, he had lost contact with the controls. *Voyager* had gone too close, and the sickening sight of the ships lighting up and firing their weapons filled the viewscreen. Even as the words left Chakotay's lips, the ship was hit and hit hard.

It tumbled wildly. This time, Chakotay was flung out of his chair. He hit the deck hard, his chin slamming into the floor and burning as it scraped the carpet. He couldn't breathe, couldn't form orders. His lungs refused to obey him. Chakotay mouthed words that had no breath behind them, stumbled up into his chair. He locked gazes with Henley, his eyes asking what his throat could not.

"We didn't get the shields up in time," she replied. She held her left arm in an odd position, and blood darkened the black on her uniform. "Damage reports coming in from decks two, nine, and eleven. Warp engines are off line. Engineering is responding, but it looks bad. Casualties reported from all over the ship."

Chakotay nodded, gasped for air. The sentinel ships were moving closer, and they fired again. The ship rocked, but the shields deflected the worst of it.

Had they been able to do it? They would have had to stay at the ten thousand kilometer distance for eight full seconds, and it sure as hell hadn't felt that long. "Bridge to transporter rooms," he gasped.

He didn't even have to finish the sentence. The disembodied voice was triumphant. "They got there safely, sir! All six of them, on three different ships!"

"Then let's get the hell out of here. Chell—"

Chell had beaten him to it. Once he heard that the mission had been accomplished, he'd already begun moving *Voyager* out of range at full impulse. The sentinel ships got off a final volley, but only one energy blast made contact. Then, the lights died, and they resumed their aimless floating once more.

"Bridge to sickbay. Be prepared for casualties. Henley, patch me through to—"

"Kim to *Voyager.*"

A slow smile spread across Chakotay's face, even though the gesture hurt his scraped chin. "Chakotay here. How was your landing?"

"A bit rough," Kim confessed, "but I've checked in with teams B and C and we all made it."

"What's the status?"

"We're just starting to investigate it now, but I'm hopeful that we'll be able to figure it out in short order. Maybe even get life support up and running."

Chakotay smothered a grin, recalling how much Harry hated the envirosuits. "I'll let your teams get on it. Check in every twenty minutes, though."

"Understood, Commander. Kim out."

"Cancel red alert," ordered Chakotay. The lights did not change. Clearly they were one of many things that would need to be repaired before they would function properly again. With five engineering crewmembers serving on the away teams, and with the warp engines being off line, it might be awhile before things were up and running once more.

"Henley, get yourself to sickbay."

"But, sir—"

Without turning around, Chakotay said, "I saw your arm. Don't make me make it an order."

"Aye, sir." She headed for the turbolift, and Chakotay didn't miss the flash of pain on her face as she cradled her arm.

The door didn't open. "Oh, just great," snapped Henley. "Nothing like crawling through a Jefferies tube with a broken arm."

"Just like the good old days with the Maquis, huh?" Chakotay grinned wickedly.

The look that Henley gave him would have put a phaser blast to shame.

CHAPTER
10

THE SUN WAS HOT ON HER BODY, SOOTHING AWAY ALL worries, all cares.

The sun-stroked stone beneath her belly was warm, too, and she soaked up its heat with a quiet sense of joy.

The little lizard looked at her with its swiveling eyes. She sensed amusement.

"Dream while you may, and soak strength into your bones for the journey."

"Janeway!"

The voice was rough, growling, almost. Janeway blinked awake, reaching for a phaser that wasn't there. The darkness was blinding. She could see nothing, but, recalling where she was and who that rough voice belonged to, she relaxed.

"What is it, Hrrrl?" She maneuvered herself into a sitting position on the soft pelts, grimacing a little as she remembered just what kind of pelts they were.

Janeway was lying on the remains of Hrrrl's father.

In this harsh environment, nothing was wasted. When a Sshoush-shin died, after the proper ritual of the *ttk ttk* had been observed, he was skinned, that his pelt might serve to keep the living warm. A great feast was prepared from the flesh, if the deceased had not been dead overlong; another way that the dead cared for the living. While ritual cannibalism still unsettled Janeway, she had to recognize the brutal necessity of it in this case.

She smelled the not unpleasant, musky odor of the Sshoush-shin leader as he approached and reached to touch her, rubbing her back in that strange circular movement.

"One of your crew is gone. I am sorry."

"Gone? What do you mean?"

"He left. He stayed up last night talking with Grrua, asking her all kinds of questions about the meals she prepared."

Janeway closed her eyes. Who among her crewmen would want to leave on his own, after having inquired about food preparation? "That would have to be Neelix."

"The little one, yes. I am very sorry. We will hold a *tkk ttk* in his memory if you like."

Janeway knew the suggestion was meant kindly, but she bristled nonetheless. "Thank you for your concern, Hrrrl, but I wouldn't count Mr. Neelix dead just yet. He had many years of traveling on his own through unfriendly territory before he came to us. If anyone knows how to take care of himself, it's he."

"But—we treated him with all respect." Hrrrl's

voice held hurt and puzzlement. "I do not understand why he would choose the wilds of Mishkara to our hospitality."

"It's not that, Hrrrl," Janeway hastened to soothe him, putting out a groping hand and touching his furry shoulder. "I told you about our friend, Kes, the girl who was kidnapped by Aren Yashar. Kes is very special to Neelix, and when he learned that we weren't going directly after her, I suspect he decided to do so himself."

"That is foolish, if you will forgive my saying so."

In the cool darkness of the cavern, Janeway smiled. "I didn't say it wasn't." She got to her feet, extending a hand above her head. She was disoriented in the blinding darkness, and didn't want to crack her skull against a forgotten overhang. "We'll have to go after him immediately."

"That is not possible."

Janeway wished she could see him. She knew Hrrrl could see her, even in this darkness, and she turned her face in the direction in which his voice came. "He's one of my crew. I won't see him harmed."

"Janeway, I have seen the scout ships. Your star-robber is looking for you. You do not move like a Sshoush-shin, you would be spotted at once." A deep, rumbling sigh. "We will scout for him ourselves, if you feel it is necessary. But I promise nothing."

"Thank you, Hrrrl. He might not have wandered as far as you think. We've got to try, at least, to find him."

The rest of the crew was waking up; Janeway heard the sounds of yawns and stretches and low conversation. She also knew they were as confused as she was. "Do you think someone could bring us some light, please?" she asked Hrrrl. The tallow candles they had been given last night—again, made from the fat of deceased Sshoush-shin—had guttered and died during the night, and Janeway knew that any attempt to ascend to the surface in this darkness would result in more injuries to her already battered crew.

"I will bring light and food and drink for your crew," said Hrrrl, rising to put action to his words. "It would be safer if you waited until nightfall to begin your quest to New Hann."

Hrrrl shuffled off in the blackness, and Janeway strained to sense where her crew was. "Good morning," she said to the darkness, aware that her voice was pitched louder than usual.

Various versions of "good morning" reached her ears. "We can't see one another yet, but I assume you all heard the news. Mr. Neelix has left us."

"Damn it," said Paris, with real heat. "Does he really think he can sneak up on Yashar all by himself?"

"Do we?" Janeway shot back. Paris did not answer. "It was unwise of him, and I'll be sure to let him know it when Hrrrl finds him, which I believe he will. Lieutenant Tuvok, how is your arm?"

"The splint provided by Hrrrl's healer, while crude, is certainly effective." *Cool as the cave itself,* Janeway thought.

She touched the bandage on her own head with gentle fingers. Hrrrl's healer, whose name escaped her at the present moment, had declined to tell her what was in the vile-smelling ointment he applied with a delicate touch, and she hadn't asked. "My injury appears to be healing as well."

Janeway turned toward the faint source of light that stretched tentative fingers into the darkness. It was Hrrrl, of course, approaching with two candles. Behind him, moving quietly down the stone steps despite their enormous bulk, came two more Sshoush-shin. Janeway recognized them as Rraagh, one of the technicians who had helped Paris and Torres with the shuttlecraft last night, and Grrua, the cook. Each of them bore large bundles, which they placed down and began to unwrap.

"Since you will be forced to spend the daylight hours, such as they are, below ground, I thought we should use the time to allow you to repair what tools you could. Also, Grrua and Rraagh will give you information about what you will encounter in your journey. I of course will come with you, as I promised, but it is well that you know how to be safe nonetheless. It is possible that something will happen to me, and then you will be on your own."

Janeway saw the uneasy looks on the faces of Torres, Paris, and Bokk. Tuvok, of course, merely raised an eyebrow. She fought back a shudder of apprehension of her own. The thought that anything out there was big enough and violent enough to bring down powerful Hrrrl was unsettling, to say the least. But she couldn't argue with the Sshoush-shin's logic.

"Hrrrl, you are a wise leader of your people," she said honestly. "They are lucky to have you."

He looked at her with those small eyes, and inclined

his head. "From what I have heard from you," he said, "I can return the kind words. I leave you in good hands. Listen well, for your lives may depend upon it."

He ascended the makeshift stairs to the surface, dropping to all fours to speed the pace. His bulk nearly filled the narrow corridor. Janeway returned her attention to the other two Sshoush-shin, who had seated themselves in front of their open bundles. Gravely, Rraagh handed some of the tools to Torres and Paris.

"We will continue the repairs we began last night while Grrua begins," he said. Bokk, Tuvok, and Janeway turned to look at the female Sshoush-shin.

"Janeway," said Grrua, "Last night, I spoke long with your friend who has chosen to leave us. He asked many good questions. I did not answer as thoroughly as I might have, as I thought he would still be here today, for the true lesson, but I did tell him much. He will be safer than most. And Hrrrl may be able to scent him, track him down for you when you depart this evening."

"Thank you, Grrua," replied the captain. "I hope you are right."

And then the lesson began.

Grrua placed before them literally dozens of plants that all looked alike to Janeway's untrained eye. Some were deadly. Some were bursting with vital nutrients. Some could stanch bleeding. Janeway wondered if her confusion showed on her face. Certainly Bokk looked hopelessly lost, and B'Elanna and Tom, when they glanced up from their tricorders and phasers and communicators, had blank looks on their faces. Tuvok, however, seemed keenly interested. Janeway hoped that his extensive background in horticulture as a hobby prepared him to detect the tiny differentiations in color, leaf size, texture and shape.

Then Grrua produced small but exquisitely detailed carvings from her pack and passed them around. Janeway held a little statuette in her hands, marveling at the intricacy of the workmanship. It was humanoid, but with a much stockier and more powerfully built torso and smaller legs. The head was enormous, and the face looked cruel.

Grrua waited until everyone held a statuette. Even Paris and Torres were requested to put down their tools for this particular lesson. "Parrris," growled Grrua, "show your carving."

Tom held up a pretty, frail-looking plant. It had a large flower at the top of a stalk, and serrated leaves continuing down to the base. At once, unbidden, the thought of Kes flashed into Janeway's mind.

"That is a kal plant. Avoid it at all costs. It is as high as you are, Parrris, maybe higher, and it smells sweet and innocent. But it likes the taste of flesh, and will as soon consume you as any bird that comes to pluck its petals for nesting."

Tom looked with renewed respect at the tiny figurine and handed it to Torres. "Flowers for m'lady?" he quipped. "Seems to me a carnivorous plant is just about your speed."

B'Elanna glared at him as she took the plant. "And yours, B—B—" Poor Grrua floundered helplessly over the name that clearly sat awkwardly on a Sshoush-shin tongue. "Torrres," she managed at last.

The chief engineer extended her right hand. Sitting in her palm was an animal that seemed to be a cross between a squirrel and a bat. Its overly large eyes and tiny features gave it a rather cute appearance, but after the plant, Janeway suspected the worst of the amiable looking creature.

She wasn't disappointed. "That is a kakkik. They will not prey upon you directly, but they will attack your thoughts—make you mad and make you do things you would not do."

"A psychic predator," said Tuvok. "Fascinating."

"Janeway, please show us your carving."

Janeway obliged, holding up the bulky, ugly humanoid. "That," said Grrua in a solemn voice, "is one of the Xians. They are takers-of-lives. It is part of their culture. They feel their race grows strong, the more blood they spill. It was their arrival that forced the guards at New Hann to strengthen their security. They introduced fear where once there was only cooperation. Be very, very careful of them. Hrrrl will do his best to steer a path that is clear of their settlements, but sometimes there are raiding parties. They are the most dangerous of any I have yet mentioned, for they are intelligent. The others, they are simple animals and plants, they cannot help what they do. But the Xians . . ." She gnashed her sharp teeth in loathing.

Janeway couldn't help but wonder how much truth there was to Grrua's statement. She certainly seemed to believe what she was telling the *Voyager* crew. But Janeway thought back to some of her history books, about how it was once thought the native people of Africa were irredeemable savages, fit only for slavery. How the Horta of Janus VI, so benevolent and intelligent, were called "devils in the dark" and killed on sight. Dreadfully, almost wickedly wrong misunderstandings that led to centuries of oppression and countless unnecessary deaths. Perhaps the Xians were so misunderstood by the Sshoush-shin.

It was not her place to intervene, however. This was no diplomatic mission, it was a fight for their very survival. She passed along the small statuette, taking one last, searching look at its vicious face before handing it to Tuvok.

"Bokk," continued Grrua. "Please show your carving."

Neelix hadn't wanted to steal food from the Sshoush-shin, but it couldn't be helped. Someone had to free Kes, and Janeway wasn't going to do it. At least, not in a timely manner, and Neelix was certain in his heart of hearts that every minute counted. It wasn't as if he'd disobeyed orders, yet still, he felt guilty. As he trudged, his feet stirring up powdery gray dust with each footfall, he fished in his pack— also "borrowed" from the Sshoush-shin—for a strip of dried meat he had snatched from the supply area. He sighed and began to gnaw dispiritedly on the filched fare.

Fortunately, the broken dome—New Hann, as his

furry hosts had called it—was so enormous, it could be seen from even this distance.

And what distance is that, Neelix? a small, unwelcome voice inside him nagged. *Don't know, do you? Just head on off, that's it, with no real supplies and stolen food—*

"Oh, shush," he said aloud, admonishing his conscience.

And Captain Janeway, and Paris, and Mr. Vulcan. Don't you think they'll be worried about you?

Neelix began to hum loudly, a traveler's tune about pleasure planets, fine food and drink, and other material delights. It cheered him somewhat, and distracted him from the fact that his legs were already, after only a few hours, starting to tire. He was not built for long hikes, and this one was going to be long indeed. His single lung labored to extract oxygen from the thin air, making the humming rather fitful.

The food sat sullenly in his belly, and he wished he'd taken a second waterskin while he was about it. As he hummed and walked, panting, he went over all the things Grrua had told him.

"Do not drink the water at the base of the four-leafed plants, for it is tainted. Do not eat the fruit of the sonnaibush, for it is poison. The dew found in the heart of the kulip is wholesome, but take care you do not touch the leaves while you are gathering the dew, for they will cause burns on your hands."

Do not, do not, do not. Neelix paused, huffing, and swallowed some water while he glared balefully at the broken dome in the distance.

It didn't look one whit closer.

Up ahead, maybe a half a kilometer, some plants grew halfheartedly about what seemed to be a still pool of water. It was a far cry from a true oasis, but Neelix decided he'd take what he could get.

"Provided," he grumbled aloud, "the water isn't clogged with the four-leafed plants."

Someone laughed.

Neelix whirled, brandishing a sharp stone he'd picked up. It made a pathetic weapon, but then, he knew that at least at this moment he was a pathetic warrior, so it at least seemed fitting. "Who's there?" he cried, trying to sound brave and fierce as any Sshoush-shin but succeeding only in sounding rather frightened.

Silence.

"I heard you laugh," Neelix continued, turning in a slow circle so as to look in all directions. His communicator was broken and he knew it, but it felt better to talk nonetheless. "Show yourself!"

Again, the mirth-filled trilling—light, like sunlight, burbling, like water. It didn't issue from a humanoid throat, but it was most certainly laughter.

Neelix whirled around again, starting to become really frightened. What if this laughing enemy was invisible to his field of vision? Or even worse, what if he'd eaten something he shouldn't have and was having auditory hallucinations?

Suddenly he heard a faint *whumph-whumph-whumph* sound and something soft brushed his face. He yelped, but managed to swing with his sharp stone. He struck nothing, but the gesture made him feel better.

The happy sound came again, and Neelix again turned around, searching desperately for its origins. This time, he saw the originator of the sound.

It hovered a few feet away from him, gently flapping its furred wings and creating the *whumph* sound Neelix had heard. In one forepaw, it clutched a berry of some sort and nibbled at the food with tiny, needle-sharp teeth. In another paw, it held a second bright blue berry. As Neelix stared at it, his jaw open, the little creature dropped the berry at his feet and flew a short distance away. It resumed its hovering and finished its own morsel. A bright pink tongue crept out to lick away all traces of blue juice from around its silver-furred muzzle. Its enormous eyes, a beautiful shade of light blue, were fastened intently on Neelix.

Neelix frowned, then, keeping his eyes fastened on the strange little flying ball of fur, bent to pick up the berry. He brought it to his nose, sniffed it, and his mouth began to water. Still watching the creature, he bit cautiously into the blue fruit. Tangy juice spilled over his tongue. It was delicious! Neelix had often found that his body knew best. If something was dangerous for him to eat, it smelled, looked, or tasted bad or off-putting, somehow. But this fruit was exquisite, and it didn't seem to harm the little furball. Throwing caution to the wind, he downed the berry.

Still in the air, the beast did a little flip and chortled happily. This time, Neelix laughed, too. What a cute little thing it was. When it flipped again, its puffy tail whipping over its head, and headed off toward the small oasis Neelix had spotted earlier, the Talaxian followed with a lighter heart than before. The creature clearly knew how to find wholesome food, and Neelix was more than willing to take advantage of the friendly overture.

By the time Neelix caught up with the little furball, it had found a perch on a large rock and was grooming itself. For the first time, Neelix realized that in addition to the furry wings the being had four paws. A six-limbed mammalian race was unusual, but Neelix had seen stranger things in his travels. Now, the creature sat up on its haunches, pulling its puffy tail through clever, four-fingered forepaws and meticulously cleaning it.

"You're a fine little guide," Neelix told it. It paused, fixed him with those beautiful eyes, and chirped happily. It then spread its wings and floated gracefully to the earth, where it began to lap eagerly at a small pool of surprisingly clear water. Following its example—it had already proven itself trustworthy with the berry—Neelix knelt and cupped up some of the precious liquid. He drank, parched from the journey, and water had never tasted so sweet.

Now the furball was off rooting around at the bottom of a bush, pausing to look back at him and chirp loudly. Neelix scrambled over to the bush, helping the creature dig. Sure enough, fat tubers extended deep into the soil, and he remembered that this was one thing that Grrua had definitely said was good to eat. He pulled them up excitedly, and grinned at his new companion. Breaking one root off, he tossed it to the creature. The furball caught it and began to nibble daintily. More exploration yielded an entire bush of the delightful blue berries. Neelix sat and munched happily, sharing the repast with Furball, who at one point clambered over to perch on Neelix's shoulder. The soft, fluffy tail tickled Neelix's neck, but he didn't mind as he popped another of the oddly crunchy, but delicious, berries, into his mouth.

The two odd friends sat in what passed for sunlight on Mishkara.

They feasted on dried leaves, brackish water, and beetles.

CHAPTER

11

COOL MIST BRUSHED KES'S FACE AS SHE ENTERED THE special room that Aren Yashar had prepared just for her. From somewhere came the splashing sound of running water. A redolent synthesis of fragrances teased her nostrils, and she closed her eyes and breathed deeply of the heady aroma. For an instant, she could forget.

"Does it please you, my little bird?"

Kes opened her eyes, returning to her reality. The light was warm and bright, as close an approximation of true sun's light as she had ever experienced, and the plants were thriving. Aboard *Voyager,* the plants had been arranged in neat, organized rows. They had been labeled, charted, studied, monitored. Cuttings had been taken, replanted, fruit and roots and leaves harvested for foodstuffs. Here, the plants had been allowed to run riot. A few Kes recognized, but most were unknown to her. Their freedom to grow as they would, without pruning or apparently even observation, almost made her heart hurt.

If only I were as free as these plants.

"Kes?" Aren's voice was concerned. "Don't you like them?"

She couldn't lie, even if she had wanted to. "Yes, I like them very much, Aren. They're beautiful." Her voice was thick as the words crawled past the lump in her throat.

"Ah, but there is so much more. Come," and he placed his hand lightly on her back, propelling her forward, navigating her through the verdant growth. Kes went where he led, partly because there was, as she had discovered, little point in fighting, and partly because she was curious. Aren stepped around some mushrooms growing on the "forest floor," pushed aside some shiny green fronds.

Before them was a small pool—artificial, of course, as everything save the plants themselves were—but inviting nonetheless. Grass grew beside **it**, and a waterfall came out of a false cliff wall to feed it. Steam rose as Kes watched.

"You have not bathed since you came here, Kes. I thought you might enjoy a pleasant place in which to cleanse yourself." She turned to look at him, surprise plain on her face, and he added, "Oh, not now. You'll have privacy if you like, of course. I merely wanted to let you know where it was, for later."

He seemed suddenly embarrassed, and his face flushed a little. Kes turned away, and buried her face in the nearest blossom. Her own cheeks felt hot.

"So I found you on the station," Aren whispered, moving up behind her with a soft tread, "hiding that sweet face in the sweetness of a flower's heart."

She tensed as he placed his hands on her shoulders, close to her neck. Out of the corner of her eye, she caught a flash of brilliant color from his finger-webbing.

"Look at this, Kes. I had to pay quite a large sum to bring this one here, but I think you will agree with me that it was worth it."

She moved her body as the subtle pressure of his hands directed, and found herself staring at a tree that might have been the model of the holographic one that had so captivated her back on the space station—the tree that had been her undoing.

Its bark was as dark blue as she remembered, and the serrated golden leaves moved in the gentle, warm breeze that circulated through the room. A giant, purple blossom, larger than her head, had opened, revealing a pale pink interior.

Almost as if drawn, Kes walked slowly toward the flowering tree. Aren's hands fell away from her shoulders, but he kept pace with her, his eyes fastened hungrily on her face, watching her. She paused in front of the tree, her small hands curling into fists.

"This one's real," said Aren softly. "They're all real. No more illusions, no more tricks with the holograms. I promise you that."

She looked over at him at that, her eyes searching his for the lie and not finding it. Kes turned back to the plant, and slowly reached out and stroked it with a forefinger.

Soft, like the skin of a child. Fragile, delicate. Kes knew that she could ruin the bloom with one strike of her hand, a gesture that would certainly show Aren Yashar what she thought of his gifts and efforts on her behalf. Yet she couldn't bring herself to do it. She couldn't destroy beauty, destroy *life,* simply to defy her captor.

The tears threatened again, and she blinked them back. Kes was not ashamed of weeping—why, even the doctor had lectured her rather lengthily on the positive effects of such a natural release of tension— but she did not know why, here, the tears came so often. This prison, of flowers and good food and soft beds and bright sunshine, and this captor, a man of grace and intellect and charm, were coming terrifyingly close to breaking her. She knew it.

Kes felt her already tenuous grip on control slip another notch as, unable to help herself, she pressed her face into the flower and breathed as deeply as if she were inhaling life itself.

No moon, no stars. Nothing to mark the difference between night and day save the most basic difference of all, light and darkness.

"It's eerie," said Bokk in a hushed whisper.

Janeway cast a glance up at the sky and nodded her agreement as she finished combing her snarled hair with her fingers. Quickly, she braided it, and tied it off. It would not be unbraided until the quest had been completed—successfully completed, she amended. With long hair, a braid was the only style that worked on long camping trips.

She made a face at the thought of equating this situation with something as comparatively pleasurable as a camping trip. Then, with a grunt, she hoisted her pack. In the flickering flame from the fire, she could see the rest of her crew preparing to embark. Tuvok's pack had been modified to be carried over his right shoulder only, because of his broken arm.

Torres, Paris, and the Sshoush-shin technicians had been able to accomplish more than Janeway had hoped. Two tricorders, three phasers, and three communicators had been repaired. Unfortunately, the tools that were found in the medikit were more delicate and complex than the others and could not be repaired with the tools—and the time—they had. Tuvok's arm remained broken, but he stood straight and confident. A reassuring sight—and she knew that all of them could use a little reassurance.

Janeway fiddled with the crude straps of leather and cinched the makeshift belt tighter, pulling her thick braid free as the pack pressed close on her back. She knew she looked a mess, and probably smelled as bad as she looked, but it couldn't be helped. Her greatest regret right now was that Hrrrl had been unable to find Neelix. Shortly after the *Voyager* crew had ascended from the cavern, he had taken her aside.

"I found his trail, but could not pursue it."

"Why not?" Janeway had whispered fiercely.

Hrrrl looked sorrowful but determined. "Your friend has entered Xian territory. I dare not trespass there, not alone. From the scent, the tracks were several hours old. I grieve with you, Janeway, for the loss of your friend."

But Janeway wasn't ready to admit defeat. "Save your sympathy," she had replied, a touch more harshly than she'd intended. "I'll grieve for Neelix when I have proof of his death. Not before."

The Sshoush-shin had been busy while she and her crew listened to and learned from Grrua and Rraagh. Each of them was presented with pelts that had been fashioned into capes, complete with hoods.

"To disguise you as well as we can," he said, draping the skin of an ancestor about Janeway's shoulders and fastening it with a sharp sliver of bone.

At once, heat began to surround Janeway. "Is this really necessary?"

Hrrrl nodded. "The scout ships will be out at night as well," he said.

Sweat gathered around Janeway's hairline, but she said nothing more. Hrrrl's caution might save all their lives, and certainly, he knew more about the habits of Yashar's pirates than they did. But the heavy cloaks would add nothing to the comfort of this particular trek.

She glanced about. "Saddled and ready?" she quipped. Her crew chuckled, and nodded. Their captain spared a moment to look at each of them. Tuvok, injured, but as calm and capable as ever. Paris, his bright eyes peering out from the shadow of the Sshoush-shin-skin cape, ready for anything. Bokk, his bulk looming large in the cape, a grim look of determination on his round, blue face. And Torres, looking fierce in the skin that was draped about her slim frame. Good people, all of them.

She spared a thought for Neelix, out alone on this

too dark night, and hoped he had indeed pumped Gruaa quite thoroughly for information. He'd need every scrap of it to survive in this place.

Hrrrl moved among them, tying a length of rope about their waists and attaching them. Janeway realized at once what he was doing. Once away from the lights of the fire, the humanoids would be all but blind. They would have to rely utterly on Hrrrl for their very survival. The ropes connected them to one another, and finally, connected their captain to Hrrrl.

The shaggy being took his position at the head of the line. "It is time," he said simply.

And they moved out, single file, into the dark Mishkaran night.

Operations Officer's log, stardate 50598.4. We have spent sixty-one hours on the sentry vessels in orbit around Mishkara, and it has been a frustrating and unfruitful time. The crew under me is in no way at fault; in fact, they're making some rather exciting and startling leaps of logic in order to try and figure out the operations of these vessels. But these alien ships are really very . . . alien.

Kim paused, replayed his entry, and shook his head. "Delete entry," he sighed. The strain was starting to show, and the last thing he wanted to do was sound like a whiny little excuse-maker in the formal log.

At least they'd been able to get life support going. That was something. It meant they'd be able to actually eat the supplies they'd brought with them. He leaned back against the bulkhead and glared sullenly at the hard, brick-like emergency rations that would serve as lunch and thought longingly of his mother's home cooking—even, to his surprise, Neelix's cooking. *Hell,* he thought with a sudden surge of resentment toward the unpalatable lump he was about to consume, *I'd take the glop-on-a-stick they sell on DS-9 over this stuff.*

Ensign Lyssa Campbell plopped down next to him, unwrapped her own block of food, and gasped exaggeratedly. Her blond hair had come loose and flopped down in her face. She tossed it back and gave Harry an enormous grin.

"Wow, Harry, look! Oh, boy, it's emergency rations again! Mmmm, mmmm!"

Despite his frustration and annoyance with himself, Kim had to smile. Lyssa grinned and punched him playfully in the arm. Her impish sense of humor had staved off many an argument over the last few hours.

Resigning himself to the taste, he took a bite of the hard, compacted food and chewed, thinking.

Why couldn't they crack it?

His dark eyes roved over the bridge. They'd been able to establish comfortable gravity and life-support, both from what apparently served as engineering. Kim wished desperately that he could have had a whole engineering crew beamed over here, but it simply hadn't been possible. He and Campbell had gone over every inch of the vessel in the last two-plus days, keeping in touch constantly with Carey and the others who were on the other two ships.

He'd been able to figure out how to operate the life–

support system with ease and in the process had learned some valuable things about the beings who had designed these ships. The mixture of oxygen and nitrogen was similar, if not identical, to that commonly inhaled by Earth-born dwellers. A slight adjustment in the mixture, increasing the percentage of oxygen and adding a bit more argon and carbon dioxide, and it was comparable to *Voyager*'s. So, it could have been Aren's people who had designed these ships.

That theory evaporated once he and Campbell had reached what served as the bridge. There were no seats at all. Kim sat down in front of one of the consoles and could barely reach it, though the bright buttons and gleaming lights indicated that beings with some sort of digits—and opposable thumbs—had operated the vessels.

They were big, whatever—whoever—they had been. And they didn't like chairs.

The gravity hadn't been too difficult to restore either. There was a vast network of forcefield generators, easily located and identified with tricorders and almost as easy to operate.

But the rest . . .

Lieutenant K'rin, over on the team led by Carey, had been badly injured on his first attempt to break into the bridge navigational systems. He'd been stabilized, thanks to a well laden medikit, but a session with the doctor was in order when they were able to return to *Voyager*, which wouldn't be until this mission was completed. K'rin had reportedly jokingly cried, "Keep delaying!" when this news was imparted to him.

Since that incident, they had all proceeded with utmost caution. Kim crunched a second bite of the dry bar and swallowed.

"I just don't get it," he said for what felt like the thousandth time but was probably only the fortieth or so. "Why could we establish life support and gravity but not be able to break into any of the controls?"

Campbell shrugged her thin shoulders and finished her own rations. She rose, and extended a hand.

"Harry, if I knew that, I'd have made Lieutenant by now. Come on. Let's take another series of tricorder readings and see if anything's changed."

"If I'd have known this would be such easy traveling, I'd have packed heavier," Neelix told his little friend. Furball was draped around his neck like a living scarf. It chirped, as if in answer, and sniffed at Neelix's ear. Its tail tickled Neelix's nose.

Giggling, Neelix pushed the friendly little creature's triangular head away. "Stop that, silly thing," he admonished, smiling.

Somehow, the air didn't seem as thin as it had before. Perhaps he'd had time to adjust to it. Furball seemed to have quite the knack for finding food and water, and had become the friendly, clever little pet Neelix had never had. He wondered if perhaps he couldn't sway Janeway into letting him keep the little fellow.

If it weren't for the knowledge that Kes was trapped

inside the desolate remains of New Hann, as the Sshoush-shin called it, Neelix could almost fancy himself enjoying this journey. He was soft from years of easy living aboard *Voyager,* and while that was nothing to be ashamed of as far as he was concerned, he found himself enjoying the sound sleep that came hand in hand with healthy exertion, and the feeling in his muscles as he pushed and stretched them to their limits.

The broken dome loomed closer now, and his heart lifted with every step. He'd rescue Kes. He'd do it if he had to choke Aren Yashar with his bare hands.

Furball stirred, as if something had made him uneasy. Absently, Neelix reached up a hand and patted his fuzzy companion. But instead of calming down at Neelix's touch, Furball rose. Four sets of small but sharp claws dug into Neelix's shoulders as the creature moved about, finally climbing atop his ride's head. It began to chirp anxiously and pulled on Neelix's hair.

"Hey!" yelped Neelix, frantically trying to dislodge the distressed animal. A claw scratched his cheek, drawing blood. "Ow! What's wrong with—oh."

And he suddenly saw just what was wrong with Furball.

Straight ahead of him, barely ten meters away, stood six humanoid aliens. They carried what looked like extremely dangerous, if primitive, weapons. From this distance, Neelix couldn't make out details, but he thought they were spears. Short, almost spindly legs supported stocky torsos, atop which were perched huge heads, utterly out of proportion to their bodies.

Their spines hunched over, as if they were somehow malformed, but there was nothing weak about them as they moved closer to him.

They were most definitely not Sshoush-shin.

"Oh, dear," said Neelix in a small voice. "Those would be the Xians, wouldn't they?"

CHAPTER

12

Tom Paris was hotter, sweatier, and thirstier than he could ever remember being.

The thin air didn't help any, either.

They were into the third day of the hike, and he felt as if he'd lost about ten kilos. He grew to dread the approaching darkness, even though it was cooler, because that meant hoisting his pack, his Sshoush-shin--skin cloak, and tying on the link rope for another ten hours of walking across soil that he couldn't see, almost falling over rocks that seemed to just love tripping him up, and stepping into a variety of things that smelled dreadful.

At one point, attempting to introduce a little levity, he looked over his shoulder at B'Elanna Torres slogging along behind him.

"Some fun, eh, Torres?" he'd quipped.

The look she shot him was only equaled by the

name she called him. Since then, Paris had stayed safely silent.

The days were better than the nights only because they weren't hiking. They still had to wear the suffocatingly hot, sweat-stiff capes as camouflage. The rations were meager, and he was pathetically grateful to Hrrrl's knowledge of the land for whatever he could find to supplement it with. Water was precious and doled out sparingly.

Paris made a cup of his hands and Hrrrl poured him his ration of water. He gulped it down, and, need driving out etiquette, licked the lingering droplets from his fingers. Next to him, Bokk was doing the same. Their eyes met and they exchanged a grin.

Torres was helping Hrrrl prepare a fire to cook the small creatures he had somehow managed to catch with his bare hands. They looked like ground squirrels of a sort, though their lack of eyes was disquieting. Hrrrl expertly skinned them, carved off pale pink flesh, and put it in a pot along with some other items he fished out of his pack.

"Blind squirrel stew," Paris said to Bokk. "A Mishkaran specialty."

Bokk giggled, sobering as Tuvok gave them both a critical glance. "In such situations as this," said Tuvok, arching a disapproving eyebrow, "I understand that humans and other humanoids enjoy humor to ease the tension. But you would be well advised not to rise to the level of insubordination, Lieutenant Paris."

"Aye, sir," replied Paris, his face blank. Privately, he thought that the rest of the crew got the better deal.

Tuvok was vegetarian; he had to eat the Starfleet rations. Blind squirrel stew somehow seemed better when viewed in that light.

Paris lifted up the cape, allowing a little bit of air to circulate and cool his overheated skin. Sweat did its job in that department as well.

There was an itching sensation along his left thigh. He ignored it, thinking it was merely his poor skin rebelling against three days of a dirty uniform and no air. The itching continued, finally metamorphosing into a hot, sharp pain. He glanced down and saw a red, multilegged insect happily chewing away on him.

"Hey, get off," snapped Paris, swatting the offending creature away irritably. He rubbed the area, which stung a little bit. "Stupid bug." Not just bad food, and dirty uniforms, but hungry bugs, too. Oh, this was just a swell away mission.

"Uh oh." It was Bokk, staring up at the sky.

"Cover yourselves!" snapped Hrrrl. The *Voyager* crew obeyed, pulling the cloaks tight about their bodies and hunching over as they sat. Paris knew even without looking, as the others did, that what Bokk had seen up in the sky was one of Yashar's scout ships. Hrrrl rose, and stretched exaggeratedly.

He's making sure they know there's a real Sshoush-shin here, Paris realized.

As he stretched, Hrrrl spoke. "Scouting parties of Sshoush-shin are not uncommon. Someone must search far afield for food, and our packs will further that illusion. I only hope it was enough."

Suddenly Paris felt a warm appreciation of his hot, smelly, heavy cloak. It might have just saved his life.

"There's a nice irony there, though," said his captain. "As long as Aren's got his scout ships patrolling for us, he won't activate the pulse. While Ja'in ships are in the sky, we're safe."

Tuvok turned to Hrrrl, who was stirring the stew. "Have you been able to scent Neelix at all?"

Hrrrl sighed, a deep rumble. "No, I have not. But neither have I seen the scavengers move with purpose." Tom's heart sank. It was clear that Hrrrl was trying to paint the brightest picture possible of Neelix's situation, but with every hour that passed, Paris doubted that he'd see his friend again.

Mishkara was brutal. That's all there was to it. He couldn't imagine trying to walk to New Hann without Hrrrl's guidance, alertness, and foraging skills. And Neelix—he may have been a survivor, but he wasn't the hardiest of the *Voyager* crew.

Isn't, damn it, Tom. He isn't the hardiest. Don't you dare start thinking about Neelix in the past tense!

He felt eyes on him, and glanced up to see Janeway looking at him with concern. "You all right, Tom?" she asked.

He nodded, glanced back down at his hands. "Just . . . just wondering how Neelix was doing, that's all."

She sighed deeply and rubbed at her own grime-streaked, sweaty face. "I should have kept a closer eye on him. He still cares for Kes."

"We all do," said Paris. A vision of Kes's pale face and blue eyes flashed into his mind. "You couldn't have known he'd have done something this—this—"

"Stupid," Janeway finished, with a bitter smile. "I think I should have. Neelix has thrown caution to the wind on other occasions. Well, we'll just have to hope our paths cross before too long. I'm certain he's heading in the same direction we are. And with a landmark like that—" she gestured toward the ruins of New Hann, which loomed on what passed for a horizon on Mishkara "—he can't get too lost."

"It's not his getting lost that concerns me," put in Torres. "It's whatever's out here that's got me worried." She shifted beneath her cloak. "Flesh-eating plants, psychic pick-picks—"

"Kakkiks," Paris corrected with a grin.

"Whatever. I mean, at least we've got tricorders, communicators, phasers. Neelix doesn't have anything. And somehow, I just can't picture him being able to fight off a horde of attacking ex-convicts with, I don't know, a pointed stick or some rocks or something."

Neelix stared down at his pointed walking stick and the rocks that lay at his feet.

Not much of an arsenal.

Neelix looked up again at the approaching Xians, who had broken into a run now, and swallowed hard.

There was nowhere to run. He had no way of communicating with them, and, truth be told, he didn't really think they were of a mind to listen to logical and reasoned discourse.

His life had begun on a pleasant, fertile moon that had been obliterated. Now, it was about to end on a planet that seemed almost as dead as Rinax.

Furball was chirping frantically, flapping about in wild circles. It flopped down on his shoulder, landing heavily, and almost knocked a startled Neelix off balance. He stumbled. The Xians came closer. He could see their hideous faces more closely now, and for an instant, his legs turned to water and he fell heavily to his knees.

Furball was going mad on his shoulders, and actually sank tiny, needle-sharp teeth into his ear. The pain jolted through Neelix. Hard on its heels came a deep, righteous anger. He rose, clutching a handful of rocks. Furball vaulted off his shoulders into the air, flapping its furred wings.

If he was going to die, it would *not* be on his knees. As the Xians came on, howling with bloodlust, Neelix bellowed out his own cry of defiance. Somewhere inside him, he was surprised by its volume and timbre. He took aim and hurled one rock after another.

The first one hit a Xian square in the throat. It stumbled, gasping. The second one caught another on the temple. This one fell. The others slowed, looking uncertain.

Furball dipped and dove among them, chattering furiously and flapping its wings in their faces but not actually landing on any of them. Neelix hesitated, not wanting to throw another stone and perhaps injure his little pet. He wished Furball would get out of his way.

Then it was too late for stones. The Xians were only a few feet away. Without thinking, Neelix hefted his pointed walking stick—he'd sharpened it earlier to help dig up roots—and howled. Holding it in front of him, Neelix met the Xians halfway.

He'd never been so angry, nor had he ever taken

such fierce joy in fighting back. Now he thrust forward with the makeshift spear, stabbing the nearest Xian in the gut and using his weight to force the point deeper into the soft flesh. The Xian cried out, a garbled, painful sound, and tried to lock its hands around Neelix's throat. The Talaxian twisted out of reach with an agility worthy of his winged friend, and tugged loose his weapon. The Xian fell to the ground, clutching his abdomen. Purple-red blood dripped onto the hard earth.

Neelix whirled, swinging the stick in front of him at the Xians who had suddenly halted. "Come on!" Neelix bellowed. "Afraid of a little man with a sharp stick? Huh?"

They backed up, though not without muttering and waving their own weapons. Overhead, watching the strange battle intently, hovered Furball.

Neelix's single lung labored for air, but he didn't dare show weakness, not now. He stepped toward the aliens, waving his stick about. "Grrua said you were really tough. Well, you're not so tough, after all, are you? Are you?"

He hurried forward, the stick in front of him, and the Xians scattered. Pausing only to pick up their fallen comrade, they fled before Neelix, yowling and jabbering in their guttural, rough tongue. When he dared, Neelix let the stick fall from his fingers and leaned down, placing his hands on his knees and drawing shallow, rapid breaths.

Blood dripped down from a wound in his left shoulder, but he didn't feel or see it. Furball plopped his soft weight down about Neelix's shoulder, cooing and nuzzling at his neck. Neelix found his breath coming easier and reached up a hand to pat Furball absently.

"Too bad you couldn't help me fight," he said wryly. "Though I appreciated the distraction."

Furball began to slide off Neelix's shoulder. Worried, Neelix twisted to catch his little companion. "Oh, no," he breathed. There was a deep slice in Furball's neck on the left side, right where the wing began. "Oh, you poor little fellow. Here, let's clean that up right now!"

He had no compunction about using the precious water to rinse the dust out of Furball's wound. The animal didn't protest, though it whimpered a little as Neelix's stubby fingers probed the depth of the injury with as much gentleness as possible.

"Well, it looks pretty clean, thank goodness. Let me just wrap it up closed . . . there we are. No more flying for a bit, though. You're not that heavy. I'll carry you till it's healed, all right?"

Furball's nose twitched and its blue eyes gazed deep into his. Neelix cradled it close to his chest, and it moved, snuggling closer. "Aw," said Neelix, stroking the soft fur. "You'll be all right, Furball. We both will."

He began walking again, his energy restored. Maybe this thin air was somehow good for him, after all. A breeze chilled his flesh, and he glanced over at his left shoulder. He was shocked to see that a Xian weapon had cut a neat incision in his coat. The flesh below, though, was completely whole.

Neelix suddenly broke out in a sweat. What had he

been thinking? He'd charged a whole group of some of the most dangerous aliens on the planet, alone, with only a stick for a weapon. And he'd won! Though it had been closer than he'd first thought, judging by that hole in his jacket. The tiniest fraction of a centimeter and he'd have been seriously injured. He'd been very, very lucky on this journey so far. What was it the Earth folks said sometimes? That you had a guardian angel looking out for you? Maybe one of their angels was having a slow day and had decided to look out for a wandering Talaxian.

Whatever it was, he wasn't going to question it.

Cuddling his pet close, Neelix continued his journey toward New Hann with a renewed spring in his step. Night was coming on, and he wanted to put a few miles under his belt before retiring.

When Aren Yashar had told Kes he could deny her nothing—except her freedom—he had apparently been serious.

Her request to see the control center had been immediately agreed to. Pleased at her interest, Aren had happily exclaimed that she was coming out of her shell and that she would be thrilled and delighted with the many interesting things to do. Down they had gone in the turbolift, until Kes was starting to become alarmed. Seeing her distress, Aren edged closer. He did not touch her, but Kes could feel his warmth, smell the wood-and-smoke fragrance with which he anointed himself.

At last, after what seemed forever, the doors hissed open.

Kes gasped.

The word enormous seemed too small for this room. She and Aren stood on a raised walkway, peering over the railing into a shadowed vault of machinery. Along the walls behind them were panels of all sorts, most of them dark. Only a few areas below were lit. Kes caught glimpses of dozens, perhaps hundreds, of monitors and video screens. The security guards, or computer operators, whatever their function was—Kes was uncertain—sat slumped in their chairs. Occasionally one would reach out a languid hand and tap something or other into the computer.

Aren cleared his throat, and chuckled a little to himself at how quickly the lethargic guards hastened to look busy. He grinned down at Kes. "An impressive array of systems, is it not?"

Kes nodded, her eyes roving over the consoles. "But why are so many of them inactive?"

"Mishkara, sadly, did not always belong to me," Aren explained as he led Kes down a winding metal stairway. "Long ago—well, long ago at least by your reckoning—this was a prison planet. The broken dome was once unbroken, and there was a greater need of terraforming technology as well as security systems. We still need security systems to operate as a Ja'in base, of course, but our requirements are somewhat different from what was necessary to effectively operate a prison."

"Who was imprisoned here?"

Aren shrugged. Kes was following him—Aren led, courteously, so that if she stumbled, he might break her fall—and the gesture drew attention to the strange knobby formations in the upper part of his back. In the dim lighting, even the slight protuberances cast shadows. Generally, Aren was careful not to turn his back on her. He seemed sensitive about letting her see the deformity. Now, though, he had no choice, and Kes looked her fill, wondering what they were and why he seemed to be embarrassed about them.

"A variety of races. If you're interested, I can show you how to research them on the computer. Do you enjoy learning about alien races?"

"I enjoy learning about everything," Kes answered honestly.

"There is much information in these computers, and most of the Ja'in are Rhulani. We have lived a long time, and have seen much. Between my people and my computers, I think you will run out of questions before we run out of answers for you."

They had reached the floor now. Kes made a quick bet with herself and won it. The moment his feet reached the last step, Aren turned around, once again positioning her so that she would not be able to see his back. He extended a hand, but Kes didn't take it. If he was irritated by the refusal, he did not show it.

"So, my little bird, what catches your fancy? Name the topic and we shall find it."

"You mentioned that this base once had extensive terraforming technology," said Kes. "Where would that be?"

Aren clapped his hands together twice. At once, the

slimmer, nervous looking Rhulani named Kula Dhad hastened up. "Great one?" he asked, bowing quickly.

"You've worked with the archives on these computers, haven't you?"

"Yes, Great One, although Shanri Shul is more—"

"Excellent. My dear Kes has expressed an interest in learning about Mishkara's past, especially the terraforming technology used by the Sshoush-shin. Can you teach her how to access those old records?"

"I shall do my utmost," replied Kula Dhad promptly.

"Then, dear one, I leave you to the attentive care of Kula Dhad. If you have any questions, he will either answer them, or find someone who can."

"Indeed, Great Kes."

"No, please," replied Kes, uncomfortable with the adjective, "I'm just Kes."

Dhad glanced from Aren to Kes and back again. Aren inclined his head slightly, and Dhad relaxed. "As you wish, Kes."

Aren turned to climb back up the stairs. Surprising herself, Kes blurted out, "Where are you going, Aren?"

He paused in mid step, and surprised pleasure lit his face. "Why, little bird? Will you miss me?"

Kes didn't know how to respond. "I—you've never left me with anyone else before. I just wondered."

"Would you like me to stay?"

"No, no, that's all right," Kes replied, wondering why polite, soothing words were slipping past her lips instead of angry defiance. "I'm sure Kula Dhad will be a fine teacher."

Aren hesitated, his purple eyes searching her face. "It is said that time away from one makes you long for one's return. I hope that is true with you, little bird. I know it is true of me." Quickly, he ascended the stairs, his booted feet making the metal ring. Kes watched him until he vanished into the shadows.

She turned and found Dhad watching her with sharp eyes. His appraising expression melted into that of the obeisant servant he had been before Aren Yashar.

"You're all terribly afraid of him, aren't you?" she asked.

"We'd be fools not to be," was Dhad's simple, eloquent reply. "He rules this base as a god rules his world. Now, Kes, you wished to see the history of terraforming on Mishkara?"

CHAPTER
13

THE SUN'S LIGHT FADED. ONE COULDN'T PROPERLY CALL it a sunset, thought Paris; you needed to be able to see the sun to watch it set on a horizon. But the light did disappear, and he resigned himself to yet another night of hiking.

He ran a hand through his hair. It was wet and greasy with sweat. Even the hologirls probably wouldn't look twice at him now. He felt incredibly filthy. Paris took a few deep breaths, gathering the wherewithal to rise.

These last few days were really taking a toll on him. He'd fancied himself pretty physically fit, but this trek, with its rationing of unpalatable food and warm, brackish water, heavy packs and cloaks, and, above all, thin air, was really taking a toll. He'd thought the hydrosailing, swimming, skiing, and mountain climbing that comprised a great holodeck break were sufficient to keep him in peak condition, but apparently not.

And that stupid bug bite. It itched like crazy. He scratched it through the material of his uniform, but that just made it itch more.

"Tom, are you all right?" Paris glanced up and realized that everyone, even pudgy Bokk, was already standing up and prepared to depart. His face flamed, and he was glad of the approaching darkness that hid his embarrassment to at least some degree.

"I'm fine. Never better," he lied, his tone of voice artificially cheery. He rose and hoisted his pack, wondering if someone hadn't mischievously slipped a few dozen kilos' worth of stones in it when he wasn't looking, and forced a smile. "Let's hit the trail!"

It was easier when you didn't think about it, Paris discovered sometime well into the fourth or fifth hour of that night's hike. Just put one foot in front of the other. Don't worry about how heavy the pack is, or how damn *hot* you feel, or how your legs are shakier than the lie you come up with when one girl catches you with another.

Instead, as he had done when he and Harry were prisoners of the Akritirians, he thought of food. A thick steak would be good along about now, Tom thought, brightening at the image he conjured up. And corn on the cob, crunchy and sweet, with a melting pat of butter on it. A tall glass of beer with just the right height of frothy head to wash it all down with. Yes, that would be just the thing.

I can almost see it . . . I *can* see it—

The thick steak that led them came suddenly to a

halt. "Quickly!" it cried, rapidly untying the rope that bound it to the other foodstuffs. "I can smell them. Get ready for a fight!"

Dazed and utterly confused, Paris stood on wobbling legs as the giant glass of beer in front of him and the corn on the cob behind him followed suit. The yellow corn turned toward him, speaking with B'Elanna's voice and waving green fronds in his face.

"Tom, what are you doing?"

He rubbed his eyes with filthy hands. The ear of corn suddenly transformed into Torres. She seized his arms and shook him roughly. He fumbled with the rope, but his fingers wouldn't cooperate. With a snarl of exasperation, Torres thrust a crude club—a Sshoush-shin weapon—into his hands.

Tom was frightened by his strange hallucination. His heart slammed against his chest and he tossed off the cloak and pack. He fought off rising panic at his lack of ability to see very far in the darkness. Stumbling, Paris hoisted the primitive but effective weapon, and hoped desperately that if he had to swing it, he wouldn't bring it crunching down on the skulls of his companions.

A gibbering howl shattered his eardrums. Paris gasped, clapping his hands over his ears as the sound seemed to vibrate right through him.

Hrrrl answered with his own bellow. Paris could just make out his shape, charging into the darkness. He stumbled forward, raising his club, determined to do something, anything, to help. He heard the whir of a phaser blast, and one of the shapes lurking in the darkness dropped like a stone.

The familiar sound lifted Paris's spirits, calmed his nerves. He could see them now, and recognized their attackers as the Xians. They were every bit as formidable a foe as Grrua had warned. Janeway, Tuvok, and Bokk were firing with their phasers, but it was so dark, and they were so hard to see—

Something seized Paris's arm, yanked him around. He had just enough time to register a horribly ugly face, foul breath, and a mouthful of sharp teeth that, somehow, he could see very clearly indeed despite the darkness, before a phaser blast caught the creature in the midsection. It fell, but didn't release its grip on Tom, and Paris tumbled down with him.

As he struggled to get free of the creature's unconscious grip—he assumed, at least, that the phasers had been set on stun—the battle continued to rage around him. He heard Torres bellow something in Klingon, heard the dreadful noise of clubs and spears hitting home. Above it all, there was an incoherent scream of pain and terror.

"Bokk," whispered Paris to himself. He got to his feet but almost fell again immediately. Nausea overwhelmed him for a moment, and he feared he was about to lose what little food he'd been able to consume. The world of dark, battling figures swirled for a moment, then stabilized.

"Help!" came Bokk's voice, shrill with horror, and Paris stumbled toward the sound. He tripped over a prone body—dear God, he hoped it wasn't one of his friends—but recovered, shuffling on like a drunken man in the direction of the cries.

When he finally spotted the Bolian, Paris wondered

for a wild instant if he was having another hallucination.

Bokk was only visible from the waist up. It was wildly comic at first, as though someone had planted him feet first in the soil and hoped he'd grow. Paris instantly realized what had happened, though. Bokk had fallen into something. Paris came closer and saw that the ensign wasn't in a hole—he was literally buried in the soil.

"Tom! Help me!" he cried pathetically, reaching out with his stubby arms. They were coated with a thick pasty substance.

The rope. It was still tied around his waist. "What happened?" Paris cried over the din as he fumbled with the knot. Not far from them the battle still raged. Wave after wave of Xians kept coming. Would it never stop?

"I was running—and then the earth, it wasn't solid below my feet—I'm going deeper, Tom, help me! It hurts—"

Quicksand. Rare enough on Earth, rarer still on other worlds, but it was one of the forty thousand or so dangers of which Gruaa had warned them. She had called it "the sand that eats." Paris was glad he hadn't come any closer or else he'd be in there with Bokk, being sucked down until he suffocated.

"Be as still as you can, Bokk," Paris called to his friend. "The more you struggle, the deeper you go. Try to float, like you're swimming."

"I can't swim!" screamed the Bolian. "Oh, it hurts!"

Hurts? Paris was utterly confused. Quicksand was frightening, sometimes deadly, especially if the victim panicked, but it didn't actually hurt you.

He'd gotten the rope loose now, and tried to recall what he knew about quicksand. It wouldn't help Bokk if he, Paris, got trapped in the gooey mess too. He could see the Bolian, still splashing about despite his warnings. Paris aimed and tossed out the end of the rope.

Bokk saw it, and ceased his flailing long enough to grab for it.

And then Paris's eyes widened with horror.

The rope began to disintegrate. As Bokk reached for it, Paris stared in shock at what was left of Bok's arm.

The quicksand was dissolving him.

The sand that eats . . .

At that same instant, a strand of quicksand reached up and tried to wind its tentacle around his arm. Paris jumped back, tripping over his own feet and falling hard on his back. The wind was knocked out of him and for a moment he couldn't draw breath. He flipped over and scuttled away. Already his arm was burning from where the acidic quicksand had brushed him.

Bokk was silent now. The sand had him. Paris forced himself to look back, and saw nothing out of the ordinary where a friend had once been.

He gasped, his lungs beginning to work again, wondering what he had seen—what was real, and what wasn't.

Paris didn't trust himself to make that kind of a judgment anymore.

Beneath the material of his uniform, the bug bite itched furiously.

At Hrrrl's harsh bark of warning, Janeway immediately threw off her cloak and rid herself of the bulky pack. She activated the wristlight—the need to see her opponent far outweighed any risk of discovery at this instant—and drew her phaser, setting it on heavy stun.

The Xians had a horrible war cry that lifted the hairs on Janeway's arms. Hrrrl's answering challenge was every bit as alarming. Before her eyes, Janeway saw her friend drop the facade of civilization like a mask. His dewlaps curled back from his powerful teeth, and Hrrrl dropped to all fours and charged the approaching attackers like a mad bull.

Janeway took aim at a dark figure running toward her and fired. The blast of energy struck it full in the chest and it fell backward, spasmed, and lay still.

She sensed rather than saw Tuvok behind her, his back to hers, using his own phaser. More Xians fell. But they kept coming, as if they were of infinite number. No wonder Grrua had spoken of them with such fear and loathing.

Three phasers firing at once were doing a good job of slowing them. Out of her range of vision, she heard Hrrrl snarling and fighting his own, more brutal, battle with his peoples' worst enemy.

Still, some made it through. Out of the corner of her eye, the captain saw one of them reach Tom. She whirled, took aim, and fired. The Xian crumpled, but

Tom fell with him. Janeway felt a surge of worry—something was not right with Paris, she knew it—but there was no time to check on him, no time to do anything but aim and fire, aim and fire, as wave after wave of troll-faced monstrosities kept coming. The sounds were awful, and Janeway fought to tune them out, to keep her concentration. The Xian scream of anger, Hrrrl's enraged bellows, Torres's defiant cry in Klingon, and someone else off to the right shrieking in dreadful agony.

In a language she understood.

It was one of her crew.

She half turned, distracted despite herself, and only barely got an arm up in time to block the blow of a heavy club. Instinctively she rolled with the movement, landing on the earth hard but getting her legs underneath her and springing up again almost immediately. The Xian was not expecting the maneuver, and his forward motion carried him a few steps before he could recover and stop. Torres was there, lacing her fingers together and bringing them down hard on the back of the creature's neck. The blow knocked it to its knees, and Tuvok's phaser sang.

Janeway found her own weapon, and made a full circle, ready for the next attack. But it didn't come. It seemed that the Xians had finally had enough.

"Captain!" The voice belonged to Paris, ragged, raw with the sharp edge of fear to it. "Bokk—"

She flashed her wristlight about in the direction of his voice. He looked terrible. He was bloody and pale and looked as though he was about to collapse any moment. She turned the light in the direction in which he pointed, but found only a dark patch of sand. Frowning, she tried to catch her breath as she stepped toward it.

Paris's hand on her arm was as unexpected as it was violent. "No! Don't go near it! Quicksand!"

"Quicksand?" asked Torres, coming up behind them.

"A bed of soft sand, saturated with water." It was Tuvok's voice, calm and soothing. "It tends to engulf unwary creatures."

"Like Bokk," said Janeway softly. She shone her light about, searching for something, anything, that would show a trace of the Bolian. But the surface appeared utterly undisturbed. "We should try to retrieve his body if we can."

"No!" It was Paris again, panicky, frightened. His face shone greasy with sweat in the light. "It's more than quicksand, it's alive!"

Janeway studied him carefully. "Are you certain, Tom?"

He thrust out his arm for her to examine. "It made a tentacle out of itself and tried to pull me in. Look."

His uniform had burned away and there was a nasty red welt on the skin. Janeway felt a quick jolt of nauseated horror as she realized exactly how poor Bokk had died.

No time to dwell on that. "Torres, you've got the medikit. Start working on Tom's arm right away. Anyone else injured?" she asked briskly.

Torres, rummaging in her pack, glanced down at her thigh. It was cut and bleeding. "This isn't too bad. I'll clean it up after I take care of the lieutenant." Her voice shook a little, but the set of her jaw was stubborn.

Janeway did a quick head count. Tom, Tuvok, Torres, herself—

"Damn it. Hrrrl's gone. Tuvok, you're in charge. I'm going to go look for him." She checked her phaser, then headed out into the darkness.

Janeway hadn't gone far before the sweep of her wristlight revealed a furry lump. She hastened up to it, fearing the worst, but then Hrrrl groaned.

"Hrrrl, are you injured?"

"No," came the reply in a voice laden with pain. "At least, not on my body." He rolled into a sitting position, and she saw that he was covered with blood.

"The blood—"

"Xian blood, not mine," he assured her. He made no further move to rise, narrowing his eyes against the artificial brightness of her light. Janeway switched it off and sat beside him in the darkness. Torres would take care of the injured for a few minutes, and poor Bokk was beyond any aid she could give. She hadn't captained the *Voyager* crew for this long without developing some intuitiveness, and right now, she knew that something was deeply troubling Hrrrl.

She waited for him to speak. At last, he did. "I took the lives of three of them." She heard him move, and sensed he was looking at his hands. "With these. I took lives with my own hands, Janeway. I cannot return to my people."

"Hrrrl," Janeway said gently, groping in the dark for his powerful, furry arm and placing her hand on it, "you did what was necessary. We all did. Gruaa was

right about the Xians. Talk would have been wasted
on them, at least in this situation, and more than one
of my crew would have died had we not fought."

Hrrrl crooned in the back of his throat. "The Xians
killed one? Janeway, I mourn with you. Who was it?"

"It wasn't the Xians. Ensign Bokk was trapped
by—by the sand that eats."

Hrrrl reached over and Janeway felt the now familiar circling of his clawed hand on her back, offering
wordless comfort. She smiled in the darkness, knowing he could see it.

"Your bravery in attacking the Xians saved many
more lives, Hrrrl."

"But I am now a taker of lives!" His voice was a cry
of anguish, and he removed his hand from Janeway's
back. "I cannot infect the Sshoush-shin with such a
contamination. I must remove myself from them."

"Hrrrl, tonight when we fought, our weapons were
set on stun. Our technology is sufficiently advanced
for us to determine what amount of force to use. But
if we hadn't been able to repair those three phasers,
we'd have had to use spears and clubs, just like your
people. And we'd have taken lives, too."

She paused, gathering her thoughts. Hrrrl was quiet
now, but she sensed he was listening.

"Under the laws of most of the worlds that belong
to our Federation of Planets, there is an understanding that sometimes, it's necessary to take a life. There
are special terms used in legal situations—man-
slaughter, self-defense, murder—that identify when
it is acceptable and when it's not."

"But my claws—"

"Hrrrl, it is possible to kill and not be a killer, to take a life under certain circumstances and not be a taker-of-lives. Tonight, you saved lives here. You didn't instigate the attack, you merely defended yourself and us. You did the right thing. No one could listen to the story of what happened tonight and think otherwise."

"Is—is this truly what your Federation believes?"

"It is," Janeway stated firmly. "And moreover, it's what I personally believe."

Again, the silence stretched between them. Finally Hrrrl said in a low voice, "It is a struggle. We were not born to be peaceful. You have only to look at our claws, our teeth, to see that. But we *want* to be peaceful. We want to help, not hurt, and tonight, I took a step away from the ideals of the Sshoush-shin. I am ashamed."

Janeway reached out a hand and rubbed his back in the fashion that he had taught her.

"You should be proud that you strive for something higher, something better, than being mere animals, Hrrrl. I'm proud of you. I still think you believe in the Sshoush-shin ideal. But you're not in a civilized world here. Perhaps someday, there won't be a need for you or your people to fight in self-defense. Perhaps . . ." her voice trailed off. Now she was handing out false hopes instead of true comfort.

"Captain," called Tuvok. "There is something here I believe you and Hrrrl should see."

"We'll be right there," called Janeway. "Are you all right?" she asked Hrrrl in a soft voice.

The big Sshoush-shin took a shuddering breath, then she heard him rise. "I will have to be, won't I, if I am to safely get you to your destination."

Janeway activated her wristlight and hastened back toward the others, Hrrrl lumbering—standing on his hind legs again—at her side. "What is it?" she asked, kneeling beside Paris.

"I am uncertain, but I believe he has become infected," Tuvok answered. They had propped Paris up against a large stone, and B'Elanna frowned terribly, her arms crossed.

"I should have concentrated on the medical tricorder," growled the chief engineer.

"Torres, we needed weapons, communication, and at least one tricorder. You had your priorities straight. Guess we'll just have to figure this out the old fashioned way."

She knelt beside Paris, who was conscious, though clearly ill. He fought to keep from trembling, but his face had lost all color and sweat gleamed on his brow. Janeway reached out a hand and pressed it to his forehead.

"Tom, you're burning up!" She placed two fingers on his neck: the pulse was rapid and thready. "Have you eaten anything that we haven't?" she asked, taking the canteen Torres offered. Gently, she placed a hand behind Paris's head—it was soaking with sweat—and lifted him up so that he could drink.

He gulped at the water, and she pulled the canteen back. "A little at a time," she admonished gently.

Paris licked gray lips. "I've eaten what you have,

and I don't think—wait a minute. There was a bug that bit me, I don't know, a couple of days ago—itched like crazy."

Janeway's heart sank, but she fought to keep her worry from showing. "Where did it bite you?"

He gestured. "On the thigh. Still itches."

Torres glanced at her captain, who nodded. Swiftly Torres knelt and with a small knife cut a slit along his left thigh.

"Oh, my God," breathed Janeway, despite herself.

The flesh was puffy and a sickly color of black green. Janeway could see the bite clearly: a dot of white tissue amid the sea of putrefaction. Beneath the harsh glare of the wristlight, she could see something else.

Something was moving under the skin.

CHAPTER
14

TORRES CLUTCHED THE SMALL KNIFE SO HARD THAT HER fingers cramped. She swallowed, once, twice, keeping the bile down where it belonged.

Tom could see their faces, and his own registered fear. "What is it?" he asked, and struggled weakly to see his thigh.

Torres moved swiftly, almost without thinking, to turn his face away from the sight. It was bad enough that they had to see it. He didn't have to. She moved to take his head in her lap, as much to be able to control what Paris saw as to offer comfort.

"It's a bad bite," she said. That much, at least, was true. She glanced over at Janeway, who, with Hrrrl, was still intent on inspecting the wound. There came the sound of a phaser; in the darkness, Tuvok was preparing to boil water. Janeway glanced up and shook her head, ever so slightly. *Don't tell him.*

B'Elanna nodded her own head in a subtle acknowledgment and waited for her captain to speak. She leaned forward and wordlessly handed Janeway the knife. The captain was going to need it. Janeway took it and said something in a low voice to Hrrrl. The Sshoush-shin clicked his teeth twice—a negative—and replied in a voice equally soft.

"What's going on?" asked Paris, sensing his captain's distress.

Janeway squatted back. The beam from her wristlight bounced off the earth, casting strange shadows. "You've been bitten by something that's obviously got some kind of poison. Hrrrl's never seen it before. It's harmless to the Sshoush-shin—their hides are a lot thicker than ours. I won't lie to you. It looks pretty bad, and we've only got the crudest of tools to work with here. Some of the flesh is gangrenous. I'm going to have to cut away the dead flesh. When we get back to *Voyager,* the doctor will be able to regenerate anything we have to—to get rid of. You'll be fine." There was a heavy emphasis on this last word, and even in the weird, partial lighting, Torres could see her captain's eyes filled with intensity.

I'd believe it, Torres thought. *I hope it's true.*

Paris took a deep breath. "Okay. Get to it." What else could he say?

"Tom," Torres said softly, "we don't have any anesthesia here. When the captain is working on the dead tissue, it shouldn't hurt, but she's going to have to go into the healthy flesh as well."

"Hey," quipped Tom, rallying as best he could,

"I've been through worse. At least this time my tongue's not falling out."

His smile was forced, and vanished almost immediately. Torres took a deep breath of her own, preparing herself. She was going to have to hold Paris down while they worked on him.

A flash of inspiration came to her. "Hey, Tom, tell me about this new holodeck program you've been working on. The one that almost got you in trouble on Oasis."

"You heard about that?"

"It's a small ship. Word gets around."

He smiled a little at that. Just at that moment, Janeway made the first cut. From where she sat, with Paris's head on her lap firmly between her palms, Torres could see the whole operation with clarity.

"It's based on Earth's history around the eighteenth century," Paris was saying. He kept his face carefully blank; Torres couldn't tell if he was feeling any pain yet or not. "Most of the action takes place on a galleon called *The Captain's Lady*. I, of course, am the dashing pirate captain."

"I'd have cast you as the scullery boy. Teach you a little humility."

"Ah, but it's my holodeck progr—*ah!*"

Torres felt him go rigid. She slipped an arm around his chest, trying to calm him and hold him down.

"Be as still as you can, Tom," she said. "You fight and the captain might cut something she shouldn't."

She felt warm breath on her cheek as, despite the agony he must be feeling, he laughed a little.

"Wouldn't—want—that," he managed through clenched teeth.

"Almost done," said Janeway.

"So," continued Torres, desperately racking her brain to come up with chatter to distract the patient, "Can I be in this pirate program of yours?"

"Oh, I have a part—in mind for you—*God! Ah!*"

"Still!" commanded Torres. Tom was bucking now, and Hrrrl came to add his own strength to keep the wounded man from hurting himself further. "Keep talking, Tom, what part do you have for me?"

Out of the corner of her eye, B'Elanna saw Janeway working busily with the sterilized knife. The captain removed a palmful of decaying flesh riddled with wriggling maggots. Torres closed her eyes.

Paris screamed again, then went suddenly limp.

"Good," muttered Janeway. "We can work faster now that he's not conscious and feeling the pain."

She finished up quickly, and poured hot, clean water into the wound, washing out the last remnants of putrefaction. Hrrrl handed her a jar of ointment. Janeway scooped out some and packed it into the gaping hole in Paris's thigh. Finally, she bound the hole with strips of clean cloth, torn earlier from their uniforms for just such a need.

Sighing deeply, Janeway sat back. Hrrrl poured hot water over her bloody hands and she washed them with great fervor.

"Is he okay?" asked Torres.

"I'm not sure," replied Janeway. She looked tired. "I got all the necrotic tissue and the larvae the insect had deposited. Tuvok theorizes that the insect lays its eggs in living flesh and the poison makes the host's flesh decay, providing food for the larvae as it's needed." At Torres's expression, she grimaced in sympathy. "I know. It's not pretty. As I said, we got the larvae and the dead tissue. I simply don't know how far the poison has spread into the lieutenant's system. And we can't begin to process an antivenom until we get back to *Voyager*. We just have to hope we got it all, and that Tom can hang on till then."

"There is the issue of transporting him," interjected Tuvok. He gestured to his arm, lying uselessly in a sling. "We have come too far to return to Hrrrl's encampment. Mr. Paris is clearly unable to walk on his own at this point, even if the poison has been completely eradicated. Ordinarily, I would have more than enough strength to carry the lieutenant and my own supplies, but the broken arm does not permit me to lift him."

"I can carry Parrris," said Hrrrl.

Janeway considered. "I'd rather you didn't, Hrrrl. We need you out front, unencumbered. You're our point man. We could perhaps make a travois—"

"I can carry him," said Torres suddenly. "I'm half Klingon, remember?"

"We've got a long way to go," Janeway reminded her.

Torres shrugged, trying not to let her concern show. "I'll let you know when I'm tiring. We can try a travois then. In the meantime, it would only slow us down."

"All right," Janeway agreed. "But don't push your-self too far, Torres. We've all got to keep our strength up." She rose, took a final swig from the canteen, and packed it away. "I'll take Tom's pack. Let's get going. We've still got a few hours left of the night."

Torres put on her own pack. Hrrrl stood beside her, holding the concealing cape. She knelt beside Paris, slipped her arms underneath him, and hoisted him as gently as he could.

For the first time she could remember, she was suddenly grateful for her Klingon blood. She could carry Tom, thanks to the strength it gave her. She could perhaps save his life. A fierce tenderness washed through her, spreading a sudden calm. She could help, because of who she was, in a way that no one else could. That was something of which to be very, very glad.

He was not much of a burden in her arms. She shifted Paris gently, trying not to wake him. Hrrrl placed the cape on her shoulders, and gave her back a quick circular rub.

Bearing her precious burden, Torres followed her captain into the night.

Kes hit a final button, and the screen went dark. She stretched and her stiff muscles popped. It felt good. She suddenly realized that she had been sitting here in front of the console for several hours, feeling no need to move or eat, intent only on learning what this alien computer had to teach her.

In another chair a few seats away, Kula Dhad lay

with his head on the table, sound asleep. He'd become quiet some time ago, but Kes had only barely noticed. She had sat, blue eyes wide and hardly blinking, her face, like a flower turned toward the sun, bathed in the radiant glow that imparted so much information.

She hadn't done much investigation into the Federation's technology of terraforming. She knew a few of Starfleet's principles with regard to such things, of course. The regulations were very strict. Planets with indigenous life-forms were not to be terraformed. The only planets that could spring to new life thanks to advanced technology must be truly dead.

But the Federation's terraforming technology operated on a planetary scale. The furry creatures known as Sshoush-shin, who had erected the protective dome of this place they called New Hann, had been able to regulate the scale on which the technology was enacted. An area as small as five square miles could be terraformed.

Kes had allowed herself to be slightly sidetracked while researching the terraforming information. She had learned about the Sshoush-shin, the Xians, and the other races who had once been imprisoned here, about some of the extremely dangerous native life that called Mishkara home. With nothing else to do for these hours other than learn, Kes had absorbed information like a sponge. Now, her body, forced to be still for so long, was paying the price.

She rose and went over to Dhad. "Wake up," she said softly, gently shaking his shoulder.

Kula Dhad sprang to alertness with an intensity

that startled Kes. He leaped to his feet, drawing his weapon. She stepped back, raising her hands. "It's all right!" she said. "It's just me!"

Slowly, Dhad lowered the weapon, looking embarrassed and still blinking himself awake. "How long?"

"I'm not sure." Kes fought to keep the mirth from her voice. "It was very interesting."

"Clearly," snorted Dhad, rubbing his eyes. "Are you finished?" She nodded. "Good. I might have the chance to get an hour or so of sleep in an actual bed before going on duty again. Come on."

She followed him up the stairs and to the turbolift. He pressed the controls, and it began to rise. For a while, they were silent, then Kes asked, "I know you're tired, but I'd like to try the bath that Aren constructed for me. I don't suppose you'd let me go on my own?"

Dhad shook his head. "You'll have privacy in the room, of course, but someone will have to guard the door. And since I did such a poor job of guarding you just now, I think I'd better cheerfully volunteer for the duty." He paused and glanced over at her. "You, er, won't mention it to Aren? That I fell asleep at my post? What with the ships out—"

He closed his mouth with an audible click. "Ships out? Why?" asked Kes, instantly alert.

"Nothing you need to worry about."

Suspicion flowered inside Kes. "What are the ships out for?" she pressed.

"There—there have been rumors of a Sshoush-shin uprising. Aren didn't want you to know—didn't want to frighten you." Dhad didn't meet her eyes.

The hope that had blossomed inside Kes died. From what she had read of the Sshoush-shin, they were a peaceable people. But she had also read about the harsh realities of living on Mishkara, and it was not difficult to believe that years of fighting to survive on this planet might have turned a race of peaceful people into violent nomads.

And it wasn't too much of a leap to think that they might focus their anger on the Ja'in.

But she had hoped that the ships were out fighting *Voyager,* and that Captain Janeway was trying, still, to find her.

The turbolift came to a halt with a squeak and a jolt. Time to come back to her reality.

Dhad, to his credit, didn't complain. He waited in patient silence for Kes to slip into a robe and gather the things she would need for her bath. He didn't even ogle her when she emerged from her rooms, merely led her to the hydroponics room, keyed open the door, and permitted her inside.

"I'll be out here if you need anything. Take your time," he said, and then the door hissed softly shut.

The light was muted in this room, but there was enough for Kes to see. For a moment, though, she simply stood, letting her eyes adjust to the dimness, enjoying the smells and the sound of splashing water.

Though he hardly knew her at all, really, Aren knew her very well indeed. She shed fear and tension here in this room almost as easily as she shed the robe, letting it fall to the floor and stepping out of it. The air was warm on her body, the light soft, calming. All around her, plants went about their business of growing, content just to be.

Perhaps I need to learn from the plants, Kes thought as she reached to caress a large, green leaf with a waxy texture. *They can't change what happens to them, so they just let it happen. Roots grow around the rocks; vines twine around the tree trunk.*

With a last pat, Kes, smiling softly to herself, stepped toward the inviting pool.

And froze in midstride.

Aren was there, his back to her. He stood waist deep in the bubbling water, letting the waterfall cascade over his long black hair. He seemed completely oblivious to her presence. For an instant Kes suspected a trap, but immediately dismissed the thought. She hadn't known herself that she was coming to bathe, and Dhad wouldn't have had time to notify his master in the brief minutes that she had taken to prepare. No, far more likely Aren was merely enjoying the simple pleasure of bathing in a warm pool surrounded by the scents of growing things.

Kes didn't know what to do. She hugged the thick towels that had been provided for her to her body, concealing her nakedness as best she could, and wished she hadn't shed the robe quite so quickly. She was about to turn, as quietly as possible, and sneak back to her room when Aren gathered up his black hair. His naked back was revealed to her, and Kes's eyes went wide with utter surprise.

The back itself was broad and knotted with powerful muscles. That much, Kes had expected. What amazed her and rooted her to the spot was finally seeing what made those strange lumps on the pirate leader's back, the lumps that he was so leery of her glimpsing even when he was fully clothed.

Tears sprang to Kes's eyes at the beauty and pain of it.

Protruding from his back, as shiny and probably as brightly colored as the webbing between Aren Yashar's fingers, were two small vestigial wings.

Not feathers, no; nor were they the leathery texture and spindly structure of bats or other flying mammals with which Kes was acquainted. These had the texture of a butterfly's wings, fragile, completely useless, but there nonetheless, a mute testament to another type of existence, another form of being. The water slicked down their length, but as she watched, Aren backed away from the waterfall and the wings fluttered, shaking off the moisture.

But one of them was incomplete, ragged and broken looking. As if someone had found that butterfly and cruelly tried to twist off those fragile wings.

Kes must have moved, must have let her astonishment find a voice, for Aren suddenly froze. He whirled, splashing in the water, to stare at her. Kes stared back, her gaze locked, unable to turn away.

For a long moment, there was silence, broken only by the sound of the waterfall.

At last, Aren spoke. "You saw," he said. His voice trembled, fraught with deep emotion.

Kes nodded. Words had deserted her for the moment.

Aren sighed heavily and sank into the water. He stayed there, his hands making sculling motions in the pool, deep in thought.

Finally, Kes found her voice. "Why do you hide them? Are you ashamed of them?"

He shot her a look, but his expression was unreadable. He gestured at her. "Why do you clutch your towels so?" he replied, not answering the question.

Kes's face flamed. The towels did little to cover her nudity, but she would feel more awkward if she turned and ran back for the robe now that Aren had made an issue of it.

"Are you ashamed of your body?" he continued.

"N-no," Kes replied. "But nakedness tends to make people uncomfortable aboard *Voyager*. One's body is one's own business."

Aren smiled. "Exactly. Our wings are . . . private. We do not speak of them; we do not display them. Especially not to aliens." He paused, then glanced up at her, and Kes's heart raced at the vulnerability in his eyes. "But you have seen. I—I think I wanted you to see, to know."

"Tell me." Kes moved forward as if drawn, easing herself down on the side of the pool. Her long, slim legs dangled in the warm water, but she still held her towels protectively in front of her. "Tell me about the wings. What happened?"

Aren ducked under the water for a moment, then resurfaced, his body, hair, and small wings glistening with wetness. He did not look at her as he spoke, and his voice was soft, filled with a strange longing.

"We are an old race, Kes; older perhaps than you

can imagine. Once, we could fly with these. But that was thousands upon thousands of years ago, when we were closer to creatures like the kakkiks than humanoids. We traded flight for mass, the ability to soar for the ability to run, to manipulate objects with our hands. The webbing," and he spread his hands to show her, "came upon us at about the same time as the wings faded." Aren paused thoughtfully.

"Let me start with some more recent history. On a fertile, gentle planet called Rhulan, there lived a people called the Rhulani. Ours was a culture rich in the arts and the sciences. With such a generous life span, any individual could learn and do so much. There was always a wealth of riches to pass to successive generations. Oh, they weren't many, granted; we were not overly fecund, not with such long individual life spans. But there were always some, bright eyed and eager, to fill the voids left by those who had passed on.

"It was . . . a long time before we noticed." He paused, not meeting her eyes. "When many families naturally have no children, it took time to realize . . . that *no* families were having children."

Now he looked up at her, and tears caught the faint gleam of light. "We are, all of us, utterly infertile. After this generation, there will be no more Rhulani."

Kes's breath caught in her throat, and sympathetic tears sprang to her own eyes. Her own people did not have lengthy life spans, but they would survive, the Caretaker had seen to that. Kes's own brush with her burgeoning fertility, and her glimpse into a possible future, complete with daughter and grandson, had told her that life did go on. There was an immortality in the faces of the children that could not be found in a long life span, and Kes now saw the pain that sat upon Aren Yashar's broad shoulders.

It took time to realize . . . that no families were having children."

"Aren," she breathed. "I'm so sorry."

He nodded in acknowledgment and continued. "I was a prominent politician then. We tried to keep things calm, tried to prove that it was all just rumors, but our scientists confirmed our suspicions. There is no political system in the universe, Kes, that can calm a people who know they are facing extinction. The world went mad. Cults sprang up overnight that preyed on the peoples' fears. Many were convinced that somehow we had offended some distant diety with our pride in our long lives, our beauty, our glorious wings and iridescent webbing. These cults had rites that demanded self-mutilation. The wings were clipped, the webbing, slashed. Some performed the self-mutilation rite alone, and bled to death. Others formed bands of roving cultists, kidnapping strangers in dark streets, sometimes in broad daylight, to perform their barbaric rite upon hapless victims. I—"

He closed his eyes and turned his face away from her. But Kes could fill in the rest.

"They found you," she breathed in horror. "They found you and they tried to clip your wings and—"

"I killed two of them," Aren interrupted savagely. "They only got one before I broke free. And somehow, I managed to flee that frightened planet. And that was when I formed the Ja'in. My people were dying. I wanted to live."

Kes wiped at her eyes. Aren Yashar had always been so proud, so handsome, so secure in his power. She had assumed he had always been a pirate leader—cruel, demanding, taking what he wanted. Now she understood, at least a little, why he had done what he did.

"What did the brief lives of aliens matter when your own race was dying?" she said softly. "Why live gently, when you had no future generations to inherit your wisdom and world?"

Aren's head whipped up and he studied her intently. He found no hint of sarcasm, and his tense posture relaxed. "You understand," he said, wonderingly.

"I see why you did what you did," Kes countered. "It's not quite the same thing."

"I gave the Rhulani hope again," he said, moving through the water closer toward her. "I made those who would join me strong, powerful. The Ja'in is the most important force in this sector, Kes. Did you know," and he laughed, "that there are tales told about us? Songs, even? And I am young yet! Think what a legacy I shall leave!"

He was beside her now, his arms resting on the side of the pool. Kes's eyes crept toward the multicolored, impotent wings and for an instant, she thought of a bird soaring in the sky.

Free.

"Oh, Aren, can't you see?" she cried brokenly. "You're as much a prisoner of your own fear as I am of you! You've got thousands of years left to live, you could be doing good and helpful things for millions of people, and instead you're a pirate. You kill and you steal and you—"

She broke off, startled. Aren had placed a damp hand on her thigh, caressing it gently.

"Teach me," he whispered softly. "Teach me then, dear Kes, how to do all these good things of which you speak. This life is fast growing empty for me, and I would have you fill it in the brief time you have allotted to you. You have already done so much. You have grown so deeply precious to me, little bird. Join me, my love."

He spread out his arms, ready to help her into the pool. Kes couldn't breathe and her heart raced. She wanted nothing more at that moment than to fling aside the sheltering towels and ease into the hot water with Aren, press her slim body against his, feel his arms encircle her, touch the heartbreakingly beautiful, broken wings. She could help him. She could take his empire and . . .

Even as she gazed at him, Kes knew it was a lie. Oh, she was certain he meant it. But Aren was who he was. He could never turn his pirates to positive pursuits. They'd turn on him, kill him, kill as he had taught them to do. And he would hate her, then, for making him lose all that he had gained.

She thought suddenly of the doctor, of Tuvok, of the captain, of her own tidy hydroponics bay, nothing like this wild jungle, no, but a creation of her own. She thought of the pain she had soothed, the wounds she had healed, the lives she had saved. Kes had a place aboard *Voyager* that she knew deep in her heart was still there for her. Warm though the water was, and beautiful—oh, exquisitely so—as Aren might be, at his side was not where she belonged.

"I'm sorry," she breathed.

"Kes—no, please, no."

Tears almost blinded her as she turned, stumbled to her feet, and broke into a run. She fled for the door, pausing only to pick up and don her discarded robe.

Behind her, she heard a cry of pain and loss and anger that she knew she would never forget.

CHAPTER
15

KULA DHAD REALLY, REALLY DIDN'T WANT TO SPEAK TO Aren Yashar about what the latest reconnaissance missions had discovered.

He'd been jolted out of his doze last evening—this morning, truth be told—by Kes's sudden emergence from the hydroponics room, her feet flying and tears coursing down her face. And he'd heard a dreadful noise issue from inside the room—Aren's voice, but so laden with pain and anger that Dhad had quickly scurried away.

He'd hoped he'd be able to steer clear of both the pirate leader and his difficult beauty, at least for a day or so. Kes he had palmed off on an underling, knowing she would be safely out of Aren's way happily ensconced in front of the computers, learning about terraforming. Aren, however, was not so easily eluded.

He squared his shoulders and requested permission to enter.

For a long moment, the door to Aren Yashar's private chambers remained closed. Then, just when Dhad was about to give up, it hissed open.

Aren stood with his back toward Dhad, the small mounds of his wings clearly visible beneath his robe of dark blue. Kula Dhad raised a thin eyebrow in surprise. More than most Rhulani, Aren was sensitive about . . . those things.

"Greetings, Great One," he began, bowing deeply.

Aren said nothing.

"There—I have—that is—"

"Say what you have come to say and get out." The voice was icy, and Dhad swallowed hard.

"You instructed me to report anything unusual, Great One."

"I know what I said." Every word was clipped and precise, and finally Aren Yashar turned around. Dhad kept his expression neutral with difficulty.

Aren looked as though he had aged four hundred years overnight. He wore the same strained, unhappy expression Kes wore. He looked—haunted.

Not for the first time, Dhad wished he had never seen Kes, never brought her to his leader's attention. Then things would be as they always had been, Aren robust and content in his casual violence, and he, Kula Dhad, a courier happily unencumbered by the honor of being the Ja'in leader's right-hand man. Silently, Dhad cursed the girl.

"There has been no luck in recovering the downed

shuttle." Dhad spoke quickly with an eye toward reporting the news and getting out as soon as possible. "We routed all the Sshoush-shin encampments that we know of and none of them appear to have assisted the *Voyager* crew. However, we've been keeping an eye on a roving band of scouting Sshoush-shin, and they seem to be heading directly for the dome area. I thought you should be notified."

Please, please, just say that's all and let me go.

But something like animation came to Aren's face and he frowned. "That is very peculiar. They have foraging parties, certainly, but—Dhad!"

"Great One!" Dhad snapped to attention.

"I want you to lead the next scouting expedition. Depart immediately. Find this wandering party of Sshoush-shin and eliminate them. I haven't commanded the Ja'in this long not to know subterfuge when I hear of it, and I feel certain that somehow they are either helping Janeway and her crew or perhaps it *is* them. How clearly did the pilots see them?"

"Ah, the usual distance," stammered Dhad. "We were looking for the shuttlecraft, not rogue Sshoush-shin," he reminded Aren.

"I want them dead. I've had enough of this. Janeway and all other ties to Kes's past life must be eliminated before she will yield. I've half a mind to show her the bodies."

Dhad kept his face from registering his shock. Aren must truly be unsettled, if he would reveal the depth of his anger to Dhad in such a blunt manner. He kept his mouth shut.

At last Aren sighed. "That will be all."

"I shall deliver your instructions, Great One." Relief flooded Kula Dhad. He bowed and turned to exit, when Aren's voice halted him in his tracks.

"You shall carry out my instructions, Kula. I want you in the vanguard to make sure none of them escapes."

Not turning around, embarrassingly aware of Aren's eyes on his wing mounds, Dhad nodded. "As you will."

This time, as he strode down the hall with a dreadful sinking feeling of apprehension, Kula Dhad was not silent when he cursed Kes.

Furball seemed to possess extraordinary healing capabilities, for by the time Neelix camped for the night the wound was closed. By the following morning, it was almost gone and the little creature was its normal, lively self.

Neelix was surprised at the relief he felt. He rubbed the animal behind its large ears with affection. "You had me worried there, little friend," he chided it teasingly.

As if in reply, Furball stood on its hind legs in Neelix's lap, reached up with a fingered forepaw, and patted Neelix's cheek gently.

Neelix melted. "That absolutely does it," he declared as Furball clambered up onto his shoulder. "When we meet up with the captain, I'm going to insist that she let me take you with us. Now," and he rose, squinting as he looked toward New Hann, "I think we can make it by the end of today. I'm feeling pretty fit, and you can fly now. Go on, that's a good fellow!" Neelix shrugged his shoulder, and Furball immediately launched itself into the air.

"I wonder if I could jog a bit?" Neelix said to himself. He certainly felt like it. He hadn't felt this good in years. "Maybe I should think of this as shore leave instead of being marooned!" he chuckled.

He decided against jogging, in the end. He didn't want to waste his energy. But he set forth with vigor and a brisk stride, the end of his quest within his reach.

After a mile or so, though, he faltered. He had no plan at all for recovering Kes once he arrived at the broken dome that served as the pirates' base. He only knew he had to try to reach Kes. Now that he thought about it, Neelix realized with a wry expression, he half thought he'd be dead by now.

"And probably would be," he said generously, "if not for my little Furball."

The creature, responding to his voice, circled his head a few times and trilled in reply.

Up ahead, to his left, something glinted in the light. Neelix's heart spasmed. He was out here with no cover whatsoever.

Shapes moved. Neelix squinted, trying to see better. They looked like Sshoush-shin. Suddenly one of them flailed. Was it dying? What—

The furry pelt sloughed off, and a shape that was most definitely human and most definitely female stretched and ran a hand over its forehead, brushing back tendrils of red-brown hair that had escaped from a braid—

"Captain!" In his joy, Neelix cried the word aloud. "Furball, we've found them. Come on!" And now he began to jog in earnest, his short little legs moving as if of their own volition. He waved his arms and his pleasure was complete when his beloved and adored captain caught sight of him and waved her own arms in return.

Tom Paris was heavier than B'Elanna had expected him to be. But she didn't say a word, instead ordered her tiring muscles to support the burden despite their objections.

He stayed unconscious for the next few hours. As the light increased, marking what passed for dawn on this planet, Hrrrl called a halt near a natural rock formation.

"This will do," he said. "Before dawn tomorrow, we will reach New Hann."

"Excellent," said Janeway. "This has all been too much like a flashback to Starfleet physical training for my liking."

Torres glanced about, trying to find the least uncomfortable spot available for Paris. He stirred in her arms, and when she glanced down at him, his eyes were open and focused.

"You know," he drawled, his voice a thin echo of his normal robust, teasing tones, "every time I thought about this scene before, I was the one carrying you."

"Shut up, Tom," she said, ever so softly.

"Shutting up, ma'am," he replied. His head lolled back over her arm; clearly, the little joke had been enough to exhaust him.

Fear shivered through Torres, but she ignored it. He'd be fine.

He had to be.

She placed him down where the soil seemed sandiest, and drew the Sshoush-shin cloak over him even though he was still running a very high fever. It was broad daylight now—well, at least as broad as daylight got on Mishkara—and they couldn't risk being spotted by a scout ship.

"How is he?" Janeway asked as Torres walked up.

Torres shook her head. "Not good. We've got to get him to the doctor soon, or . . ." She didn't complete the sentence.

Janeway nodded, but said nothing. With a sigh, she shrugged off her heavy cloak in order to rid herself of the pack. Tuvok, as he had done every time they halted, was busily running a tricorder scan of the area. He raised an eyebrow. "Captain—"

But Janeway had beaten him to it. "My God," she breathed, a slow grin spreading across her face, "It's Neelix!"

Torres straightened and gazed where Janeway had indicated. Sure enough, a tiny humanoid blip on the horizon was charging into view. Torres found she was smiling. She hadn't realized how worried she had been about the little Talaxian until now, when he turned up, somehow, apparently safe and sound.

Neelix came puffing up happily, and in his enthusiasm flung his stubby arms about everyone. "Oh, goodness, am I happy to see you!" Before she could protest, Torres was enfolded, squeezed, and released.

"Neelix," began the captain. "We're glad you're safe, of course, but—"

"Aii!" Hrrrl's wordless cry caused them all to whip around, taut, ready to fight or flee. The huge Sshoush-shin was pointing in horror at an airborne animal about the size of a small housecat. The thing dipped and dove like a hummingbird, chirping and squeaking all the while. Its huge eyes, the color of the sky back on Earth, blinked rapidly. It appeared to be as afraid of Hrrrl as the big Sshoush-shin was of it. Yet it didn't flee.

Not more than a few days ago, Torres herself had held a small carved figurine that might have been modeled after this specific creature. What was it? She searched for the name. Pick-pick . . . kiki . . .

"Kakkik!" cried Hrrrl. "Quick! Your phasers! Blast it, blast it!"

"Don't you *dare* hurt him!" came Neelix's indignant yelp. "Furball, come here!" And to Torres's shock, the creature immediately folded its wings and dove for the safety of Neelix's arms. "There, there," the Talaxian soothed.

"Neelix," and Janeway's voice held that icy calm that immediately riveted her crew. "The creature is dangerous. It's a psychic predator."

"Pish-posh," scoffed Neelix. He rummaged about his person with one hand while the other still cradled the kakkik. "He's a pet, Captain, and a sweet one. He helped me find—ah, here they are. Look at these berries—don't they look delicious?"

Torres stared, as did the others, at the handful of dead beetles Neelix proffered.

"I think," came Tuvok's calm voice, "that we are all somewhat mistaken." He had his tricorder out and aimed it at the animal. "Mr. Neelix, the kakkik has tricked you into eating beetles, not berries. Close your eyes, clear your mind, and look again at your hand."

Confusion was plain on Neelix's face, but he did as the Vulcan instructed. When he glanced at the "berries," he gasped and dropped the handful of beetles in horror. "But—but—" he spluttered.

"You see? It clouds the mind, tries to poison you!" cried Hrrrl. "Evil, wicked creatures!"

"On the contrary," said Tuvok, his eyes on the tricorder's readings. "These beetles are extremely dense nutritionally. There is absolutely nothing harmful about them. If the kakkik urged Neelix to eat them by persuading him that they were a more appealing foodstuff, then we must assume two things: the creature is intelligent, and it is not hostile—possibly even benevolent."

"Furball?" asked Neelix, glancing down at his pet with wide eyes.

"The kakkiks?" echoed Hrrrl, his voice a rumble of skepticism.

"Then why isn't our communicator translating its noises?" asked Torres.

"Not every intelligent creature communicates through a verbal process," Tuvok reminded her.

"Given its ability to influence thoughts, it is probably a pure telepath. The sounds it makes are more likely kin to our sighs and other non-verbal noises than to actual speech." He turned to Janeway. "Captain, I believe it is trying to establish a mental link with me."

"Janeway," rumbled Hrrrl, "they have long been mistrusted by my people."

But Janeway was regarding the small creature with narrowed eyes and a thoughtful expression. "That may be, Hrrrl. But with all due respect, perhaps you simply misinterpreted a friendly overture as an attempt at mind control. I leave it to you, Lieutenant. Perhaps Furball has some information that could help us."

Neelix looked utterly bewildered, but handed the kakkik to Tuvok. The Vulcan sat on the earth, the little winged creature sitting on its hind legs in his lap. It placed its forepaws on Tuvok's chin.

They waited, quietly. Neelix caught sight of Paris, and turned to Janeway with a question on his lips. Janeway put her finger to her own lips, indicating that he shouldn't break Tuvok's concentration, and Neelix nodded. He moved quickly to Paris's side, knelt, and took his hand. The pleasure on Tom's face, despite his own agony, made Torres turn away quickly in embarrassment. She directed her attention instead to Tuvok.

Emotions flitted across the Vulcan's dark face: pleasure, fear, amusement, determination, all with a rapidity that was startling, especially on Tuvok's normally composed features. His lips moved, but no words came out. Instead, strange murmurings, yips, and crooning sounds issued forth. At last, he broke contact, and Torres noticed that Tuvok stroked the little being gently before tossing it into the air. It at once took flight and hovered about them.

"It is as I suspected," said Tuvok, appearing once again his normal, composed self. "I couldn't even get a name—just an image of wind rippling the water of a still pool. They are native to Mishkara, extremely intelligent and playful, and have been greatly pained by the fear of the Sshoush-shin, whom they believe to be intelligent and whom they know they can help."

"Amazing," breathed Hrrrl, looking with renewed respect on the airborne telepath. "They tried to contact us. We feared their manipulation of our thoughts."

"They are incapable of communicating in any other way. Even with me, the images were not truly coherent, nor did they resemble any language I have ever encountered." He turned to Neelix, who with a last smile for Paris had come up eagerly to listen. "Mr. Neelix, the kakkik—whom I shall call Wind-Over-Water for simplicity's sake—is very fond of you. He thinks of you as a beloved pet."

Torres was hard put not to laugh at Neelix's shocked and mortified expression. Even Janeway had to turn away to hide a smile. "But—but—Good heavens," said the Talaxian at last.

"He—for it is indeed a male—took care of you. To get you to eat food that would succor you, he made you think of it as something you knew you liked. He helped you fight off the Xian scouting party by making you think there were far fewer of them, and giving you artificial courage. He also flew among the Xians and made *them* see *you* as an extremely fearsome opponent. He healed your wound and lent you some of his strength. It is my belief that you owe him your life several times over."

Neelix blinked rapidly. Wordlessly he held out his arms and Wind-Over-Water came to him at once. "Good little Furball," Neelix whispered. "Thank you so much!"

Hrrrl reached out a mammoth paw and, tentatively, stroked the kakkik. It glanced up at him and blinked solemnly.

Neelix cleared his throat. "Captain, what's wrong with Tom?"

"He was bitten by a native insect," replied Janeway grimly. "The poison seems to have spread throughout his system. I don't think we can dally here too much longer." She glanced over at the prone lieutenant. "He's been running a high fever and having delusions. We've got to get into New Hann soon."

"May I make a suggestion?" said Tuvok. "Before Mr. Neelix and his companion arrived, I had taken some tricorder readings of the surrounding area. We are directly above the outermost limits of the ancient mines. It is possible that we might be able to use our phasers to penetrate the earth and rock. It would be cooler below ground, and it would also be more difficult for Aren Yashar's scout ships to discover us."

"I don't know about that. We'll be making an announcement that we went underground if they notice the hole we've dug. It may be leaping from the frying pan into the fire. Hrrrl, your people worked in these mines once. What do you know about them?"

Hrrrl shrugged his massive frame. "That was many years ago, Janeway. No one living has ever ventured near these mines. However, I do know that there were once tunnels that led from the mines to New Hann."

"Tunnels that probably collapsed long ago," replied Janeway. She glanced up at the sky. "But even a place to hide during the day would make it worth our while. Neelix, I want you to monitor the tricorder. Don't take your eyes off it. The minute we know there are any scout ships in the area, we stop digging, put on those cloaks, and become Sshoush-shin. Understood?"

"Aye, Captain!" He snapped rigidly to attention.

"We'll take one more set of readings to determine the best spot to begin digging, then—"

"No!" shrieked Paris. He stumbled to his feet, wildly attacking an invisible enemy. "Get away from me. No, no, God, no, stop it!"

Torres raced to him. Tom's eyes widened in horror, as if she, too, were something dreadful and dangerous, and he took a wild swing at her. She caught his arm and pushed him down. "Tom! Tom, it's me!"

He struggled beneath her, finally exhausting what little strength he had left, then blinked and focused. "B'Elanna?" he whispered. "Is it you? The Xians— they had tentacles and poison—"

"Tom, it was a hallucination. You're sick. You're seeing things that aren't there."

He was silent for a moment, and she eased off him, catching her breath.

"B'Elanna." The word was barely audible.

"Yes, Tom?"

"I don't want to die." His eyes were closed, and when he opened them, there was a dreadful fear in their blue depths.

Torres's gut clenched. "You're not going to die," she told him firmly, hoping even as she spoke them that the words were true.

"I've—I've been there. I've been dead before. I know what it's like. I don't want to go there again, not yet, not like this. You can't imagine how—" He turned away, his throat working.

Torres couldn't think of anything to say. Instead, she reached out and touched his cheek gently. It was as hot as fire. Biting her lip, she rose.

"Got that fix yet, Tuvok?" she asked, covering her concern with brusqueness. At his answering nod, she adjusted her phaser to setting eleven and stepped forward.

"We should keep a safe distance," advised Tuvok. "There is some likelihood that there will be poisonous subterannean gasses that our phasers could ignite. The tricorder has thus far detected nothing, but we should be cautious."

The earth and rock quickly surrendered to three phasers used in conjunction. As the phasers sang out, a smoking hole began to emerge beneath the powerful rays. A little less than six minutes later, they had penetrated to the mines beneath.

"This is the shallowest point," said Janeway, "But it's still a good eight-meter drop." She stepped forward and shone her wristlight into the dark depths. "Seems solid enough." She backed away from the heated hole. "Still damned hot, though. Let's take a break and let it cool down while we prepare for descent."

"Captain!" Neelix's voice was strangled. "We don't have time. Five ships are approaching."

"Quickly!" snapped Janeway. "Put on the skins! They may think this is some kind of natural volcanic activity." Torres knew it was a slim chance, but it was the only one they had. Hurriedly they flung on the cloaks and bowed down. Seconds ticked by.

They heard the rumble of the scout ships, closer than they had ever come before. Then suddenly, a rock a few meters away exploded.

The scout ships were firing on them!

"Let's go!" cried Janeway. "Hrrrl, you first. Get the packs and the skins down there. It'll help break the fall. Let's move, let's move!"

Another explosion, this time closer. Torres risked a glance skyward and her heart leaped into her throat. They were right there! She flung her pack and skin down into the still-smoking hole and raced back for Paris. He was curled into a tight ball, almost catatonic, but he didn't struggle as she scooped him up into her arms and carried him toward the hole.

There was no climbing down. The mouth of the just-blasted entrance to the mines would burn at the touch. They'd be lucky if the soles of their boots held. As she ran, she saw Hrrrl leap into the entrance, followed by Tuvok and then Neelix. The little kakkik fluttered down next to his friend.

Janeway was there, calling out something, but Torres was deafened by the scream of energy weapons and the explosion of rocks and soil. One hit too close and knocked her off her feet. Paris didn't even move to catch himself and hit the earth hard. Nearly blinded by dust, Torres scrambled to her feet and tried to grab him.

Paris squirmed out of her grasp, his eyes wild. Baring his teeth in a savage growl, he turned to her and landed a solid punch to her jaw. Torres was taken utterly by surprise. She staggered backward—

And fell into the mine.

CHAPTER 16

Kula Dhad could not believe what was happening.

It had started so well. The *Voyager*s had perhaps once been careful, but they had been caught without their Sshoush-shin disguises and even if they had not been, Dhad would have obeyed Aren's orders to slay the Sshoush-shin.

Dhad had once held a palmful of a strange material called *luris,* a substance that naturally occurred on several worlds and that had strange properties. He could hold the liquid-solid in his palm, but it was impossible to pick up, and if he tried to tighten his grip on the peculiar substance, it oozed defiantly through his fingers, slowed only by the webbing.

For all the success he was having in taking care of the *Voyager* crew, they might as well have been fashioned of that damnable substance. As he watched, dismay twisting his features, they dove, one by one, into a crevice they had opened in the earth. Frantic, he fired randomly before they all disappeared, and his companion vessels did likewise.

Charmed lives, these Alpha quadranters led. Before a minute had passed, they were all gone. Dhad opened his mouth to order a cease fire, but before he could utter the words, someone had fired on the crevice, causing it to cave in.

Dhad swore violently. What was he going to tell Aren? He thought yearningly of his little vessel, big enough only for two, and his carefree days as a simple Ja'in courier.

He pulled up and came in for another run, just to be certain. Yes, the crevice was certainly sealed off. And—wait. One of them hadn't made it. He was stumbling about, limping badly, waving his arms, and crying something Aren couldn't hear. His left leg was wrapped up and blood stained the bandage. Paris, wasn't that this one's name?

Before anyone could fire, Dhad punched the inter-ship communicators. "Hold your fire! I'm going to take this one alive!"

The lie was already forming. He would share it with his colleagues. Dhad was certain they'd go along with it; their necks were in as much danger as Dhad's own. He hadn't actively killed the humans, no, but sealed up in that abandoned mine, they were surely as good as dead. He settled the vessel gently on the earth, puffing up clouds of sand. Paris, clearly delusional, walked up to the ship and began stroking it fondly.

Dhad punched a button. The door hissed open and he hurried out. "Good girl," Paris was saying. "What a pretty filly!" He turned to Dhad, smiling. His eyes were bloodshot and vague. "You have a lovely horse, Mr. McCain."

"Yes, I do," said Dhad, drawing his weapon. A quick burst of energy, and Paris spasmed and fell. Dhad hooked his hands beneath Paris's armpits and began to drag him aboard.

We were entirely successful, Great One, he began to rehearse. *All of the Alpha quadranters and their Sshoush-shin collaborators were utterly destroyed. The only survivor was—*

"—this one, who is, as you can plainly see, far too ill to pose any sort of threat. I thought you might wish to use him for leverage, if *Voyager* refuses to leave quietly."

"Dhad, you amaze me!" approved Yashar. He bounded up out of his soft chair with an enthusiasm that made Dhad's heart lift. This was more like it. "Somehow, I thought you'd manage to mess this up. I have never before been more delighted to be mistaken."

Two guards supported the limp body of Lieutenant Tom Paris. His head lolled and his face was flushed. A thin green tendril of poison had worked its way along his cheek. "Scarlet death bite, I see. Take him to the hospital and begin treating him. Just enough to keep him alive. He's not as good a bargaining chip dead."

The guards nodded and dragged Paris away. Aren

turned his approving smile full on Kula Dhad. "A perfect job, Dhad. I am so pleased they are dead. We may indeed need Mr. Paris. *Voyager* refuses to leave. Twice, they have ventured close enough to the sentinel ships to trip the mechanisms. They have even fired upon them. With Janeway and her team out of the way, and Paris to show them, they might be more amenable to simply departing. Prepare all ships for attack in twelve hours."

"As you will, Great One!"

Kes didn't glance up as the shadow fell across the screen, so engrossed was she in what she was learning. Her eyes still scanning, she held up a hand in a just-a-moment gesture. At last, finished, she turned to greet her visitor.

"What—oh. Hello, Aren."

"Hello, Kes." The warmth, the need she had seen in his face a few hours earlier was nowhere to be found. His face was friendly, cordial, but revealed nothing—the true visage of a Ja'in commander. "I trust you are learning whatever you like?"

"Oh, yes," replied Kes. "This is all fascinating. Kula Dhad showed me how to interlink and cross reference. Do you think we might be able to try a terraforming experiment sometime soon?" Kes was not an accomplished liar, and it was difficult to keep her face open and guileless. Anyone who knew her well—Tuvok, the doctor, Neelix—would have sensed immediately that she was not being truthful. For a heart-stopping second, Aren's thin eyebrows drew together as he scrutinized her, then nodded, as if confirming something. His body posture relaxed a bit but, Kes noticed, he was careful never to show his back to her.

"It pleases me that you are happy here, with the computers."

"I am. Aren, about last night—"

He held up a commanding hand, the webbing flashing brightly. "No more words on last night. It is done. I vowed I would not force anything upon you. If you prefer the company of the computers to that of my person, I accept that. I hope, as always, that you will change your mind. I wanted to let you know that I will be very busy shortly, but my duties shouldn't take long. Other than this brief interlude, if you wish my company, you have but to ask. I command all here save you. You, dear Kes, command me."

He placed his hand on his chest and bowed. Kes regretted the necessity of the lie, but did not regret the lie itself. He backed away until the shadows fell upon him. Only then did he turn around, safe in the darkness where she could not glimpse his wing mounds.

Kes watched him go, dry eyed. She had chosen her path, and was set upon it. There would be no more tears for herself, or for Aren Yashar. Only a determination, hitherto smothered in soft pillows and nearly drowned in warm waters, to concentrate on escape.

She had ceased looking at terraforming technology. Under Dhad's absent-minded guidance, Kes had applied her quick brain and computer skills to cracking the security codes without anyone being the wiser.

She already had a good idea of the layout of the base, and was now concentrating on the weapons and defense systems. Somehow, some way, she would find a way out of here. Kes had reached a decision: she would rather die in the harsh wilderness of Mishkara than live out her life in the opulence of the pirate base.

She had allayed Aren's suspicions. The guards didn't see her as a threat, just as a playpretty for their master. Kes would use that underestimation to her advantage.

She touched the screen with a forefinger and continued her study.

Torres woke to pain. She lay face down in a pile of animal pelts, breathing in dust and their musty scent. Every bone in her body had been rattled, and there was an awful burning on her back. For an instant, she couldn't recall where she was, and the darkness, broken only by a few paltry beams of white light, made her try to rise with a growl.

"Easy, B'Elanna," came the soothing voice of her captain. "You've had a bad spill and those burns are nasty."

Torres felt Janeway's calming hands on her, cutting away the uniform. The air felt cold on the burns. When Janeway began applying an ointment, Torres hissed in agony, but clenched her fists and teeth and managed to remain still. Janeway continued to talk.

"You hit the side of the chasm when you fell, and burned your back. I'm putting on an ointment which will dull the pain and help seal in moisture. You'll be the first to see the doctor after we—when we get back."

Another sort of pain crashed over Torres. Tom. She'd left Tom on the surface, for the Ja'in to find and kill. Unless—

"Did Tom make it down?" It hurt her swollen mouth to form the words.

She felt her captain's hands still for an instant, then resume their ministrations. "No." Janeway was blunt. "He attacked you, you fell, and then fire from the Ja'in ships sealed the tunnel. Mr. Paris is more use to Aren alive than dead, if they need to bargain with *Voyager*. We can hope they captured him rather than killed him."

Tears stung Torres's eyes. She blinked them back. She couldn't afford to waste the moisture.

"How is everyone else?" she asked.

"We're a pretty sorry crew," replied Janeway. She began to apply clean cloths—as clean as they could get, anyway—to the burn area. "You can't be moved with this burn. Tuvok's further damaged his arm and suffered a concussion. And Neelix's leg is broken."

Torres remembered climbing with Neelix and Paris on the Sakari homeworld. He'd broken his leg then, too. "He doesn't seem to have much luck with falls," she said. "Are you all right? What about Hrrrl?"

Janeway chuckled. "I'm fine. When I fell, I landed on Hrrrl. He wasn't happy about it, but he's all right. Now. Can you sit up at all?"

"I think so." With Janeway's help—and a great deal of pain—Torres maneuvered into a sitting position, careful to resist the urge to lean against the rock wall of the mine. She glanced around at the rest of them. Janeway was right. What a sorry lot they were.

"Here's the situation." Janeway sat cross-legged in front of them. She turned her wristlight on herself, so that they could see her face, throwing her features into grotesque angles and shadows. "It's bad, but not hopeless. Aren Yashar knows where we are. He probably thinks we're dead—I would, if I were him. We're trapped beneath tons of rock, with every entrance sealed. Lieutenant Paris is either captured or dead. Everyone else but myself and Hrrrl is too injured to continue. Here's what I propose.

"You three remain here with the food supplies. I'll take one canteen of water, but everything else I'll leave with you. We can punch a hole through to the surface, which should provide enough air for you to breathe for several hours. I'll leave a phaser with you, just in case you need to widen the hole or to defend yourselves.

"I'll take a tricorder and two phasers. I should be able to find my way in to the complex. Hrrrl will come with me in case we run into any trouble. Any questions?"

The only reply was a ululating croon, presumably from the kakkik. "Captain," and Neelix's voice was ragged with pain, "What about Furball?"

Janeway glanced at the little creature. "He's helped us an awful lot already. I hate to ask him to do more, but . . . Neelix, do you think he can ease your pain, heal your injuries?"

Neelix stroked the small animal, his face going slack for a moment, then smiled. "Furball wants to do anything he can to help."

She rose and went to kneel beside the Talaxian. Furball stared up at her with his beautiful eyes, blinking solemnly. Janeway stroked him between the ears. "Thank you, Wind-Over-Water. I think your greatest opportunity to help will come shortly, if all goes well." With a last pat, she rose, slung the tricorder over her arm and checked her phaser. "Neelix, Torres—you've got to keep Tuvok conscious. Maybe the kakkik can help with that, too. He can't be allowed to fall asleep, not with that concussion."

"Captain, I do not think that will be a problem. My mental disciplines—"

"—might not be enough," Janeway interrupted, "and don't tell me about shutting down to heal yourself. That might have worked with the arm, but not with damage to the brain." She turned to Hrrrl. "Let's go," she said.

"Captain?" said Torres.

Janeway turned around. "What is it, B'Elanna?"

"Good luck."

Janeway smiled. "I normally don't believe in luck," she replied, "but at this point, I'll take whatever help I can get. Take care of yourselves. I hope to have us all out of here within a few hours."

With that, she and Hrrrl were gone, disappearing down the twining labyrinth of tunnels.

"Well," said Neelix with forced cheerfulness. "How about a game or song to keep us all alert? Let me think . . ."

It was going to be a long wait.

First Officer's log, stardate 51975.3. The teams aboard the sentinel ships are having no luck whatsoever in their attempts to deactivate the vessels. Ensign Kim and his teams have performed admirably, but we have been forced to beam them back once already after they ran out of supplies, with some not inconsiderable damage to the ship as a result. We're going to try it again.

Wherever she is, I hope Captain Janeway is more successful at whatever she's attempting than we are.

"I'm seriously beginning to hate this place," said Kim.

Lyssa Campbell nodded without comment. She looked better now that she'd had a chance to sleep in a bed for a few hours and eat some real food, but she still looked haggard. Gone was the chirpy, mischievous friend who'd kept monotony at bay for several days. Circles darkened her eyes and her lips were set in a grim line. Kim imagined he didn't look much better.

They were on the bridge of the alien vessel, and Kim's eyes roved over the scene with something approaching active hatred.

"Where should we start?" The unspoken word *again* lingered in the air.

Kim took a deep breath. "Where we started last time, I guess. You take that station, I'll take this one. Start recording."

There came a few beeping, blipping sounds as

Campbell activated her tricorder. Kim did likewise, just in case something—anything at all—happened.

He placed his hands on the console, trying to drum up the wherewithal to try, again, and activate the damned things. He was just about to start when suddenly the console lit up with vibrant colors in strange patterns.

"Harry—"

"I know, I'm getting it too." Kim couldn't keep the excitement from his voice.

"What the hell did you do?"

"Nothing!" As he watched, dumbfounded, incredibly grateful that all of this strange activity was being recorded, hums and clicks issued forth.

"Carey to Kim. Something's going on with—"

"I know, Carey, we're getting it over here as well. Record it and let's just see how it plays out before we do anything."

To Kim's stunned delight, what was clearly a code began to scroll across the screen. Kim couldn't stop smiling. Someone from the planet was activating the ships, and once he had that code, Kim suspected he could override any commands from here.

Finally, something was going right for a change. He hit his commbadge. "Kim to *Voyager*. Commander, I've got some very good news."

Kim's news was indeed very good, and Chakotay felt the smile, unbidden, stretch its pleased way across his face. "Well done, Harry. But keep playing dead. I don't want to tip our hand unless it's absolutely necessary. Be ready to jump when I tell you."

"How high, Commander?" The voice on the other end of the commlink was as full of delight as Chakotay's own.

"I'll let you know."

"Commander," and Henley's voice was urgent. "The field and the ion storm have been deactivated. The Ja'in have launched six ships, sir." She glanced up at her commander. "They're finally coming for us."

"And their timing couldn't be better," Chakotay replied instantly, although the smile had vanished from his face. He leaned forward, his body taut and alert.

For just a moment, he had a flashback to his harsh days as a Maquis commander. He, more than any of the original crew of *Voyager,* had a good idea of how the Ja'in and Aren Yashar would think and operate. Perhaps it was a blessing in disguise that the bridge was now staffed not with Starfleet-trained officers but with former Maquis.

Set a thief to catch a thief, Chakotay mused wryly. He spoke his thoughts aloud, so that his crew would be privy to the process.

"They're launching six ships now, plus they think they've still got control over the three sentinel ships they've just activated, which, as we've seen, are pretty formidable," he said. "What they don't know is we've beaten them to the punch. Henley, hail the lead vessel."

At once, Aren Yashar's smirking, handsome countenance filled the screen. "Ah, Commander Chakotay. I'd say what a pleasure it is to see you again, but I think it would have been best had you left while you still had a chance."

"I wouldn't overestimate myself, Yashar, if I were you," replied Chakotay.

Aren's lips thinned and his purple eyes flashed anger. "Surrender and prepare to be boarded. I have had enough of toying with you. The game is about to end."

Chakotay lounged in the command chair, his body posture bespeaking utter confidence. He laughed aloud. "I don't think so."

Aren locked gazes with Chakotay for a moment longer, then made a motion with his right hand. Another Ja'in came forward, and Chakotay felt his body tense as he saw what—who—Aren's crewman thrust toward the screen.

It was Paris. He looked dreadful. Pale, eyes glazed, there was an unhealthy green tendril twining its vile path up his collar and across his face. His lips were white, and he clearly could not stand on his own.

Aren maneuvered into center stage again, thrusting his face close toward the screen. "Janeway. Tuvok. Torres. Neelix. Bokk. Paris." He ticked them off on his fingers as he spoke. "We have them all. Lieutenant Paris was the only one even left fit to stand. Make no mistake, Commander. I will kill them if you do not cooperate."

Chakotay's throat went dry, but long experience kept his body from betraying his thoughts. Paris looked awful. Aren Yashar and the Ja'in had a reputation for violence in this sector, and there was a good chance that the threat was real.

But there was also a good chance it wasn't. *What would I do in this situation?* Chakotay thought, his mind racing.

Why not show us all of them? It would be effective, wouldn't it, to show us all the wounded, to drive the point home. He hasn't got them, that's why. Somehow, he's only managed to get Paris.

A few years ago, that wouldn't have meant much. But Paris had changed, and so had Chakotay, and seeing the lieutenant in such bad shape—

Chakotay made his decision. Yashar was bluffing about having the others.

And he was bluffing about killing Paris. He still needed him, if things took a turn for the worse.

Chakotay shrugged his shoulders, made his face nonchalant. "Kill him. He means nothing to me."

"Gee, thanks," gasped Paris.

At once, the screen went dark. Aren's face vanished, to be replaced by the image of the three Ja'in vessels closing in in what was clearly attack formation.

"Commander—" Chell's voice betrayed his dismay.

"He was bluffing," Chakotay snapped. "I know it when I see it. I've done it often enough myself. Shields up, red alert!"

Chakotay had a perfect view as red energy built up on all three of the Ja'in ships, swelled, and was released. *Voyager* shuddered beneath the first volley.

At least, I hope he was bluffing. . . .

CHAPTER
17

HUNGER GNAWED AT KES, BUT SHE IGNORED IT. SOMEthing was going on. She feared the worst when Aren told her he would be unavailable. Something told her that she couldn't spare a moment away from the computers, not if she were to be able to free herself and perhaps help the *Voyager* crew.

The computers were activated and operated by touching the screen. Kes's fingerprints had been keyed in as acceptable, and working one link at a time, she'd been able to enter where she ought not to have been. She licked dry lips, her eyes roving over the screen, touching, connecting, moving.

There were many ways out of this major building in which Aren had her imprisoned. Unfortunately, all but the main entrance were sealed off with the highest priority security codes. She'd need more time if she were to be able to work her way past these, and time was suddenly very important. She could sense it. If she hurried too much, though, Kes knew she'd eventually make a mistake and expose her presence in restricted areas. And that would eliminate all access to the computers.

So, instead of concentrating on the most obvious exits, Kes had begun exploring some of the older areas of New Hann. There was a labyrinth of tunnels beneath and extending from the base area itself. Many of these were still active. Kes touched the screen and picked up signals: traces of directed energy technology used to bore through the rock here, the signal of a communication device there. Far too active, then, for her purposes.

Again she touched the screen, tracing the twining path of the mines. The area in which the Ja'in seemed to be concentrating on harvesting was to the west of the base. There was a great deal of activity there. She guessed a full shift was hard at work right now. Touching the screen, Kes investigated to the north. Nothing. Further probing yielded the disappointing news that, though there was no Ja'in activity occurring at this site, it was because there was no site at all. The tunnels here had long since collapsed. Any exits and entrances were sealed by tons of rock. No security code she could enter would make those doors functional again.

Kes gnawed her lip in disappointment. She shrugged her tense shoulders, their stiffness indicating that hours had passed. Kes allowed herself to rise and stretch, luxuriating in the feeling, then sat back down to work.

She had done enough investigating to realize that at this point, the mines were the only way she could possibly escape. She directed her attention to the east. A possibility here. Some tunnels had collapsed, but there were indications that at least a few of the mammoth doors that sealed them would still respond to her signals.

Better than nothing.

Kes now turned her attention to the south, and hope grew within her. This was more like it—only a few areas had collapsed. Most of the doors were still active, and there was no trace of the Ja'in energy signature to—

Wait.

Something was radiating from that area.

Kes frowned, for the thousandth time touched the screen, honing in on the signal. It was some kind of radiation, but it was not any of the traces she had seen connected with the Ja'in.

Blip. Blip.

It was moving. Now to the left, now to the right, circling back, stopping, moving forward again. Though it was taking a circular, strange path, it was clear its ultimate destination was the center of the base. Kes watched it for several long minutes.

Blip. Blip.

A pattern she recognized. Joy flooded her, and she put a small hand to her mouth to keep the burst of happiness from breaking free and giving her away.

The pattern in which the radiation emissions were released formed a Starfleet code. Someone from *Voyager* was coming to the base.

Coming for her.

Her tense muscles forgotten, Kes immediately began to concentrate her efforts on the south of New Hann, figuring out how to open doors for her unknown friend. She would not sit idly, waiting to be rescued like some princess in a tower, not when she had the controls at her fingertips.

She pressed the screen, and somewhere in the long-forgotten mines of Mishkara, a door slid open.

Janeway leaned against the cool stone and wiped sweat from her brow, sparing a smile of encouragement for her large friend. Hrrrl was a comforting presence, his huge bulk and sharp claws ready to defend her. For now, though, it was work that was both danger and drudgery, phasering their way through rock, finding the right turn, and somehow, keeping their lungs going. For a brief moment, she wished she'd let the kakkik come with them. She was sure that with Furball curled around her shoulders, her heart wouldn't be pounding quite so fast, her lungs working quite so hard.

Concentrate on the task, Kathryn. Don't waste time and energy on worrying about how little air is left.

Another half a mile of twisting and turning. She glanced upward, shining her wristlight at the ceiling. Provided, of course the tunnels didn't collapse in on them. The light glittered off the spark of gemstones and veins of precious minerals, twining through the rock in almost obscene profusion. Yet the Ja'in had sealed off these branches. That must mean that what they did mine must be even richer, even easier to access. It was a staggering thought.

The tricorder showed no life signs. It didn't look as if they'd have to fight any time soon. That, at least, was a relief.

They had come to what was clearly a door, marking a differentiation between tunnels. Janeway felt along the smooth metal, searching for a way to activate it. There was nothing on the door itself.

"Hrrrl, can you check for—"

Suddenly there came a deep, groaning noise. Janeway's heart climbed into her throat as the door opened unexpectedly.

Phaser at the ready, she threw herself back into the darkness of the tunnel, flattening herself against the rock. Hrrrl did likewise, his dark fur blending smoothly into the shadows.

She waited for the rush of guards, the blast of directed energy fire. Nothing happened. She flipped out her tricorder. No signs of life for several meters in any direction.

"I don't understand," she said aloud to Hrrrl. "Someone opened the door for us, but there's no welcoming committee from Aren Yashar."

Hrrrl looked nervous as well. "It seems as if it would have to be a trap, but—"

"For right now, I'll take what breaks we can get." She gestured with her phaser. "But I'm not taking any chances. The only way in is through here. Let's keep moving. We have injured people waiting."

The Ja'in fired again. Aren Yashar's ship broke free of formation and dove toward *Voyager* in a run both rash and daring. It was small and quick enough that Chell couldn't respond in time and *Voyager* almost did a complete rollover as it fired back. Chakotay nearly took a tumble out of his seat, and many of the bridge crew didn't manage to stay at their posts. It was for naught; the phasers missed Yashar's ship completely.

Voyager righted itself as red pulsed through the bridge. Smoke billowed and there was the sound of crackling and burning. Henley dove for the extinguisher and tried to tame the flames that roared along the console.

"Chell," cried Chakotay, "you remember what we did that first time we attacked the Cardassian convoy?"

"Aye, Commander!" Chell yelled back.

"Execute on my command!"

"Aye sir!"

"Bridge, brace yourselves. It's going to be a bumpy ride!"

The ships now converged, and began another run. *Voyager* bore hard to port, firing as it turned. The phasers went wide of their marks, striking a single, glancing blow to only one vessel. The ships, like wolves attacking their prey, veered to the other side and fired simultaneously.

Voyager took the attack full on, spinning almost completely around with the force of the shots and finally coming to rest in a dangling, awkward position.

"Henley," snapped Chakotay, "seal off and shut down life support to all unoccupied areas of the ship."

"Aye, sir!"

"Bridge to engineering. Dalby, start venting plasma from the port nacelle. I want us to look as bad as we possibly can."

"Aye, Commander."

"Commander." It was Henley. "Casualties are being reported from all over the ship. It won't be that hard to look bad, sir."

Chakotay nodded quickly. "Mr. Chell!"

The Bolian sat up straighter. "Sir!"

"Punch me in the jaw as hard as you can."

Chell's brow furrowed in utter confusion. "Sir?"

"That's an order."

"But—"

"Don't make me repeat myself," snapped Chakotay, rising and walking down to the conn. Chell also rose, looking dreadfully uncomfortable. "And if you pull that punch, I'll put you on report."

Chell nodded, still looking miserable. He drew back his arm, muttered, "Sorry, sir!" and let fly.

Chakotay wheeled backward, surprised at the power behind the punch. He felt as if Chell had smashed him in the face with a rock. He raised his hand to his mouth, touched it lightly. Pain shrieked through him, but he was satisfied—there was a copious amount of blood. Chakotay wiped off a generous amount of crimson fluid, dabbed it onto his ear. He looked every bit as knocked about as he had hoped.

"Well done, Chell," he said, though moving his

mouth was agony. He spat a tooth into his palm. "Henley, hail Yashar's ship."

He sat down in the command chair and held his left arm tightly, awkwardly, with his right. Aren Yashar's triumphant visage filled the screen.

"Changed our minds, have we?" gloated the pirate.

Exaggeratedly, Chakotay licked his bloody lip, tasting hot, coppery blood.

"What are your terms for surrender?"

Yashar's smile grew. "I am pleased and disappointed at the same time, Commander. Somehow, I thought you'd put up a better fight than that."

Chakotay went cold inside. Was it possible Aren suspected a ruse? Chakotay narrowed his eyes and called Aren a vile name, while at the same time touching his bloodied mouth, sending exactly the wordless message he wanted to send: *I don't want to do this, but we're too badly hurt not to.*

Aren threw back his dark head and laughed heartily. "You do have spirit, don't you," he said in a tone that was almost admiring. "I respect that in an adversary. There are many planets within the Ja'in sphere of influence; perhaps, if it pleases me, I will set your crew someplace that is not too hostile."

"Your graciousness is overwhelming," sneered Chakotay.

"Disabled as you are, I could blow you to bits," Aren reminded him.

"You want our ship. You wouldn't do that."

"Perhaps not. But only my good mood is preventing me from killing all of you the moment I set foot on the vessel."

"Do I have your word?" Chakotay sat upright, feigned anxiousness.

"You do. I shall not harm you or your crew."

"And what of your prisoners? Show me Paris!"

"You have but to ask." Aren gestured, and again Tom Paris was brought to stand, swaying and sick, before the screen. "It is a good thing this battle was so one sided, Commander Chakotay. I just didn't have time to execute them." Aren's smile widened, and he lifted his arms in an expansive gesture. "Have no fear. Those who cooperate find I am a generous master. Prepare your vessel for boarding." He moved a hand, and the screen went dark.

Almost at once, smaller ships launched themselves from the larger Ja'in vessels. Each larger vessel, it seemed, had at least four or five of the smaller ships. The screen was filled with the small ships, bearing down on *Voyager*.

Chakotay smiled through the pain. He didn't miss the anxious look Chell cast, covertly, over his shoulder, nor the tense silence on the bridge.

"Bridge to Kim."

"Kim here."

"You played dead very well." Chakotay kept his eyes on the screen. Closer they came . . . closer . . .

"Commander, the boarding vessels are now within forty kilometers and closing," said Henley.

"Mr. Kim." Chakotay leaned forward. *"Jump!"*

Suddenly, like great beasts of legend awaking from a deep sleep, the three huge sentinel ships came to life. Lights sparkled, and they moved with a speed and purpose that filled Chakotay with keen pleasure.

At once, they began firing on the small boarding ships, disabling them almost casually. Every burst of fire-power sent a small ship spiraling off course to tumble to rest and hang limply in space.

"Engineering! Let's move!"

And then *Voyager,* too, powered up, hardly the defenseless vessel she had feigned to be. She joined the three sentinel ships, and the odds were now four to six. Half of the crew of the Ja'in vessels were vulnerable in their small boarding ships. Chakotay did a quick count. Eighteen of those smaller ships were completely defenseless now.

"Captain," said Chell, "two of the larger Ja'in vessels are breaking formation. They're fleeing. Shall we pursue?"

"Negative," replied Chakotay. "Let them go. It's Yashar I want. Concentrate on those still left."

The battle continued.

"This can't be happening!" whispered Kula Dhad, staring at the viewscreen from the main control center. All about him was chaos. A few Ja'in still remained at their posts, stubbornly loyal in the face of unlooked-for catastrophe. They shouted orders that were disobeyed, frantically pressed webbed, clawed, or padded fingers to screens in a futile effort to avert the inevitable. Others had long since fled, fearing the worst, taking their own ships and getting out before the conquerors arrived.

By Dhad's horrified estimate, twenty-two of the little raider ships had been either destroyed or disabled past the point of continuing the fight. Two of the big ships had peeled off, heading who knew where, deserting their commander in his most desperate hour.

Which, Dhad thought with ignoble honesty, *is not such a bad idea.*

Somehow, the Alpha quadranters had been able to surprise them at every turn. Their captain had refused to yield Kes with good grace. They'd refused to die when their ship was shot down. They'd allied with those smelly, nasty Sshoush-shin, they'd managed to take over the Ja'in's own sentinel ships, they were decimating the most powerful pirate fleet in the sector with an almost careless ease, and Kes—

He'd watched the crack in his dreams begin the minute he'd brought word of Kes's beauty to Aren Yashar. Bit by bit, the comfortable fortification he'd built for himself had crumbled, and now, it was all collapsing on top of him.

When Aren returned—and the way Dhad's luck was running recently, the commander would somehow manage to wriggle his way out of this one as he had so often before—he would come with anger the likes of which Dhad had never seen. His fleet was decimated, he would have lost more than half of his servants, and who would he blame?

Kula Dhad, of course. Not Kes, who was the cause of it all; not the Alpha quadranters, with their soft morals and unexpected rock-hard spirits; and certainly not himself. He would come with anger, and he would most certainly kill Kula Dhad.

Dhad hesitated just an instant, then, with the rest of the traitors, abandoned his post.

He found Kes exactly where he expected her to be. Dhad had no idea why he was detouring when every second was precious, but there he was, staring down at her as she was bathed in the luminous glow of the screen.

She looked up at him, victory shining in her eyes. Did she know?

"Things are not looking good for the commander," Dhad said bluntly. "Your people are pressing him hard. But I have known Aren for nearly two millennia, and I have never seen him beaten yet. He will return, and he will be angry. I'm leaving. I wanted—I wanted to warn you." He paused, rubbed the webbing between his fingers in a nervous gesture. "I can't take you with me. I'm sorry. But if he returned and you were gone, he would follow me to the ends of the universe."

Kes smiled, that soft, haunting smile of hers. "It's all right," she said. "I don't know what's going on up there, but it doesn't matter."

"You should find a means of escape," Dhad urged, wondering why he was so concerned.

Her enigmatic smile grew. She pointed to the screen. There, Dhad saw a blip that he didn't recognize.

"I already have," said Kes.

He looked down at her with amazement. "What are you?" he whispered. "You have broken him! Aren Yashar has ruled this sector for centuries, and none have opposed him. He has been with hundreds of women, some of them more beautiful even than you, and yet—" Realization broke upon him. "He loves you, Kes. I have never seen it in him before, but—he loves you!"

Kes swallowed, but did not lower her gaze. "I know," she replied.

"Do you—did you love him?" Somehow, this was very important to Dhad.

"I could have," said Kes. Now she did avert her eyes, gazing at something Dhad could not see. "I could have."

"The walls are tumbling about us, Kes," said Dhad. "Take care that they do not crush you."

He turned and hurried away, more unsettled than he had ever been, and raced for the comfort of his familiar little ship.

Better to be a fugitive with a vengeful Aren on his heels than to stay a minute more with Kes.

Far, far better.

CHAPTER
18

"Mr. Kim, target their defense systems. I want their shields rendered inoperable," ordered Chakotay. Kim, he knew, had access to the complete layout of the pirate vessel. From his post Kim could fire where it would do the most damage with the least loss of life. Angry as he was at Aren Yashar, Chakotay had no desire to take more lives than was absolutely necessary.

The sentinel ship fired. It was a direct hit. Aren's vessel spiraled out of control, finally slowing and coming to a stop.

"Shields are completely inoperable!" shouted Henley, barely able to control her excitement.

"Security, send up some people *now*. Transporter room, lock onto the entire bridge crew of the lead enemy vessel. On my command, beam them directly to the bridge." A few seconds later, five security guards, phasers at the ready, emerged from the just repaired turbolift.

"Now, transporter room!" ordered Chakotay. There came the familiar hum and shimmer, and Aren Yashar, four other Ja'in, and Tom Paris materialized on the bridge. Aren went for a weapon, but one of the guards stepped in quickly and placed a phaser to the pirate's throat. Aren opened his hands in a placating gesture.

He looked over at Chakotay. "You tricked me, Commander," he said coolly. "Well done."

"You've lost, Yashar," and Chakotay's voice was as cool as the pirate commander's. "You might as well cooperate. Your fleet is scattered, your people fleeing, and I've got you right where I've wanted to get you since the moment we entered orbit about this planet." He stepped closer, pushed his face to within inches of Yashar's. "Instruct your people to deactivate the ion storm and the deflector shield."

Aren's smile widened. "No."

"We may not be killers like you," growled Chakotay, "but for someone who lives as long as you do, I'd think that spending the rest of your life in a brig would be intolerable."

"Captain," interrupted Henley. "Someone from the pirate base is hailing us."

"On screen," said Chakotay. He wasn't sure what he expected—a surrender, or an exchange of hostages.

He did not expect to see Kathryn Janeway's

bruised, bloody but ultimately triumphant face. "I see you've got our bad boy," said Janeway.

"Captain," said Chakotay, "It's good to see you." He had never meant any words more than he meant these.

"The feeling's mutual. What's your status, Commander?"

"As you see, we've got Aren Yashar and his bridge crew, and those pirate vessels that are not severely disabled have fled."

"Captain," and Kes's voice floated to Chakotay from somewhere off screen, "I think I've got it."

"Excellent. Chakotay, we're going to deactivate the storm and the field from here. We've got injured to beam out. Stand by."

Chakotay couldn't help giving Aren Yashar a good imitation of one of the pirate's own smug smiles.

"How's Mr. Paris?" asked Janeway as the doctor scanned her with the medical tricorder.

"I've been able to process an antivenom and have begun to administer it," replied the doctor. "He is responding quite well. Though I don't like to admit it, Yashar's intervention may have saved his life. Lieutenant Paris had already undergone a certain primitive level of treatment by the time we beamed him aboard." He flipped the tricorder closed and eyed her. "I don't suppose I could convince you to rest for a few hours?"

Janeway rose. "If it's an option, then no. I'm off for a shower and then down to Mishkara." Her lips thinned. "And I have something special in mind for Aren Yashar."

"Captain." Kes turned from B'Elanna's side. "May I come with you?"

Janeway's eyes narrowed, and out of the corner of her eye she saw the doctor stiffen with disapproval. "Why, Kes?" she asked, keeping her voice soft. "I would have thought you'd had enough of Aren Yashar to last for quite some time."

Kes's face was composed when she replied. "I have some things I would like to say to him. Doctor, all the patients have been treated, there's not much here for me to do. Please, let me go to the surface with the Captain."

"Kes," he began slowly, fiddling with his tricorder, "I had wanted to wait and discuss this with you in private, but—you have just undergone an extremely traumatic experience. There is a strong likelihood that you may have suffered from Stockholm syndrome while under Yashar's influence. If that is the case—"

"Doctor, I'm familiar with Stockholm syndrome, and I'm not suffering from it, I assure you." As ever, her voice was gentle, but her eyes were hard. "This is something I need to do. Please."

He glanced over at Janeway, who inclined her head slightly and shrugged. "Very well. But Captain, I expect you to keep an eye on her."

"Don't worry, Doctor. Kes, meet me in Transporter room one in forty minutes, and don't be late. Mr. Tuvok, how are you feeling?"

The Vulcan was already sitting up. "My head aches, but other than that, I appear to be ready for duty."

"Then clean up and get to the bridge, if you're up to it. I wanted to let you know, your idea of the radioactive isotope may have saved all our lives. Kes was able to recognize it and guide me in from the control room. Well done."

Tuvok inclined his head, then winced at the gesture. "Thank you, Captain. As always, I hope to serve you and this vessel well at all times."

Janeway gave him a final smile and then turned her attention to the rest of the away team. "Mr. Paris," she said, striding over to where he lay beneath the diagnostic arch of the biobed. "You're looking less green around the gills. The doctor's treatment seems to be working."

He did indeed look better, though he was a long way from well. Paris arched an eyebrow, and for just an instant, she saw the old, healthy Tom Paris superimposed over this very ill patient.

"Thank you, Captain, I'm feeling a little better. Though next time you see a spider near me, remind me to step on it. Vigorously. With both feet."

She smiled. "I will." She glanced at the nearest bed. "B'Elanna, how do you feel?"

The half Klingon grimaced. "Doctor says I'll be good as new soon. He better be right, or I'll scramble his program. Tom? Now that you're awake, something's been bugging the hell out of me regarding that pirate program of yours."

"Oh. That."

Janeway shook her head in amusement. From the other bed, she heard Neelix chattering happily to Kes. The Ocampan's face was alight with pleasure and affection for her friend as he spoke. She had heard, of course, of Neelix's brave, if foolhardy, gesture in striking off on his own to rescue her. "And then, Furball led me to this beautiful stream . . ."

Janeway patted Torres's hand. "I'll stop in again when we've dealt with Yashar. Meanwhile, everyone, rest up."

Janeway was almost halfway out the door when she heard Torres's enraged cry: "You cast me as a *what?*" The door hissed closed behind her, so Janeway never did hear how Tom managed to talk his way out of whatever he'd gotten himself into this time.

Kes was smiling. The doctor was annoyed. Tuvok was composed. Neelix was chattering. Tom and Torres were arguing.

All was back to normal on *Voyager* again.

Captain's Log, supplemental. The few Ja'in who remain on Mishkara seem to be a frightened, sorry lot and were more than willing to go with the prevailing wind, to borrow a phrase. Hrrrl has sent the kakkik Wind-Over-Water back to his people, to convey the news that interspecies communication and cooperation is now welcome. As I had predicted to Wind-Over-Water, the greatest opportunity for him to help will come later, in building bridges between races. The Sshoush-shin technicians are already starting to recover some of the forgotten knowledge of their ancestors, and together with the last remnants of the Ja'in, should be able to get much of New Hann up and running in a short time.

Now that the Sshoush-shin are able to control the ion storm and the distortion field, the surface of Mishkara is receiving much more light than before. When combined with judicious terraforming projects, the transformation of this world, first a prison and then a hell, should be complete.

Meanwhile, I have decided what to do about Aren Yashar and the other Ja'in who did not willingly surrender. I think justice is about to be served.

Janeway's gaze traveled over the gathering of Sshoush-shin, their happy murmurings punctuated by the sounds of engineering crewmembers working on the shuttle. Things were radically different from the last time she had been here, injured, suspicious of the huge aliens, fearful of the sudden pulse that would cause instant disaster, and feeling like a helpless victim of Aren Yashar's treachery.

Yashar was here now, closely watched by two security guards with drawn phasers. The tables had been turned with a vengeance.

"I don't know how many years you ruled Mishkara," she said to Aren, though her gaze was on the Sshoush-shin and their new friends, the kakkiks. "I don't know how long you blocked out the sun, how long you made a peaceful people suffer for your own purposes."

"Captain, in my own defense, making the Sshoush-shin suffer was not my goal," replied the Rhulani, his voice still as honey smooth as ever.

"That makes it even worse," Janeway replied at once. She turned to face him, hands on her hips. "Your reign is over. This planet belongs to those who evolved here, and to those who were brought here against their will centuries ago and who have survived to make it their home. It is not a planet for conquerors and pirates any longer.

"For centuries, you were in charge, they were the vanquished. I think it's time to reverse those roles."

The color drained from Aren's face. "You—you're turning me over to the Sshoush-shin?"

"You catch on quickly, Yashar."

"Captain, I protest—"

"You're in no position to protest anything, Yashar. I don't have the time, rations, or inclination to haul you along with us on our journey. You made this your planet, fine. Stay on Mishkara, in the hands of its new masters." She allowed herself a small grin. "If you had bothered to learn more about Sshoush-shin culture, you wouldn't be so worried. They are a fair and decent people. There's no word in their language for murder. But there's no fine cuisine, no soft pillows, no holorooms for your pleasure here. You'll work hard for a change. It's time to start undoing some of the damage you have wrought. And," she added, enjoying twisting the knife a bit, "you've got so much time on your hands now, don't you? Or would you prefer it if we dropped you somewhere in the wastelands where you can take your chances against kal plants, the Sand-That-Eats, and the Xians?"

"Why, Captain," and the mask was back in place, "You can be almost as ruthless as I. How charming."

He inclined his head. "I accept your offer," he said, as if they were sitting at a negotiating table.

Janeway didn't rise to the bait. She would have the last laugh. That was enough.

She turned to Hrrrl, who stood patiently beside her. "What's the latest news, Hrrrl?" she asked.

"Very good indeed," the Sshoush-shin leader replied with a trace of pride in his rumbling voice. "The sight of the sun seems to make almost everyone want to cooperate. The kakkiks have already given us much information about new crops to harvest, once we have tamed Mishkara. We do not know if our homeworld survived, and we may not know for a long time. But this, as you say, is our home now, and we will make it a happy one. We have much to thank you for."

He reached and rubbed her back in the gentle, circular motion she had come to enjoy. Janeway did the same to him, smiling up at the large creature at once so formidable and so benign. "We wouldn't have survived to help you had you not helped us first," she reminded him.

"A good lesson, and one we will teach the children."

Out of the corner of her eye, Janeway saw Kes's face grow sad at the word *children*. The captain was confused, but said nothing. "Kes, are you ready to leave?" she asked quietly.

"Just a moment, Captain." Kes smiled uncertainly, then went to Aren Yashar. For a long moment, the tiny woman gazed up at the former Ja'in leader, scrutinizing him in great detail. His mask stayed in place for a while, but at last, his expression changed.

Janeway was surprised to see genuine caring on his handsome face.

"This doesn't have to be a punishment," Kes said softly.

Aren laughed at that, a hard, unpleasant sound. "Doesn't it?"

"No, it doesn't," Kes said firmly. "For a long time, you've acted out of pain and anger, Aren. You hurt so badly, you wanted to hurt others, too. You wanted to drown the sorrow in pleasure, bury the anguish with riches and power. You wanted to tame your own fear by inspiring fear in others. And because of that, you have blood on your hands."

She reached out and touched the hands as she spoke, spread his fingers with her own small ones, stroked the beautiful, rainbow-hued webbing between them.

"Be proud of your wings," she said. Janeway was surprised. Those odd lumps on his back that Aren was so careful that no one saw—wings? "Let them remind you that once, your people could fly."

"No one will fly anymore," he said harshly, snatching his hand back and curling it into an angry, impotent fist.

"There may never be any more Rhulani children," Kes continued, relentless in her gentleness. "But there will be kakkik children, and Sshoush-shin children. They will remember, and pass those memories on to their own children. You would have gone down in history as an evil man, Aren. You have centuries left to undo that. And when someday the Rhulani are at last truly gone, those here on Mishkara may well

speak of them as great allies, not great enemies—
friends who shared the wisdom of centuries. Memory
is a powerful thing. Take it. Use it." She stroked his
cheek softly. *"Fly!"*

Aren's throat worked, and his eyes grew bright. He
turned away. Kes stepped back beside her captain.
She stood straight, composed and dry eyed. "I'm
ready now, Captain."

The last thing that Janeway saw as the world
shimmered around them was Aren Yashar turning,
for one last look, at the brief-lived being who had so
radically changed his life.

The doors hissed softly as Captain Janeway entered
the hydroponics bay.

She wasn't sure why she was here. She'd meant to
go to her quarters, fortify herself with a cup of coffee,
and begin writing the eulogy for poor Bokk. Instead,
her feet had led her here, as if of their own volition.

Was it only nine days since she had stood here with
Kes, chatting happily as the Ocampan exclaimed over
the cymarri flower, pondering the delights in store for
them on Oasis? It felt more like nine years. The trip to
Oasis had taken its bitter toll.

And yet the cymarri flower was mute testimony to
the brevity of the time. It was in full, proud bloom
now. Janeway knew that in a day or two, it would start
to fade, its radiant purple dimming to gray and then
black. Its blooming period was brief indeed, and yet,
for those few short days, it could not be ignored.

Janeway thought about Kes, whose lifetime was so
incredibly short by human standards; about Aren,

whose life was almost inconceivably long; about the very different paths the two had chosen.

And then Janeway knew why she was here. She wouldn't write a eulogy, stiff and stilted and impersonal. She'd just speak about Bokk, speak simply and from the heart. And she would take this flower with her, let it serve a healing purpose before its petals fluttered to the floor and it died.

There never seemed to be enough time, did there? Not enough time to rest, to think, not enough time to tell those who mattered to you that you cared. You had to make the time, had to take a step or two out of your way sometimes—had to visit the hydroponics bay instead of heading to your quarters.

It's too brief. No matter how long you have, it's always just too brief.

Captain Kathryn Janeway stepped forward, stroked the incredibly soft petals, brought her face to the flower's heart, and breathed deep.

About the Author

Christie Golden got hooked on *Star Trek* in the fifth grade and has been a fan ever since. Her first Voyager novel, *The Murdered Sun,* was very well received and led to her being invited to pitch story ideas for the show to Paramount.

Golden is also the author of two original fantasy novels, *Instrument of Fate* and *King's Man and Thief,* both from Ace Books, as well as having launched the TSR Ravenloft line with the very successful *Vampire of the Mists.* Golden went on to write two more books in the Ravenloft series, *Dance of the Dead* and *The Enemy Within.*

She is presently hard at work on more ideas for *Voyager,* the novelization of the animated television show *Invasion America,* an "epic fantasy historical thriller," a mystery series, and the first novel of a new fantasy series. Readers are encouraged to visit her web site at http://www.sff.net/people/Christie.Golden.

STAR TREK®
THE NEXT GENERATION™

THE
CONTINUING
MISSION

A TENTH ANNIVERSARY TRIBUTE

♦The definitive commemorative album for
one of Star Trek's most beloved shows.

♦Featuring more than 750 photos
and illustrations.

JUDITH AND GARFIELD REEVES-STEVENS
INTRODUCTION BY RICK BERMAN
AFTERWORD BY ROBERT JUSTMAN

Available in Hardcover
From Pocket Books

POCKET
B O O K S

1413-01

Coming Next Month from Pocket Books

STAR TREK

ASSIGNMENT: ETERNITY

by

Greg Cox

Turn the page for an excerpt from
Star Trek: Assignment: Eternity...

Kirk seized the armrest of his chair to keep from being thrown to the floor. On the opposite side of the chair, McCoy was not so fortunate. The ship's doctor staggered, then began to pitch forward. He fell toward the hard duranium floor, only to be rescued at the last second by Spock, who somehow managed to take hold of McCoy's arm while maintaining his own balance. *Good work,* Kirk thought as he struggled to keep standing. "Red alert!" he called out to his crew. Uhura, tightly holding on to the communications console, responded at once to his command. Red warning lights began flashing all around the bridge, accompanied by a high-pitched siren that drowned out the gasps of the other crewmen.

The vibration lasted several seconds, during which Kirk could feel the throbbing of the floor through the soles of his boots. Then the shaking began to subside, and the bridge gradually righted itself as the *Enterprise* stabilized its course. Kirk dropped back into his chair. "All stations report. What the devil was that?"

"Captain!" Ensign Chekov called out. "Sensors report a transporter beam of *astounding* power, a hundred times stronger than anything we've got!"

A transporter? Kirk thought. He had never felt a transporter beam like that, except for— His brain resisted the notion that occurred to him. *But that was three centuries ago!*

Spock's mind seemed to be racing down the same channels. "As I recall, Captain," he said, releasing his grip on McCoy, who had regained his balance, "we have experienced this phenomenon before—"

"Captain, look!" Chekov interrupted as two outlines suddenly materialized at the front of the bridge, only a couple of meters from Sulu's station at the helm. The figures were blurry at first, composed of a swirling blue energy, then quickly defined themselves. Alerted by his memory, Kirk recognized the intruders even before they fully solidified.

It was Gary Seven and his attractive young sidekick from the twentieth century. What was her name again? Kirk quickly retrieved the data from year-old memories. *Roberta Lincoln, that was it.*

But what were they doing aboard the *Enterprise* in this day and age? Kirk had never expected to encounter the pair again, let alone in his own time and on his own ship. Even their clothing, he noted, belonged on Earth a few centuries ago. Seven wore an antiquated suit and tie, while his female companion had dressed more casually in a loose-fitting, motley-colored shirt and a pair of faded denim pants. They both looked as if they had stepped out of some sort of historical costume drama.

Chekov leaped from his seat and drew his phaser. Sulu looked ready to do the same. Even McCoy instinctively placed his hand on the medical tricorder hanging from a strap over his shoulder. "Don't move," Chekov ordered the newcomers, "or I will fire."

Seven ignored both the young ensign's weapon and the blaring alarms. "Hello again, Captain Kirk, Mr. Spock," he said calmly. As usual, Kirk noticed, Seven had his cat with him. The sleek black animal nestled against Seven's chest, unruffled and undisturbed by its journey through time and space. By contrast, Roberta Lincoln looked around with wide-eyed astonishment; Kirk guessed she'd never seen the interior of a starship before. "Forgive the intrusion," Seven stated, "but I need your assistance."

"Captain?" Chekov asked, sounding confused. He kept his phaser aimed at the intruders. "Do you know these people?"

"You can stand down, Ensign," Kirk replied, rising from his own chair. Flicking a switch on the command functions panel on the starboard armrest, he deactivated the siren and blinking red lights. "Cancel red alert status." It occurred to him that few of the crew had actually met either Seven or Roberta; only he and Spock had actually beamed down to Earth during that mission. "I don't think you'll need that phaser. At least I hope not. Meet Gary Seven and Roberta Lincoln. They're time travelers from twentieth-century Earth, or so I assume."

Cradled in Seven's arms, the cat squawked, as if angry at being overlooked. Kirk didn't even try to remember the pet's name, although he found it slightly odd that Seven never seemed to go anywhere without the cat. *At least it's not a tribble,* he thought.

"Good Lord," McCoy said, staring in amazement at the strangers on the bridge. Kirk wondered if the doctor was remembering his own harrowing trip to Earth's Depression era, McCoy's only firsthand encounter with the twentieth century. "Kind of a long way from home, aren't they?" the doctor said. "In time *and* space."

That was certainly true, Kirk thought. Earth was hundreds of light-years away from their present location, not to mention a century or three removed from Seven's own time. *This must be serious,* he thought. Seven wouldn't have come all this way without a strong reason.

"Excuse me, Captain." Lieutenant Uhura spoke up from her post at the communications station. She pressed a compact silver receiver firmly against her ear. "Chief Engineer Scott is hailing you from Engineering. He wants to know what's happening."

"Tell Scotty the situation is under control," Kirk instructed.

"I'm glad you think so," McCoy grumbled. The doctor gave his captain a dubious look.

Kirk shrugged, then turned his attention to their unexpected guests. "All right, Seven, what's so important that you had to shake up my ship to get here?" His fists clenched at his sides. *That damn beam almost shook my ship apart,* he thought. Last time around, the *Enterprise* had intercepted Seven's transporter beam by accident. *Don't tell me that this was just another coincidence. I won't buy it.*

"I'm here on an urgent mission, Captain, the nature of which I can't fully disclose. Unfortunately, in this century, I don't have access to all the resources I had in your past, so I need the *Enterprise* to help me complete my mission."

"You'll have to tell me more than that," Kirk replied. He walked across the bridge, stepping up from the command module and circling around the navigation console until he was less than a meter away from Seven and his companions. "I suppose you are still working on behalf of some mysterious alien benefactors—"

Seven nodded.

"—whose nature and location you're still unwilling to divulge?"

"Exactly," Seven confirmed. "I trust you appreciate the delicacy of my position, Captain. As a visitor to your era, I don't wish to disturb future history any more than absolutely necessary. At present, your Federation remains unaware of my sponsors. Thus it is imperative that I do nothing to change that situation."

Kirk shook his head, scowling. "That may have been good enough back in the twentieth century, but not anymore. Your activities in the past are a matter of history; there's nothing I can do about them. But this is my era now—my present—and you're the one who doesn't belong here. And I don't like the idea of you, or the aliens you represent, meddling with our affairs. Humanity's grown a lot since the twentieth century. We don't need any cosmic baby-sitters these days."

"Actually, Captain," Seven replied, "that's exactly why I need your help. In this century, the human race has indeed graduated to a higher level of civilization, and no longer requires the intervention of my superiors."

"Well, bravo for us," McCoy said. He had remained within the circular command module, keeping one hand on the red guardrail just in case the ship lurched again. "Hear that, Spock? Modern-day *Homo sapiens* isn't nearly as primitive as you think."

"No matter what level of advancement, Doctor," Spock answered, not far from McCoy's side, "there is always room for improvement. Especially with regard to humanity's frequently unrestrained emotions."

"What's wrong with emotions?" Roberta blurted out. Her gaze, Kirk noted, kept drifting back to the points of Spock's ears. *Just wait till she sees an Andorian,* he thought. *Blue skin and antennae are even more eye-catching.*

"Please, gentlemen," Kirk said to Spock and McCoy. "Not now." He turned back to face Seven. "What are you saying? That the Federation is outside your jurisdiction now?"

"More or less," Seven said in a noncommittal manner. "That's why there is no organization or infrastructure in place to assist me in this era. My superiors, and my successors, are occupied elsewhere in the galaxy, safeguarding the development of sentient races that your civilization will not encounter for generations to come." Seven calmly stroked his cat's head as he spoke. "Given time, I could certainly acquire a starship of my own, and whatever equipment and personnel may be required to complete my mission, but time is exactly what is at stake."

"Meaning what?" Kirk demanded, growing annoyed by Seven's cryptic remarks. He was exhausted, the ship was facing a difficult rescue mission, and the last thing he needed now was a meddlesome time traveler with a secret agenda. True, Seven had proved trustworthy the last time they met him, but that didn't mean Kirk was ready to turn over the *Enterprise* just at Seven's insistence. *I need more than that,* he thought. *A lot more.*

Seven paused, weighing his words carefully. "I can tell you that I'm here to untangle a temporal paradox that threatens both our futures."

Kirk didn't like the sound of that. He knew, from painful experience, just how fragile the timeline could be. Memories of Edith Keeler came unbidden to his mind. "What sort of paradox?" he demanded. "Is something going to happen to change the past?"

"No," Seven said. "But your own future could be changed—has been changed—unless action is taken immediately. I have reason to believe that an event damaging the proper procession of history will originate several hours from now, at a specific location within this quadrant. Trust me, that's all you need to know, except for the coordinates of our destination."

"I need to know a good deal more than that," Kirk protested. "This ship is not going anywhere, except on its current course, unless I hear something better than a couple of ominous hints and warnings."

Seven refused to give in. "Think about it, Captain Kirk. Do you really want to know your own future?"

Look for STAR TREK Fiction from Pocket Books

Star Trek: The Next Generation®

Encounter at Farpoint • David Gerrold
Unification • Jeri Taylor
Relics • Michael Jan Friedman
Descent • Diane Carey
All Good Things • Michael Jan Friedman
Star Trek: Klingon • Dean W. Smith & Kristine K. Rusch
Star Trek VII: Generations • J. M. Dillard
Metamorphosis • Jean Lorrah
Vendetta • Peter David
Reunion • Michael Jan Friedman
Imzadi • Peter David
The Devil's Heart • Carmen Carter
Dark Mirror • Diane Duane
Q-Squared • Peter David
Crossover • Michael Jan Friedman
Kahless • Michael Jan Friedman

#1 *Ghost Ship* • Diane Carey
#2 *The Peacekeepers* • Gene DeWeese
#3 *The Children of Hamlin* • Carnen Carter
#4 *Survivors* • Jean Lorrah
#5 *Strike Zone* • Peter David
#6 *Power Hungry* • Howard Weinstein
#7 *Masks* • John Vornholt
#8 *The Captains' Honor* • David and Daniel Dvorkin
#9 *A Call to Darkness* • Michael Jan Friedman
#10 *A Rock and a Hard Place* • Peter David
#11 *Gulliver's Fugitives* • Keith Sharee
#12 *Doomsday World* • David, Carter, Friedman & Greenberg
#13 *The Eyes of the Beholders* • A. C. Crispin
#14 *Exiles* • Howard Weinstein
#15 *Fortune's Light* • Michael Jan Friedman
#16 *Contamination* • John Vornholt
#17 *Boogeymen* • Mel Gilden
#18 *Q-in-Law* • Peter David
#19 *Perchance to Dream* • Howard Weinstein
#20 *Spartacus* • T. L. Mancour
#21 *Chains of Command* • W. A. McCay & E. L. Flood
#22 *Imbalance* • V. E. Mitchell
#23 *War Drums* • John Vornholt

Star Trek: Deep Space Nine®

Star Trek®: Voyager™

Flashback • Diane Carey
Mosaic • Jeri Taylor

Star Trek®: New Frontier

Star Trek®: Day of Honor